THE SINISTER STUDENT

A 1930s MURDER MYSTERY

Kel Richards

Marylebone House

First published in Great Britain in 2016

Marylebone House
36 Causton Street
London SW1P 4ST
www.marylebonehousebooks.co.uk

British Library Cataloguing-in-Publication Data
A catalogue record for this book is available from the British Library

ISBN 978–1–910674–32–1
eBook ISBN 978–1–910674–33–8

Typeset by Graphicraft Limited, Hong Kong
First printed in Great Britain by Ashford Colour Press
Subsequently digitally printed in Great Britain

eBook by Graphicraft Limited, Hong Kong

Produced on paper from sustainable forests

For Shane and Sarah

THE TIME: 1936 (in the short break between the end of Hilary term and the start of Trinity term).

THE PLACE: The town and university of Oxford.

ONE

~

'Morris,' a voice bellowed from behind me. It was the kind of voice it's impossible to ignore, sounding rather like the explosive roar of a large bull that has just spotted a long-lost friend in a distant meadow.

At the time I was just leaving the White Horse pub, stepping into the Broad and heading in the direction of St Giles, where I was due to meet the editor of the *Oxford Mail* with a view to gainful employment.

The voice roaring 'Morris' came from the entrance to Blackwell's bookshop, just over my shoulder, and it was one I recognised.

Turning around I saw the beaming, ruddy face of my old tutor C. S. Lewis.

'Jack!' I cried (all Lewis' friends call him 'Jack' – the self-chosen name he's carried from childhood).

'Why aren't you in Bath?' roared Jack, striding towards me shifting a pile of books from one arm to the other. 'You ought to be in Bath. You ought to be terrifying the maiden aunts of Bath with blood-curdling headlines.'

'I'm not that sort of journalist,' I protested.

'Then what sort of journalist are you?' he boomed, still in that lecture room voice of his that could be heard from one end of the Broad to the other. 'What does the *Bath Chronicle* employ you to do?'

'I'm a feature writer and a leader writer – mainly a leader writer.'

'And what does a "leader writer" actually write?' he asked, falling into step beside me, a welcoming grin still on his face.

'I write the unsigned editorials – usually expressing the newspaper's outrage at the latest absurd policy adopted by the government.'

'I know the sort of thing, although I never read them myself,' chuckled Jack. 'Opinions on any subject under the sun, tuppence a yard, choose your own pattern and colour.'

'Pretty much,' I agreed.

'And what pattern and colour does your proprietor require his editorials to be?'

'Generally we fulminate over government expenditure – any government expenditure on any item. And we don't like the Germans very much, and we shake our inky fist at their increasing militarisation. Oh, we don't like "the land that gave the world Shakespeare falling under the puerile influence of Hollywood". That sort of thing.'

'I see that you've already developed the hardened journalist's carapace of cynicism,' chuckled Jack.

'Well, one does try to fit in, you know, take on the colour of one's surroundings.'

'And what brings you back to Oxford?'

'A job application. The *Oxford Mail* is looking for a journalist who can churn out my sort of stuff and I thought I'd like to return to the scene of my undergraduate triumphs – so here I am, to meet the editor of said journal in about half an hour from now.'

'And when do you return to Bath?'

'Not for a week,' I replied. 'I thought I'd seize this opportunity to catch up with old friends.'

'Instead of which, old friends have caught up with you. Are you free tonight?' he asked, and before I could reply added, 'The Inklings meet in my rooms at Magdalen tonight – and you are hereby invited as my special guest.'

This, of course, was what I'd been hoping for and so I agreed with alacrity.

'And you, Jack,' I said, 'you appear not to have changed at all during my year in Bath.'

And he hadn't. He still wore the same baggy flannel trousers and the old tweed jacket with a battered felt hat jammed down firmly on the crown of his head. His brother, Warnie, was always more neatly dressed, as befits an ex-military man, and often complained of Jack's general carelessness of his appearance. Jack, he said, had invented his own sartorial style, which Warnie labelled 'contemporary scruffy'. At his worst, Warnie had once complained to me, Jack could look like a parrot that had been dragged backwards through a hedge and then left out in the rain all night.

'Who else will be there?' I asked, referring to the meeting of the Inklings.

'Well, Warnie, of course. And Tollers. Probably Dyson, Coghill and Fox . . . and whoever happens to turn up. Oh, and a student of mine, young chap named Willesden, asked if he could come along, so he'll be there. You'll come?'

'Wild horses couldn't drag me away, not that they're likely to try, I suppose. It's hard to imagine any assembly of untamed horses taking an interest in my social life.'

'Where is this appointment of yours with the editor of the *Mail*?'

'Well, his office – the modestly named "Newspaper House" – is over in Osney Mead, on the far side of the railway line, but he's offered to meet me in town – so I nominated our favourite pub.'

'The Bird and Baby?'

'None other.'

'So if you're on your way to the Eagle and Child, what are you doing emerging from the White Horse, as I saw you doing?' Jack asked. 'Have you become a dipsomaniac during your year in Bath?'

'Meeting a friend for lunch,' I explained. I didn't want to explain to Jack that I was meeting a young woman. Penelope had stayed on as a tutor at St Hilda's after we both graduated. Our meeting over lunch had been slightly awkward but encouraging. Definitely encouraging.

When I knew I was paying a visit to Oxford I'd called St Hilda's and arranged to meet Penelope for a pub lunch and a glass of cider at the White Horse.

The thing you need to understand about Penelope Robertson-Smyth is the profile. She has a hauntingly beautiful profile. The sort of profile you see in magazines and that chaps dream about. A rather superior, haughty profile, it's true – one that suggests a vicar's daughter who has just ticked off the villagers for failing to bring enough pumpkins to the harvest festival. Haughty, as I say, but stunningly beautiful and utterly unforgettable.

And there it was, that stunning profile, sitting opposite me over lunch. We reminisced briefly about our undergraduate days, but it quickly became apparent that she didn't want to dwell on the past, so I asked her about St Hilda's. This produced a detailed account of the failings of the principal, the chaplain and all the senior dons. At least, I think it was all of them – I don't think she left a single reputation intact.

'Gosh,' I exclaimed, trying to make an intelligent contribution to the conversation, 'sounds as though they ought to put you in charge.'

'Just give me time,' she replied smugly, hinting at her role in the web of college politics. 'One can't rush these things. Now, tell me about yourself.'

I did so – trying to play up the glamour of the inky world of newspaper journalism. This produced nothing better than a rather superior sniff, so I quickly added, 'Of course, this is just temporary. It just pays the bills, don't you know, while I work on my real goal of becoming a novelist.'

At this her eyes lit up and she leaned forward. I thought she was about to ask me to tell her more about my dreams and schemes, but instead she launched into a passionate lecture on the short-comings of the modern novel and what I should do to fix it.

'Have you read *Spindrift* by Florence Craye?' she asked. I responded by looking baffled. 'Then you should,' she continued. 'That's the model you should follow. Florence is a friend of mine. You can borrow my copy if you wish.'

After I'd paid the bill and we were climbing the short flight of steps up to street level I asked if I could see her again – and she actually reached out, touched my hand, and said with a smile that she'd love to.

So as I entered the Broad I was rather floating on air when I was summoned back to earth by Jack with his bellowed greeting – but I've already told you about that bit. Which sort of brings us back to where we came in.

'So – tonight, then?' said Jack, raising his voice. And as I drifted out of my cloud of reminiscence I realised he was saying it for the second time.

'Oh . . . yes, yes, tonight in your rooms. I'll be there. Sorry, Jack, my mind was elsewhere for the moment.'

'Your mind, young Morris,' Jack chortled, 'was so far away I would have had to send a pack of bloodhounds to track it down. Tonight, then.'

By now we had passed Balliol and had just reached the church of St Mary Magdalen. As I looked up at the ancient facade I turned to Jack and asked him if he remembered our long running debates of the past.

'Of course I do, young Morris. Rich and fruity discussions they were.'

'Well, at the risk of starting another – that's what I most dislike about Christianity.' As I spoke I pointed to the cross on the church building. It was only a small cross on the roof of the chancel, but it had attracted my wandering eye.

'The cross, you mean?' Jack asked.

Precisely, I agreed, it was the cross that I objected to.

Jack asked why and I said, 'It's a symbol of death, of execution. The Romans, being less civilised than us Britons, who only hang people, executed thousands by crucifixion. When I was your pupil we talked about that form of execution once, remember?'

Jack nodded. 'And you explained,' I continued, 'that crucifixion killed its victims by asphyxiation – that as they hung on their cross, often for days, they first supported their weight with their feet and legs, but as they tired they sagged forward. This prevented their lungs from expanding and they, in effect, suffocated. A horrible death. That makes the cross a symbol of an extremely cruel form of execution. And this, in turn, makes Christianity a death cult.'

'My dear Morris,' said Jack heartily, 'you have, in fact, got hold of the truth, but you are looking at it exactly upside down. Christianity is not a death cult, but a life cult – Christians belong to the life squad, not the death squad.'

'But just look at that, Jack,' I protested. 'You might as well use a hangman's noose as the symbol of Christianity, or a guillotine, or an electric chair. It *is* a symbol of execution – you can't deny that.'

'I don't. In fact, I glory in it. The death, the execution, of the One who died is what Christianity is all about . . .'

He was about to say more, but at that moment I looked at my watch and saw the time.

'Sorry, Jack, I have to run. Mr Rainbird, the editor of the *Oxford Mail*, will be waiting for me.'

We repeated our promises to meet again in his rooms that night as we parted and I hurried up St Giles.

There I plunged from the glare of the street into the gloom of the oak-panelled walls of the Eagle and Child. In the back of the pub, in the parlour, I saw a man who looked like a world-weary bishop with bulging eyes and an unusually bad case of indigestion.

'Mr Rainbird?' I inquired.

'You're Morris, I take it?' he wheezed. 'Sit down, sit down, dear boy . . . or rather . . . actually, before you sit down, my boy, you can get each of us another pint from the bar.'

A moment later, equipped with a glass in each hand, I sank down onto one of the overstuffed leather benches opposite my potential future employer.

He was a stout man with a round face and several more chins than were strictly necessary. As he demolished a large plate of fried eggs and chips he complained about the constant battle he fought to keep his weight down. During the course of lunch he cleaned up his plate and downed two more pints. Whether this meant he had run up the white flag in his weight control battle, or whether his lunch counted as only a modest snack – just a small something to keep him going until dinner – was not entirely clear.

As he ate and drank he interviewed me for the job of leader writer with the *Oxford Mail*. As least, I think that's what happened. The interview consisted mainly of a rambling, but emphatic, monologue from Mr George Rainbird on the deplorable state of the modern newspaper industry. At the end of this, without having asked a single question, he leaned back from the table and gave a deep, sad sigh – making him resemble a rather glum bishop who'd just heard his mother-in-law was coming to stay and would be in the house for at least a month.

'I can tell you, John,' he said. 'May I call you John?'

'If you wish, but my name's Tom.'

'Tom? Ah, yes, Tom. I can tell you, Tom, that I've been very impressed by your understanding of the problems facing modern journalism.'

I thanked him politely and he rose to go – this being a major logistical operation involving a good deal of squeezing and sideways shuffling. He then shook my hand and said it had been very pleasant meeting me, adding, 'You'll be hearing from me very soon, Ron.'

'Tom.'

'Tom. Very soon.'

And then he waddled out of the Eagle and Child.

TWO

~

That night, as I mounted the stairs of Magdalen College's New Building towards Jack's rooms, I could hear loud voices and laughter drifting down the staircase towards me. The weekly meeting of the Inklings, it appeared, was already under way.

The door to Jack's room was standing half open – always an indication that more guests were expected – and I was immediately welcomed by Jack's brother, Warren (Major, British Army Supply Corps, retired), known to one and all as Warnie.

I was ushered into the large sitting room, where Jack and I had had our tutorials when I was his pupil. It was a handsome room with high ceilings, eighteenth-century oak panelling and broad sash windows looking out onto Magdalen Grove and the deer park. The furniture, however, did not quite come up to the standard of the room. In fact, I always thought the very modest, rather shabby furniture looked slightly embarrassed to be here – as if it thought it belonged in the back parlour of a bus driver's cottage in Brixton and was rather surprised to find itself in such a fine old room.

Sprawled in the worn but comfortable armchairs and on the ancient Chesterfield sofa were Jack himself, Nevill Coghill – who had lectured us undergraduates in Chaucer – and a man I didn't know in a clerical collar.

'Ah, Morris, delighted you could come,' boomed Jack. 'You remember Coghill, don't you? And the chaplain of our little literary group is Adam Fox.'

The cleric smiled and rose to take my hand. 'Actually, Dean of Divinity at this college,' he explained.

'And sitting modestly in the corner there,' said Jack, waving his arm at a young man I had not so far noticed, 'is Willesden – a visitor like yourself to our circle of muses and amusement. Willesden, this is Morris – he once occupied the exalted position you now enjoy, namely of being one of my pupils.'

Have you ever met someone you instantly disliked for no discernible reason? That was my response to Willesden as he rose from the armchair in the far corner to shake my hand. The handshake was limp and his eyes were half closed as he sank back into the chair. Beneath his slicked back yellow hair his face was a mask – somehow a vaguely unpleasant mask. What it was hiding I couldn't really know, but, for some reason, I felt the mask covered a vast sense of self-importance and superiority. He gave the impression that he believed the whole room and everyone in it smelled of onions – and onions that had been fried with garlic and then left in the pan for several days. But perhaps I was being unfair to the young man. No, no, upon reflection I was being entirely fair. Leaping to judgement is what we journalists do, and so I leapt with delight: the man was a pimple.

A plain table stood in the middle of the room, bearing the scars of much usage. On this was an enamel beer jug that I knew, from previous visits to the Inklings, Jack would have obtained earlier in the day from the college buttery. As Warnie poured me a mug of beer and I settled into an armchair the loudest bell in Oxford, Old Tom at Christ Church, began to chime, as it did every night at five minutes past nine. Although Tom Tower was a quarter of a mile or more away from Jack's rooms the giant bell sounded clearly as it rang out its one hundred and one strokes – supposedly representing the original one hundred scholars of Christ Church College, plus one. It was called the 'door closer', since it's always been the signal for students to return to their colleges and for porters to hastily lock gates, compelling latecomers to climb walls. All part of the fun of Oxford.

As the chimes were still ringing in the air the door swung open again and a dapper man in a neat grey suit entered.

'Tollers!' cried Jack with delight. 'Glad you could make it. You remember Tom Morris, don't you?'

Professor J. R. R. Tolkien smiled as he shook my hand.

'I certainly remember the difficulty I had beating Old English and Old Norse vocab into his young brain,' he said, in the quiet, precise, rather rapid way he had of speaking. 'What brings you back to Oxford?' he asked with a welcoming smile.

'The possibility of work,' I explained and told him about my meeting with Rainbird and the prospect of employment at the *Oxford Mail*.

Tolkien accepted a mug of beer from Warnie and took a seat, unbuttoning his jacket to reveal the startlingly yellow waistcoat underneath.

The revelation that my profession was now journalism triggered off a rattle of conversation around the room. Coghill expressed the view that the only sort of journalism worth the energies of an intelligent man was literary journalism – book reviewing and the like.

'Chesterton,' he said, 'showed how well that sort of thing could be done.'

Fox lamented the lack of moral scruples he detected in the modern press, Jack said he never bothered reading newspapers and didn't understand why anyone would, while Warnie took the view that one had to read the papers to keep informed: 'Dark clouds gathering in Germany,' he muttered, 'a chap has to keep up.' Tolkien agreed with Warnie, saying that despite his own German name he was depressed by some of the news coming out of that 'once great nation', as he put it. Willesden, I noticed, said nothing but kept his own counsel.

'Now,' said Jack, 'who has something to read to us?' as his brother, the most hospitable man I've ever met, circled the room topping up everyone's mug of beer and handing around a jar of nuts.

In response, Tolkien pulled a sheaf of papers out of his pocket.

'Aha!' Jack cried with delight. 'More *Hobbit*?'

'The final chapter,' said Tolkien, 'at long last.' The pages he held, I noticed, were thickly covered with his small, neat handwriting.

As pipes and cigarettes were lit and beer sipped, Tolkien spread out the pages on his lap and was about to read when Jack interrupted him.

'For the benefit of Morris and Willesden, Tollers has written the most wonderfully inventive new fairy tale since George MacDonald or William Morris. And now, Tollers, can you assure the group that it's about to appear in print?'

'Perhaps. It's not certain yet. One of my old philology students, Susan Dagnall, is working in a publisher's office in London and she's encouraging me to send them the typescript. Do you remember Dagnall, Jack? You did some tutorials at Lady Margaret Hall, didn't you?'

'All I remember, Tollers, is how earnest the young ladies were. Far more so than slackers like this pair.' With a wave of his hand and a grin on his face he indicated the grim and unlikable Willesden and the completely adorable Tom Morris (I speak modestly but truthfully – all us Morrises being painfully truthful people). 'Now,' Jack added, settling back into his chair and relighting his pipe, 'let's hear how the adventure concludes.'

Not knowing the back story, it took a while for Willesden and myself to pick up on the narrative – but Tolkien's strangely musical voice was soon carrying us along. In fact, it reminded me of the times when, in a lecture, Tolkien would begin reciting a passage from *Beowulf.* He started quietly, but a magisterial rhythm would quickly develop that was positively hypnotic, and carried us all along as only great storytelling could.

And something along those lines was happening again. The point at which he picked up his tale appeared to be in the aftermath of a great battle. His hero, if 'hero' is quite the right word, was someone called Bilbo Baggins – 'companion of Thorin the Dwarf', as he called himself. And at the moment when the story resumed he was temporarily invisible, for a reason I never quite understood.

There followed the tale of the victors in the battle settling matters and making preparations to move on – all told in the best manner of the great epics and myths.

Whatever that battle was about, and wherever it had happened, the story soon turned into a tale of a journey homewards. On this journey Bilbo was accompanied by a wizard named Gandalf. On the way they stopped at the dwelling place of elves, at which point Tolkien recited a poem that he said was an elf song. I'd heard some of Tolkien's verse before – when I was an undergraduate – and I'd always been impressed. The verse that Tolkien wrote bore no resemblance whatsoever to modern so-called poetry. It was what I called *real* poetry: strong rhythms and rhymes and sounds and sense.

And although I was coming in at the very end of the story, it wasn't long before I was feeling Bilbo's deep longing for his home. But when he did arrive back he found his possessions being auctioned off on the presumption that he, being gone for so long, must be dead. So caught up was I in the tale that I shared Bilbo's sense of outrage.

This Bilbo, by the way, was something called a Hobbit. So as the final words left Tolkien's lips and he laid down the last page of his manuscript, I asked, 'What's a Hobbit?'

'A cross between a human being and a rabbit,' Warnie replied.

This produced a scowl from Tolkien, so Warnie quickly leapt in to add, 'Well, what I meant to say, Tollers, old chap . . . that is . . . I mean, I've always pictured them as small people with hairy feet who lived in holes rather like rabbits . . . or . . . or something along those lines.'

Just at that moment the door was thrust open and a large, energetic man burst in. Seeing the manuscript in Tolkien's hands he immediately howled, 'Not more ruddy elves, is it?'

The man joining us had a round, cheerful face – in some ways not unlike Jack's, but thatched with a rather thicker mop of hair.

'Morris, Willesden,' said Jack, 'this disreputable specimen is Hugo Dyson. He does what he pretends is teaching English literature at Reading University. Dyson, these two are pupils of mine – one present and one past.'

'So I not only have to suffer elves,' laughed Dyson, 'I also have to put up with youngsters who'll applaud every word Jack utters!'

'Actually, your timing is impeccable, Hugo old chap,' said Adam Fox, 'since Toller's reading of his manuscript has just concluded.'

'But our discussion of it has not,' Coghill added. 'So fetch yourself a beer and pull up a chair in silence like a good chap, while we weigh up the evidence and reach a verdict.'

Asked to volunteer his own opinion as a pipe opener to the discussion, Coghill replied that the chapter was excellent and very neatly rounded out the whole mythic adventure. Adam Fox was also generous in his praise – in particular heaping encomiums on Tolkien's verse.

Jack agreed. 'Excellent! Excellent! Beautifully done . . .' he boomed.

'But . . . ?' said Tolkien. 'I heard that upward inflection, Jack. You have a qualification to add, haven't you?'

'Well . . . wonderful though the chapter is, I must admit that I believe it has too much Hobbit talk in it.'

Tolkien laughed pleasantly and said, 'My problem, Jack, is that I *like* Hobbit talk. So does my youngest, Christopher. The way Hobbits talk amuses us both. But the two older boys agree with you – less Hobbit talk and more action they say. So I shall bow to the collective wisdom of you and my elder sons and rewrite the chapter.'

From this the conversation veered off in several directions with sharp insights and awful puns being mixed in equal measure.

At one stage someone asked Dyson if he was doing any research at the moment.

'I'm trying to prove,' he boomed back, 'that Bacon owed Shakespeare money.'

'The point being . . . ?' Coghill asked.

'To explain why Bacon went to the trouble of writing all those plays only for Shakespeare to get all the credit and all the dough. I believe Will was a bookmaker at the bear baiting and Francis had backed a string of losers!'

A collective groan greeted Dyson's joke, and the conversation fragmented again for some minutes.

Jack brought the room back together, and onto a new line, by announcing in his lecture room voice, 'Young Morris here has decided he is repelled and offended by the Christian symbol of the cross.' Each word was very precisely enunciated and weighted – I had the impression that Jack almost always spoke in italics.

Hugo Dyson spun around to face me. 'Where's the offence, Morris?' he demanded. 'Where's the repulsion?'

'It's a symbol of death,' I said somewhat defensively. 'It's an instrument of execution. Could you imagine a new movement getting started in modern-day America, say, and using as its most ubiquitous symbol the image of the electric chair in Sing Sing prison? Why celebrate death?'

Dyson roared with laughter. 'Have you ever seen a photographic negative, young Morris?' he asked. Then he answered his own question: 'Of course you have. Everyone has. Well, that's what you're looking at in your mind right now. All you're seeing is the preliminary stage. When the picture is fully processed and becomes a positive print, black becomes white and white becomes black, and the image is reversed – the cross comes to be seen as a symbol not of death but of life. What do you see when you look at the cross, Tollers?'

Tolkien pursed his lips thoughtfully and replied, 'I see a treasury, a storehouse.'

'Holding what?' Warnie asked.

'A treasury of grace, and generosity and forgiveness.'

'That's rather good,' Warnie said, nodding. 'Rather good. I wouldn't have thought to put it in quite those words myself, but I like that way of seeing it. Don't you, Jack?'

Jack agreed, but before he could add his own insightful footnote Warnie resumed, 'I must tell you chaps about an outrageous accusation that's been made against Jack.'

Having seized our complete attention he announced dramatically, 'Jack has been accused of stealing a book from the Bodleian Library!'

Jack raised a hand in protest. 'It hasn't been put quite as bluntly as that, Warnie.'

'As good as,' blustered Warnie, his moustache bristling with indignation. 'As good as. It appears that a first edition of *Paradise Lost* has gone missing from the stacks at the Bodleian and Jack's name is down in their records as the last reader to have had the volume in question in Duke Humfrey's Library. So they're asking him to explain what's happened to it. The hide of them! Outrageous!'

A babble of conversation broke out, most of it along the lines of someone in the Bodleian having slipped up, and the library's inclination to blame a reader rather than a staff member.

'How dare they suspect Jack?' Warnie continued to rumble. 'I intend going to the Bodleian myself tomorrow to conduct my own investigation.'

Then he turned to me and said, 'If you have some time on your hands in Oxford, young Tom, why don't you come with me?'

And I agreed that I would.

'We shall,' I said, 'boldly confront the dreaded Bodleian together.'

THREE

~

At the end of a long night of conversation, beer and laughter Willesden and I found ourselves making our way down the steps of New Building and into the fresh evening air together. I felt positively invigorated by the sparkling conversation of the Inklings – and intrigued by the glimpse I had been given into Tolkien's powers as a storyteller.

For a short distance we walked in silence down the long, straight path between the New Building and the main quad.

'Well, now you've been to a meeting of the Inklings,' I said, breaking in on the sound of echoing footsteps. 'What did you think?'

'Vastly overrated,' Willesden replied, barely able to keep the sneer out of his voice. 'They have a reputation in certain circles in Oxford as an important new literary circle.'

He paused for a moment on the path and looked up at the full moon that was filling the lawn around us with an elvish, blue light – changing it into something out of Tolkien's magical landscape.

'Can't see it myself,' he concluded. 'For my money they are rather common – clever, but common. I just can't see what's supposed to be so remarkable about them.'

This comment so surprised and baffled me I felt as though the clear night air had suddenly been filled with fog. Or as if a dragon had breathed choking, dark smoke into the magical blue world around us. I had spent an evening in a world of wit and wisdom and imagination, and this man just couldn't see it? Willesden was an Oxford student and therefore, clearly, intelligent. He had just heard the same sparkling conversation, the same riveting story I had, and yet he couldn't see it?

'You're joking with me, aren't you?' I managed to splutter out, as surprised as a canary that's discovered it's sharing its cage with a cat.

'I never joke,' he replied, in the voice he probably used when instructing the waiter to take back an inferior bottle of wine.

I thought for a moment and then quietly muttered, 'Perhaps that's the problem.'

'What's what?' he snapped. 'What did you say?'

'Joking requires a lightness of spirit. It also requires the ability to see unexpected or surprising connections.'

'Are you accusing me of lacking a sense of humour?' His tone now was rather sharp – as if he was accusing the upstairs maid of short sheeting his bed.

'Well, since you said almost nothing all night I have no way of knowing whether or not a sense of humour is one of your attributes. But it was you, yourself, who proclaimed just now that you "never joke",' I pointed out.

'I was referring to present company. Joking is something that only happens between equals,' he growled, thrusting his hands into his pockets. 'But I don't know why I'm even bothering to speak to you.'

At that point my earlier leap to judgement became entirely justified: the man was a pill, he was a gumboil of the ripest sort.

'But since Lewis saw fit to invite you to what, I gather, is normally a private club,' Willesden continued, 'I will take the trouble to explain.'

'Please do,' I responded. And even in that bright moonlight I don't think he saw my smile.

Slowly and patiently, as if spelling things out to the local village idiot, he said, 'My father is Sir James Willesden.'

'Ah, the former Chancellor of the Exchequer.'

'Since you're a journalist I suppose that I shouldn't be surprised to discover you know a little about politics. Yes, as you say, the Pater is the former Chancellor. And since I am a younger son I won't inherit the title or the estate. So what the Pater has planned for me is a career in the diplomatic service. That's why I'm at Oxford. Not to play at silly games – even literary games – but to prepare for a diplomatic career.'

'I see,' I said, dragging out the vowels, playing at acting the village idiot he imagined me to be. 'Given your skill at relating to people, the plan is that the Foreign Office will send you off to any country we wish to sever diplomatic relations with. Should work.'

Willesden turned to face me and raised a fist. 'Now, listen . . .'

'Only joking, only joking,' I said hastily. 'You know what I mean – a joke . . . one of those things you say you don't understand.'

'Oh, I understand the jokes of civilised people all right.'

Before what I had intended to be a brief, pleasant chat descended further into a swamp of personal abuse I said, 'But back to tonight's meeting of the Inklings. If you think about the level of scholarship, of wit, of wisdom we heard in that room tonight . . .'

'You heard that – not me. You must be easily impressed.'

'Well, take the manuscript Tolkien read to us.'

'What about it?'

'It was vivid storytelling in the classic tradition of the great epics, the great myths, of the human race.'

'My dear boy – it was a fairy tale! It belongs in the nursery, not in Oxford. And now, if you don't mind, I'll bid you goodnight.'

We had, by now, come through the archway and were standing in the cloisters of the north quad. Here we parted company – since Willesden was on staircase three and I was on staircase two.

I was tempted to make a final learned and intelligent thrust by saying, 'Go boil your head,' but thought better of it, and we parted in silence.

Walking slowly and thoughtfully down the cloister – turning over in my mind the self-centred unpleasantness of that young man – I entered staircase two. But as I mounted the steps a door flew open on the landing just ahead of me, and standing in the doorway was David Bracken.

Now, this David Bracken needs a little explanation, and I see I've got my storytelling a bit mixed up at this point by not introducing him to you earlier.

That morning, when the porter showed me to the room Jack had arranged for me, the first person I met on my staircase was this David Bracken. He's a foreigner, with an accent I can't quite place. He was just coming out of his door as I walked up the stairs to drop off my bag, so he introduced himself. He told me he was a traveller and a student of history.

'Just here for a couple of weeks to work in your wonderful Bodleian Library,' he said in that odd voice of his.

'It's not exactly *my* Bodleian,' I responded. 'I'm an old graduate just visiting for a week.'

'So why stay here at Magdalen, rather than the Randolph or the Eastgate or one of the other hotels?' (What I quickly discovered about David Bracken was that he asked endless questions. He should have been a journalist, not a historian. I kept expecting him to whip out a notebook and jot down what I said. Sometimes I wondered if he went back to his room and did exactly that – make notes. Odd man.)

I explained that my old tutor had organised a room at Magdalen for me for the week. And then came the next question: who was my old tutor? When I said it was Jack, this David Bracken's eyes widened like saucers.

'You studied under Mr Lewis?'

I agreed that, astonishing though it was, this was the truth. Then Bracken asked if I could introduce him to Jack. Why, I wondered.

'Why?' I asked.

'Well . . . his reputation . . . it would be a real honour . . . and I have a great interest in . . .' but he couldn't find the words to explain exactly what he meant.

Well, that's all the background that I should have given you earlier. So now we're up to date, and back on the staircase, just after midnight, as I'm climbing up to my room. And I must have made a small noise because David Bracken shot out of his door like a jack-in-the-box.

'How did the meeting of the Inklings go?' he asked, his face alight with curiosity. I'd forgotten that I'd told him that afternoon about the meeting I was attending.

I opened my mouth to answer (I'm not quite sure what I would have said) but before I could speak he continued, 'Come in for a nightcap.' He stepped back, holding his door open and gesturing me inside.

When I hesitated he said, 'I have rather a nice old port here – come in for at least one glass and tell me about your evening.'

It felt rude to refuse so I stepped into the room. Bracken bustled around finding a couple of glasses and pouring a generous measure of port into each.

'Was Tolkien there?' he asked as he did so.

'Yes, he was there. You know Professor Tolkien, do you?'

'Know of him, rather. Never met him personally. Although that's one of the things I'm hoping to do during my short time in Oxford. Meet both Tolkien and Lewis, that is,' he explained, sinking into an armchair facing me. And then he added one of those odd expressions that I'd heard him throw into his conversation before. 'If the cap fits,' he said. It was as if he'd learnt a set of common clichés but didn't know exactly what they meant or quite how to use them.

'Was anything read at the meeting? At the Inklings, I mean?'

'Oh, so you know they read their work in progress to each other?'

'Yes, yes. That is to say, I'd heard that's what they do. Who read? And what did they read?'

There he was again with his endless questions.

'It was Professor Tolkien actually.'

'Really?' His enthusiasm and interest seemed to be wound up to a new level by this announcement – it was as if I had just been handed the sealed envelope and was about to say, 'And the winner is . . .'

'A great writer,' burbled Bracken. 'Professor Tolkien, that is. A great writer.'

'I wasn't aware he'd published very much,' I added cautiously. 'So I'm a little surprised at your knowledge.'

'Ah, well . . . I suppose . . .'

'In fact, the only thing I know that he's published is an edition of *Sir Gawain and the Green Knight*. And that's a scholarly edition of a medieval text – hardly a good guide as to his writing style.'

'Ah . . . can I top up your glass?' asked Bracken, looking slightly awkward, as if he had made a social gaffe.

I let him refill my glass of port, and then sat silently waiting for him to take up the reins of the conversation.

'I must have heard, I think, about Tolkien's writing, I mean . . . from someone who'd heard him read . . . or who he'd loaned a manuscript to.'

'Well, there certainly are such people around – fellow dons and former pupils. So that must be it.'

'So what did Professor Tolkien read tonight?'

'A sort of fairy tale, or epic, or mythic adventure – it's a bit hard to classify really. During a lull in the conversation Coghill told me it's called *There and Back Again*.'

'Ah, his first tale about Hobbits!'

'It's his *only* tale about Hobbits as far as I know,' I corrected. 'And I'd never heard of Hobbits before tonight, so where on earth did you hear about them?'

'Ah, well . . . same source, I suppose . . . whoever talked to me about Tolkien's writing must have mentioned Hobbits . . . can't remember just who it was, though. More port?'

'I'm fine, thanks.'

'So what part of the Hobbit story did he read tonight?'

'What is this: *Twenty Questions*?'

'Twenty Questions? Ah, yes, a radio panel show. No, no, I'm not trying to guess a secret answer. I'm just very interested in the Inklings – who they are and how they function. Can I just say how much I envy you – I really wish I'd been at that meeting tonight.'

He chatted on for a bit longer, and I remember answering a series of questions in a sort of sleepy haze. My answers steadily got shorter and shorter and I felt the approach of the sandman, who was about to sock me over the head and send me into dreamland.

At last Bracken got the hint.

'You're looking tired, and I'm keeping you up. But we must resume this conversation another time.'

I promised to answer any of his questions at some future date – preferably at a time when I was under a total anaesthetic – and I went up to my room and climbed into bed.

FOUR

~

The next morning as I emerged from staircase two, intending to make my way to breakfast, a scout was just coming out of staircase three with an anxious expression on his face.

'Excuse me, sir,' he called. I paid no attention, my mind having flown off to the enchanted land of eggs and bacon where I was busy wondering if there would be kidneys as well, so he had to say it again, a little louder this time. 'Excuse me, sir . . . do you happen to know Mr Willesden, sir? Is he a friend of yours?'

'Friend is not the word I would have chosen,' I replied, as I returned, reluctantly, from the land of the breakfast sausage to the stone cloisters of Magdalen. 'Why do you ask?'

'He told me specially that I had to wake him up this morning to catch the London train, but I can't rouse him . . . and I'm afraid to knock on his door any harder than I already have, sir.'

'Let me try,' I volunteered. 'I have no fear of incurring Mr Willesden's displeasure. In fact, making Mr Willesden annoyed would quite please me.'

The scout led the way up staircase three and pointed out Willesden's door.

I pounded on this happily. If that gumboil had overslept, I would take great pleasure in waking him.

'Come on, Willesden – rise and shine. Your scout is here trying to wake you in time to catch your train,' I bellowed. My voice echoed up and down the staircase. There was no way an occupant within could have failed to hear it, but there was no response. I repeated this performance twice more, gleefully imagining a bleary-eyed Willesden dragging himself from his bed and staggering complainingly to the door.

But no dragging or staggering occurred.

So I crouched down and put my eye to the keyhole.

All I could see was a small patch of rug, but sprawled across it was a hand and part of an arm.

'Your name is Harman, isn't it?' I said, scrabbling in my memory from undergraduate days. His reply was a nod. 'Does the porter have a key?' I asked. He nodded again. 'Tell him Mr Willesden appears to be unwell and he'll have to unlock this door.'

I waited as the scout sped off to the porter's lodge and returned a few minutes later with Murray, our rotund and dignified head porter, puffing in his wake.

'Well, Harman,' wheezed Murray, taking off his bowler hat and fanning his red face. 'Which room is it?'

'This one, sir.'

'Stand back, please,' wheezed Murray, addressing his words to me as well as the scout. Murray was clearly one of those porters who believed what he'd read in so many Oxford books about the head porter being the most important person in any college.

He played with the keys on a large, metal ring, selected the right one, turned it in the lock, and tried the door.

'Still won't open,' he said, pointing out the obvious after a minute of struggling. 'Mr Willesden must have shot the bolt. What do we do now, sir?' he added, turning to me.

I suggested he take a look through the keyhole and confirm my observation that there appeared to be something wrong. With some difficulty Murray bent his portly frame to keyhole level and squinted.

'You're quite right, sir,' he grunted, straightening up and catching his breath. 'There's nothing for it – we'll have to break the door down.'

This turned out to be a task much easier to suggest than to enact. I tried my shoulder against the door, followed by Harman the scout, followed by both of us together, but the door refused to budge.

I asked Murray to join in a three-person attack on the recalcitrant door, but he declined.

'Not at my age, sir,' he said, squinting at me ferociously. 'My doctor would never allow it. Not with my lumbago.'

In the end the door was broken down by two young, beefy gardeners. As it swung a little way inwards from its shattered bolt, Murray ordered everyone else to stand back – as if he alone knew the proper order of precedence, including the fact that he, as college head porter, should lead the procession.

Murray stepped around the door that was hanging half open on its hinges. Seconds later he stepped back again. His round face had turned pale and he was holding a hand to his mouth.

'What's wrong?' I asked.

But the only explanation the porter could offer was a moan, 'Oh . . . oh . . . oh . . .'

I stepped past him and entered the room – and the same wave of shock and revulsion that had hit the porter hit me. Unlike most young men of my age I had seen violent death, and murder, before. But nothing prepared me for this.

For a start there was the blood. There was a great pool of blood across the floor – pints and pints of blood. It had flowed from

Willesden's neck – or, rather, where his neck would have been if he still had a neck. Most of it was missing. His neck had been severed just above the shoulders. He had been savagely beheaded.

I took several deep breaths and looked around the room for a weapon that might have inflicted such a dreadful blow. There was none.

And the other thing I noticed was . . . there was no head!

There at my feet was Willesden's decapitated body – but the head had not only been removed from the body, it had been removed from the premises.

Back out on the stairs I found the porter still pale and starting to tremble. He was obviously in no state to provide any help, so I turned to the scout.

'Harman,' I said. 'Go to the porter's lodge and telephone for the police. The number will be on the wall of the lodge – I've seen it there in the past, along with all the other emergency numbers. Call the police and tell them to come at once – there's been a murder.'

Harman gulped, his jaw dropped, and he stared at me.

'At once!' I barked. 'Now!' And he scuttled away to do as he'd been told.

I turned to the two young gardeners who had broken down the door. They were still waiting at the foot of the stairs in case they were needed further.

'You two,' I commanded, 'help Mr Murray back to the porter's lodge. He's had an awful shock. He needs to sit down and rest. And he probably needs a stiff brandy.'

Is brandy the right treatment in such circumstances? I had no idea, but it was all I could think of. St Bernards always look to me like very intelligent dogs and I'm sure they would have recommended brandy. In fact, they probably would have supplied a small cask.

Murray was led away, with a young gardener on each side to support his weight as if he was a sagging rose bush. I turned back towards the half-open door. I had said 'murder' to the scout and that was my instinctive reaction. How could a beheading be anything other than murder? It was impossible to imagine someone committing suicide in that manner – much less how it could be achieved. As for accidental death – well, how on earth could that ever happen?

As I stood guard, facing the stairs, blocking the entrance to Willesden's room with my body, footsteps sounded down the staircase. Presently one of the dons who occupied the upper rooms appeared.

From my undergraduate days I remembered his name was Mallison. He was a history don.

'Anything the matter?' he asked gently, squinting over the top of his glasses with a slight smile on his face.

'Mr Willesden appears to have . . .' What should I say? 'Met with an accident, sir. The police are on their way.'

'Dear me, oh dear me,' Mallison muttered. 'How unfortunate, how very unfortunate. Anything I can do?'

'The matter is all in hand, sir. There's nothing you can do here. Why don't you go on to breakfast?'

'Well, if you're quite sure . . .'

'Quite sure, sir,' I said firmly, at which Mallison tottered down the staircase and headed across the quad to the Hall for his breakfast.

In my self-appointed position of guardian-of-the-corpse I waited for the police to arrive.

After a couple of minutes I wondered if I should take another look at the murder scene. After all, I told myself, once the police arrived they would chase me, and everyone else, well away. If I was to have any opportunity to make useful observations, this was it.

Making sure there was no one else approaching on the stairs, I stepped inside once more. This time I was prepared for the ghastly scene that met my gaze. Knowing the importance of not contaminating the crime scene I stood just inside the door, and penetrated no further into the room. I did, however, drop down to my knees so that I could see under the bed and under the desk.

There was no sign of the severed head.

It had certainly not just rolled away and come to a halt underneath the furniture. There was a wardrobe on the far wall, but its doors were closed. I suppose a murderer with a Grand-Guignol sense of the macabre might have removed the head and put it in a hat box in the wardrobe. No, surely not! Not even a psychopath would do something as bizarre as that, I told myself.

Hearing voices at the foot of the stairs I hastily stepped out of the room again, and took my post in the doorway. Harman was standing there, but refusing to come any higher. Stamping up the stairs towards me was a tall, broad-shouldered young man in a constable's uniform.

'Now, what appears to be the trouble, sir?' he said indulgently. 'Another student prank is it, sir?'

I suppose I was still young enough to look like an undergraduate. By way of reply I stepped aside and waved him into the room. He was there for about five seconds, I should estimate. He staggered out, looking as if he had aged five years in those few seconds.

'Inspector Fleming will have to be told,' he said in a hushed voice, speaking more to himself than to me, taking off his helmet and running agitated fingers through tousled hair. 'The inspector will have to come and take over.' And with those words he hurried back down the staircase. As he reached the bottom he called back over his shoulder, 'If you can stand guard for just a little longer, please, sir. Thank you, sir.' Then his footsteps could be heard on the stone paving hurrying away.

Oxford Police Station was, I knew, in St Aldates, just down from Christ Church. The constable must have telephoned rather than run to the station, and the reinforcements must have come by car, because less than ten minutes passed before I heard the sound of voices and footsteps.

A small group of men, some in uniform, approached me up the stairs. At the back of the group was the constable I had met earlier. With him were two men with different shoulder stripes indicating different ranks.

The senior of the three, judging by his grey hair, reached me first.

'And who might you be, sir?' he asked.

'Morris is my name. Tom Morris. I'm staying here in Magdalen for a week. Not here but on staircase two.'

I went on to explain how I'd been summoned by the scout and, consequently, had found the body. The officer stepped forward and glanced around the half-open door. He had been warned what to expect and didn't gaze for long on the scene of carnage.

'Do you happen to know the name of the deceased, sir? Is he a friend of yours? Do you know him well?' he asked, returning to my side. I explained about having met Willesden last night for the first time.

He barked an order to his sergeant to fetch the police doctor, a photographer and fingerprint man, then introduced himself.

'Fleming,' he said, 'Inspector Fleming. Did you hear any sounds – a disturbance of any sort – during the night?'

'None, I'm afraid. Whatever awful thing happened here, it was not loud enough to wake me.'

'From your knowledge of the deceased, do you know if he had any enemies? Anyone with a motive to do something as . . . as . . . savage as this?'

'I really don't know him well enough. As I said, I only met him last night.'

The inspector seemed to be working his way through the Policeman's Handbook of Standard Questions in Cases of Murder. I suppose he had to, but given the bizarre nature of Willesden's death I doubted that any standard handbook would know what questions to ask. As I was musing along these lines, the inspector was asking another question: 'I take it you have no plans to leave Oxford in the next few days, sir?'

'I'm here for a week at least.'

'In that case, it might be best if you go about your affairs. We know where to find you when we need you.'

FIVE

~

It was a relief to get out of the crowded staircase and into the fresh air. And the first thing I did was to turn my steps in the direction of Jack's rooms in the New Building. I walked down the long path, clearing my lungs by taking deep breaths of the fresh morning air.

When I knocked on the door it was opened by Warnie. 'Hello, Morris old chap . . . didn't expect to see you so early this morning . . . but it's nice to see you, old boy . . .' he mumbled in his usual cheery way as he threw the door open.

'I didn't expect to be coming – and I wouldn't have come if it weren't for Willesden.'

Jack was at the table in the large sitting room just pouring three cups of tea – three because, to my surprise, Professor Tolkien was there. I discovered later that the professor had come around early to collect his precious manuscript of the final chapter of his Hobbit story. This, it turned out, he had loaned to Jack to reread overnight.

All that detail I found out later, and you don't really need to know it just here. I'm sure you'd much rather I just got on with the story of the murder and of what happened next.

'What's Willesden up to now,' asked Jack, handing me my tea, 'that he's sending you around on errands before breakfast?'

'Well, he's not up to very much at all,' I explained, 'largely because he's dead.'

This dramatic announcement got the stunned reaction I was hoping for. Why is it that we take such pleasure in being the first to break startling news to our friends? It's a pleasure we all share, but one I don't quite understand. Is it that we like to be the 'insider' – the one with knowledge others don't have?

Slowly, and in graphic detail, I told the story of my grisly find that morning, and its official aftermath.

When finished I was greeted by a prolonged silence of stunned disbelief.

It was Tolkien who broke this by saying, 'Astonishing. Utterly astonishing. We saw horrible things in the trenches in the Great War, didn't we?' He looked at the Lewis brothers as he spoke. 'But what you've told us equals any of those things in sheer, appalling horror.'

'Willesden, of all people,' rumbled Jack. 'He always seemed so far above the rough and tumble of normal student life.'

There was another silence while we all drank our tea and tried to come to terms with this sort of thing happening in Oxford.

'A Frenchman,' Warnie said at length. 'He was killed by a Frenchman.'

'Now how do you make that out, old chap?' Jack asked.

'Beheaded,' said Warnie. 'That's how the French do it. Very fond of the old guillotine, the French. Now, if he'd been strung up in a hangman's noose, I'd be inclined to say it was an Englishman who'd done it. Or fried in an electric chair, well, I'd say then it was an American. But, his head whipped off . . . got to be a Frenchman.'

This theory was received in gloomy silence.

Eventually Tolkien finished his cup of tea and rose to his feet. 'I just can't take it in. It seems so unreal – more like a dark story that belongs in a folktale or a legend,' he said, speaking rapidly in his usual clipped manner. 'And thank for you this,' he added, scooping up a sheaf of manuscript pages and sliding them into a rather battered old brown manila envelope. 'I'll read your notes with great interest, Jack. Now, I really must be getting back to Pembroke. They won't believe me when I tell them.'

He walked to the door then turned to say, 'Willesden, eh? And to think that we all saw him only last night.' He shook his head as he added, 'It's like something out of a bad nightmare.' Then he left.

'I think we all need another cup of tea,' wheezed Warnie, pushing back his chair and rising from the table.

'What do you make of Willesden's death, Morris? And the manner of it?' Jack asked, focussing his intelligent, penetrating gaze on me.

'I have no idea what to make of it, Jack,' I confessed. 'I walked back with him to the quad after our meeting. He impressed me as an odious, rather self-important young man. But people are not killed because they're odious and self-important, are they? If that were so, who should live?'

Jack sighed deeply and then said, 'Perhaps, Morris, you and I should get involved.'

'Involved?'

'Conduct our own investigation – or, at the very least, keep track of how close the police are to success. That, you understand, is not something I would normally suggest, but we two have had some little experience in such matters and, as much as I trust the police in their professional skills and their diligence, the method of death suggests this is far from being a straight-forward matter.'

'I agree,' I said as Warnie brought a fresh pot of tea to the table, 'but you, Jack? Why do you feel an obligation to keep track of the investigation – or, even, investigate yourself?'

'For two reasons. In the first place, I was his tutor, and as such I did stand *in loco parentis* to some extent. If a student is behaving irresponsibly, or failing to prepare for exams, or facing the prospect of being sent down, I do try to speak to the young man and save him from the dangers of his own behaviour. This is the first of my pupils to be violently murdered, and I feel that I must, at the very least, keep close track of the police investigation. I have some responsibility to see that his murderer is brought to justice.'

'And the second reason?' Warnie asked, having resumed his seat at the table.

'Secondly, I suspect that we will turn out to be the last people to have seen him alive.'

'By "we" you mean the Inklings, I take it?'

'Precisely. All who were here twelve hours ago will be witnesses to Willesden's last night on earth. You especially, young Morris, since you left with him. And that makes his death an Inklings murder mystery.'

'It's certainly a mystery,' I agreed. 'I looked around the room and I could see no sign of a weapon that could behead a man. Nor could I see any sign of the head.'

'What?' burst out Warnie, almost choking on his tea. 'What? There was a headless body in a locked room, but no head?'

I told them the little I had been able to see when I'd stepped back, briefly, into the room before the police arrived.

'That is certainly a puzzle,' Jack agreed. 'A puzzle worthy of the collective intelligence of the Inklings.'

With these words Jack returned to drinking his tea. He had the largest teacup I'd ever seen. In fact, Jack had said to me more than once that there could never be a cup of tea too big or book too long for him.

The horrific scene I had encountered in Willesden's room kept flashing back upon what Wordsworth would have called my 'inward eye'. In particular, I kept seeing all that blood.

'Death is a horrible business,' I muttered grimly.

Warnie chipped in to say, 'Anyone who'd been in the trenches would agree with you, my boy.'

'And that's why,' I said, turning to face Jack, 'it's so appalling that Christianity has as its chief symbol something that spells death – an instrument of execution. Every death is awful in one way or another. There is no such thing as a good death.'

By way of reply Jack rumbled, in his deep and thoughtful voice, 'Not all deaths are quite the same. I once had a pupil whose older brother had been awarded a posthumous VC at the Somme. There'd been an advance from our side but the British troops had been pushed back to their trenches by heavy machine-gun fire from the Germans. One soldier lay in no man's land in between the muddy trenches – badly wounded but clearly alive. My pupil's brother dashed out to save him – knowing he was risking his own life. And that valiant rescuer *did* die – took a machine-gun bullet to the chest. But he saved the wounded man – at the cost of his own life. Is there nothing good, nothing admirable, nothing praiseworthy, in such a death, young Morris?'

'I suppose if the man he rescued lived, then he gave his life for the life of another. Did he live, by the way?'

'The young man I tutored was the young man who was rescued – so, yes, he lived.'

'In other words, this posthumous VC winner gave his life to rescue his younger brother?'

'Precisely. Would you condemn such a death?'

'But . . . but . . . hang on . . . in the Christian symbol of the cross we're not talking about that sort of death, we're talking about a judicial execution . . . now . . .'

But I got no further, because at that moment there was a sharp, loud knocking on the door.

Warnie rose to open it, and two police officers entered.

'Mr Lewis?' said the grey-haired man. 'I'm Inspector Fleming and this is Sergeant Packer – we are from the Oxfordshire and Thames Valley police.'

Jack introduced himself and his brother, and then Fleming noticed me.

'Mr Morris . . . we meet again. You are a friend of the Lewises', I take it?'

A light of suspicion went on behind the inspector's grey eyes. This (I could hear his primitive policeman's brain saying to itself) is starting to look like a conspiracy. Just wait, I thought, until he discovers that we were the last to see Willesden alive – then he'll be really suspicious.

'I've come to see you, Mr Lewis,' he said, reluctantly dragging his eyes away from me, 'because of the death of Mr Aubrey Willesden – although I take it that your friend Mr Morris has already told you about that?'

Jack nodded.

'And I am also told,' the inspector continued, 'that you were Mr Willesden's tutor.'

Another nod from Jack.

'I need some help, Mr Lewis, in understanding the deceased. What kind of young man was he?'

'I found him amiable enough,' rumbled Jack thoughtfully, 'although I suppose that may not be universally the case. You shall have to ask others about that. As a pupil he was diligent. Always had his weekly essay prepared. Always seemed to get his set reading done. But the sort of pupil who never read beyond the recommended list. Not an inquiring mind, I would have said. Diligent, rather than intelligent. He struck me as a young man working towards a goal, and determined to reach it.'

Sergeant Packer was jotting all this down in his notebook.

Inspector Fleming scratched his head. I gathered that the Policeman's Handbook of Standard Questions in Cases of Murder didn't help him at this point. Either that or he'd forgotten what page of the textbook he was on.

'Did he ever talk about his social life or private life at all?' asked the inspector.

'No, never,' Jack replied firmly. 'I don't encourage that. We have little enough time in our designated hour once a week together – certainly not enough time to waste on trivialities. And I also got the impression that Mr Willesden was not one of those men who are eager to share. I would even go so far as to say that he was reserved to the point of being secretive.'

'Aha!' gasped the policeman, seizing on this. 'So you would describe him as a young man who had secrets, would you?'

'Not exactly what I meant, inspector,' said Jack with a chuckle.

The toing and froing continued for another ten minutes and then the inspector asked, 'When did you last see the deceased, Mr Lewis?'

'Last night.'

I thought the inspector was about to leap out of his chair. He was suddenly electric with tension. Here, he clearly thought, was something that counted as a lead.

'What time was this?'

'The meeting began shortly after nine.'

'Was that usual? For you to see a pupil at night?'

'He wasn't here as a pupil. We had a meeting here last night, of a small literary circle called the Inklings. Willesden had heard of our group and asked if he could attend – and I said yes.'

'The Inklings? The Inklings, eh,' muttered Inspector Fleming. 'Can't say I've heard of your little group or circle or society myself.'

'Hardly!' snorted Warnie. 'You're town not gown. If you're not part of the university community, you're hardly likely to have heard of any of the literary or discussion groups, are you now?'

The inspector chewed his small, grey moustache in thoughtful silence for a moment and then said, 'Well, you'd better tell me, Mr Lewis, about this secret society of yours.'

SIX

~

I thought Warnie was about to explode. He took on the personality of a hand grenade after the pin has been pulled. His face went bright red and seemed to swell – like a child's balloon at a birthday party being rapidly inflated.

'Secret society? What balderdash is that?' Warnie grumbled.

'Well, if it's not a secret society,' growled Inspector Fleming, 'what is it?'

Clearly his Policeman's (Standard Issue) Suspicion Meter, operating on a scale of one to ten, had suddenly shot up to eleven and was making a pinging noise inside his head.

'The Inklings is a group of like-minded friends,' spluttered Warnie indignantly, 'who meet to read to each other from their latest writings, and to critique and praise each other's work, and generally chat and make jokes over beer. We are not, I can assure you, inspector, a secret cell of bomb-throwing anarchists.' Pieces of outraged shrapnel were scattered all over the room by that particular detonation.

Sergeant Packer wrote Warnie's statement down in painstaking detail while the inspector said thank you, sir, very helpful, sir. Obviously deeply cynical, so great was the man's sense of suspicion that he must have been compensating for some childhood trauma. Perhaps his mother had dropped him on his head in infancy, and the old wound still hurt on frosty mornings, so he had become a policeman in order to inflict his suspicious nature on the world.

With a growl that implied he never believed anything anyone ever told him, the inspector then asked what kind of writings the group indulged in. Politics, perhaps? he asked hopefully.

Jack laughed heartily – a big, resounding laugh that must have shattered Fleming's hopes of uncovering a secret Bolshevik cell set on undermining Western civilisation as we know it.

'A less political group you could never hope to find,' Jack boomed with a huge grin on his face. 'We may occasionally conspire over who should be elected as Professor of Poetry at this university, but our scheming and caucusing doesn't extend beyond the dreaming spires of Oxford.'

'If you say so, sir. At last night's meeting, for example, what kind of writing was read aloud to the group?'

'A fairy tale,' I volunteered.

The inspector spun around and turned a deeply sceptical eye on me. To have the switch thrown from political plotting to fairyland so swiftly had sent him reeling off balance.

'Now you're having a lend of me, aren't you, sir? Asking me to believe that Oxford dons write, or read, fairy tales. Now, come along, sir, play fair – what was really read aloud at this meeting of yours last night?'

'I tell you it was a fairy tale,' I insisted. 'Or perhaps it could more properly be called an epic adventure, or even a mythic adventure, entitled *There and Back Again*. Professor Tolkien read it to us – apparently he's been writing it for some time. And jolly good it was, too.'

The inspector turned back to face Jack and Warnie and asked if this was true. They said it was, and this was duly recorded in the sergeant's notebook.

'And this young Willesden chap did not normally attend meetings of your group . . . the . . .' he glanced over his sergeant's shoulder to look at his notes '. . . the Inklings?'

'No, it was his first time among us – as an interested observer,' said Jack. 'My impression was that he was looking at us rather as a zoologist might study a rare species. Perhaps he was considering writing an essay on the convivial eccentricities of middle-aged dons.'

'Who write fairy stories,' said Sergeant Packer, suddenly coming to life.

Ignoring this observation, the good Inspector Fleming soldiered on: 'And what sort of mood was young Mr Willesden in last night? Did he share any particular concerns with your group? Did he seem disturbed or apprehensive at all?'

'Not in the least, old chap, not in the least,' Warnie responded. 'He sat back in that corner chair, over there, and contributed very little to the evening. I think he looked a bit disappointed when he left – as if he had expected us to be a rather more entertaining pack of performing monkeys. I think he found the circus not worth the popcorn.'

'Did he leave alone?'

'No, I went with him,' I said.

This led to a close examination of my walk with Willesden from the New Building to the quad. Since this was a stroll down one straight path over a short distance that took only a few minutes, there was not much I could say about it. But Inspector Fleming had me say it over and over again – step by step and word by word – until he finally seemed convinced that this provided no clues to the subsequent murder.

As he rose to leave, the inspector turned to the Lewis brothers and said, 'Will you be staying in college over the weekend?'

'Normally we'd pop back to our house,' said Warnie, 'out at Headington. Is there a problem with that?'

'It would be much better for our investigation if you two could be immediately available, should we need you again. Would you mind staying in college for the weekend?'

Jack and Warnie looked at each other, then Jack said, 'If that will help, we will certainly comply. Although,' he added, looking at Warnie again, 'we'll have to telephone Minto and Maureen and let them know.'

As the door closed behind the two policemen, Warnie rolled his eyes and said with a deep sigh, 'Here we go again.'

'At least this time,' said Jack, 'we are on home ground. So we have what I believe is called among the sweaty, sporty types the home ground advantage.'

Feeling irritated by this latest encounter with police procedures and police methods I stood up and paced back and forth over the threadbare rug down the length of the room for a minute or two. Then I walked over and stood at the inner window of Jack's large sitting room – the one facing the main Magdalen college buildings. To my surprise the lawns between New Building and the older quad buildings were filled with uniformed police officers, some of them with sticks, some of them bent double. All clearly searching the place. They were working in a line across the whole expanse of the lawn, apparently examining it inch by inch.

'They look like the widow in the story who lost one coin out of ten and swept and searched until she found it,' I said.

Jack joined me gazing down on the 'hunt-the-thimble' brigade filling the lawn.

'What do you think they're looking for?' I asked.

'They're trying to get ahead,' Jack replied with a straight face. After a pause he added, 'I am normally reluctant to apologise for puns, since puns are a noble form of humour. However, on this occasion I probably should apologise.'

'Yes, I rather think you should,' I replied. 'But pun or no pun, you're quite right – they must be looking for the missing head.'

'And for any small clue of any sort that the murderer may have dropped going to or from Willesden's room. And probably for the missing murder weapon as well. Presumably there must be some sort of large, very sharp blade that inflicted the fatal blow. From your description it must have been something very powerful.'

'What a way to die!' I muttered grimly.

'Ah, yes, now then – we were talking about the ways in which people die, and the reasons why people die, when that policeman interrupted our conversation.'

'Yes, we were,' I said, turning to face Jack. 'And you were defending that deadly instrument, the cross, as the symbol of Christianity on the grounds that it is possible for a death to be a good death.'

'I think I'd choose my words rather more carefully than that. Calling any death a "good death" is putting together an adjective and a noun that rarely if ever belong together. I would prefer to speak of an admirable death.'

'Oh, ah, yes. You told me about that posthumous VC winner – the soldier who gave his life to save another.'

'That's one example of what I would call an "admirable death". Or do you object, young Morris, to that expression?'

'I'm still thinking about it. Give me another example.'

'Well, given the unusual and horrific manner of Willesden's death, *A Tale of Two Cities* springs to mind – set in Paris at the time of the French Revolution when the guillotine was being very heavily used.'

I agreed that Dickens' novel was one of his ripest, and was not inappropriate to Willesden's death. Then I rattled off the opening words: '"It was the best of times, it was the worst of times, it was the age of wisdom, it was the age of foolishness, it was the epoch of belief, it was the epoch of incredulity, it was the season of Light, it was the season of Darkness, it was the spring of hope, it was the winter of despair, we had everything before us, we had nothing before us, we were all going direct to Heaven, we were all going direct the other way . . ."'

'In other words,' said Jack, 'a time very much like our own. And in that grim context Sidney Carton, the barrister who happened to resemble French nobleman Charles Darnay, saved Darnay's life by dying his death – by freeing Darnay from prison and going to the guillotine in his place.'

I nodded. 'The book ends with the guillotining of Carton, and that famous speech of his: "It is a far, far better thing that I do, than I have ever done; it is a far, far better rest that I go to than I have ever known." I grant you that this is an example of an admirable death. But even so, if there was, let's say, a club devoted to the memory of Sidney Carton, would they really use an image of the guillotine – the implement of his death – as their symbol?'

'It might depend, might it not, on just how admirable, how powerful, how important, his death was? And what you're failing to see about Christianity is that the death of Jesus is at the heart of it all.'

'That's the crux of the matter, you mean?'

Jack slapped me on the shoulder and said, 'You have chosen exactly the right word. We talk about something being "the crux of the matter" or of being "crucial". Look at both those words – they are both formed from the word "cross". Because of the central role Christianity has played in our culture, in our civilisation, and in the formation of our language, earlier generations understood the central importance of the Cross in the story and the impact of the death of Jesus. The result of that understanding was that if anything was so significant as to be comparable to the Cross in its importance and its impact it was, to that extent, "cross like" – it was "crucial". It was "the crux" of the matter.'

'But surely the teachings of Jesus, and the example of Jesus, matter far, far more than the manner of his death!' I protested.

'They do matter,' Jack agreed. 'But the death matters much more. It is crucial, it is the crux: the Cross – the death – is at the very heart of the Jesus project.'

'Granted he died heroically, died a martyr,' I began, but my voice trailed away because the expression on Jack's face had changed, had become more earnest.

'The purpose of God was in that death,' he said. 'No way of viewing the Cross which regards it primarily as a tragedy, a martyrdom, or the like is adequate.'

'But . . . that still doesn't explain why Christianity acts like a "death cult" by glorifying the death of its founder,' I protested.

'Think back to the death of the posthumous VC winner I told you about,' Jack said gravely. 'A young man dying on the battlefield to save the life of his younger brother. Think too of Sidney Carton taking the place of Charles Darnay and dying his death. To remember such things with admiration is not to join a "death cult" – because in each case a life was saved. The death of Jesus is all about the saving of lives. It is the exact reverse of what you imagine, young Morris – far from being a death cult, it is the world's ultimate life cult.'

SEVEN

~

The next morning I stepped through the college gates into the High Street and found Warnie there consulting his pocket watch. Warnie had to be equipped with a timepiece since Jack refused to wear a watch (on the grounds that he could never remember to wind it). Now that he was retired from the army Warnie seemed to have two main tasks in life – compiling a history of the Lewis family, and keeping Jack organised. The latter, I think, took most of his energies.

'Ah, Morris, young chap!' cried Warnie when he spotted me. 'I was just debating with myself whether to go up to your room and dig you out. I'd like your assistance with a little matter.'

I said I was free at the moment and I'd be happy to volunteer in whatever capacity I could be useful.

'Excellent! Excellent! Our goal, young Morris, is to clear Jack's name. We need to conduct our own investigation and find out the truth.'

'Into the murder, do you mean? You intend to retrace the steps of the police?'

'No, no, old chap. Leave the murder to the experts, that's my view. What I have in mind is this outrageous accusation made by the Bodleian against Jack. Mind you, they haven't had the courage to come out and say it openly, but they clearly suspect Jack of having purloined a valuable first edition of Milton. Complete rubbish, of course, and you and I are going to prove it!'

Despite his snorting disapproval of the Bodleian, Warnie was in a much more cheerful frame of mind than when I had last seen him exploding in the general direction of Inspector Fleming. In the morning light he looked like a jolly major out of a cartoon in *Punch* – one who had just bought a round of drinks in the officers' mess and was about to suggest another.

I had, up until that moment, been planning to head in the general direction of St Hilda's to see if I could manage a 'casual' visit with Penelope. But however much I wanted to see her, the prospect still made me nervous – so I fairly happily abandoned a tongue-tied and embarrassing performance in Penelope's presence to fall in with Warnie's plans.

'They're just clerks, of course,' grumbled Warnie as I fell into step beside him. 'Mere pen-pushers. Only rather dull-minded, dull-eyed, flat-headed pen-pushers could ever assume that Jack was capable of anything improper.'

We walked up the High Street, turned right at the University Church of St Mary the Virgin, passed the Radcliffe Camera on our left and found ourselves at the grand arched entrance to the Bodleian Library.

As we stepped into the shadows of the archway, we saw Professor Tolkien walking towards us, a sheaf of papers under his arm.

'Tollers, old chap!' Warnie cried with delight. Tolkien looked up, woken from his scholarly reverie by the major's hearty greeting.

'Good morning, Warnie, good morning, Morris. You two about to indulge in a spot of research?'

'You could say that. We're researching the Mystery of the Missing Milton – with the aim of clearing Jack's name,' I explained.

'An admirable project. Silly of them to suspect Jack of even the smallest impropriety.'

'May I,' said Warnie, 'ask a favour? If you have a few minutes, would you come with us to speak to the Bodleian authorities? When questions are asked by a professor they carry more weight than when asked by the suspect's brother and ex-pupil.'

Tolkien glanced at his watch (which, unlike Jack, he always remembered to wind).

'Yes, why not? It's the least I can do for Jack. Lead the way, Warnie, I'm right behind you.'

In fact he wasn't, he was beside us, as we three marched across the Bodleian quad to the main building and the reception desk. Behind that desk, or just stepping out from behind it carrying an armload of books, was a young man I recognised. Gooch had been an undergraduate during my time. Looking up at us 'three musketeers' approaching, he recognised me first.

'Morris,' he said, blinking in a startled way. 'You're back in Oxford.'

He thus managed to coordinate his eyesight with his geographical knowledge and display a level of mental acuity he had rarely shown as an undergraduate.

'Well spotted, Gooch, old chum,' I responded. 'And you, I take it, have never left.'

He explained that he had only managed a second class in his degree so he'd stayed on to add a BPhil to his MA in hopes of qualifying for either a fellowship in Oxford or, more likely, a spot in one of the redbrick universities.

'But why all this?' I asked. 'Why do you masquerade as a librarian?'

'I work here part-time – just a little cash to keep the tins of baked beans on the breakfast table.'

Gooch's whole person having now emerged from behind the reception desk, I saw he was wearing plus fours in a startling chessboard pattern. I was tempted to say 'pawn to queen four' but instead I said, 'Is this standard dress for librarians today?'

'Oh, the plus fours, you mean? No, I finish at lunchtime today and I've lined up a game of golf for the afternoon.'

'You mean you're going to wear that in a public place? You're a braver man than I thought, Gooch.'

'Why? What's wrong with my plus fours?'

'Apart from the fact that such an eye-popping pattern is likely to induce a migraine in anyone who sees them? Just don't go near the clubhouse, old chap – we don't want the older members of the Oxford Golf Club writing angry letters to the *Oxford Mail* complaining about the disgraceful tastes of the younger generation.'

Gooch looked goggle-eyed and was trying to calculate how serious I was, so I hurried on to make the introductions: 'Professor Tolkien you know and this is my friend, Major Warren Lewis.'

He nodded a greeting as I explained that we were there about the missing Milton.

'The Milton? Oh, yes, the Milton. First edition. Quite valuable. Last reader it was signed out to was a don . . . ah, name of . . .'

'Lewis,' Warnie said, supplying the name Gooch was struggling for. 'My brother, in fact.'

'Surely, young man, you don't suspect a don of having stolen the book?' said Tolkien, in his precise, clipped voice. What he said carried considerable authority. Gooch laid down his bundle of books on the reception counter and tried to explain: 'No, not stolen, exactly. Perhaps mislaid. Or something of the sort.'

He seemed to be hinting at something peculiar, and exactly what that was we were about to find out.

'Do dons often mislay books?' Tolkien demanded.

'Well, no, not often. In fact, hardly ever,' the hapless Gooch stuttered. 'But in this case . . .'

'In this case,' Warnie fulminated, 'you've chosen to imply that my brother has been either dishonest or unbelievably careless!'

'Not me,' Gooch protested, his eyes as wide as saucers. 'It was the general opinion among the staff that since we had no name to consider other than the last known reader of the volume . . .' He looked like a small cat that had wandered down an alleyway and suddenly found itself surrounded by a gang of bulldogs with murder on their minds.

'Where did it go missing from?' Professor Tolkien asked.

'From Duke Humfrey's library, I suppose,' Gooch replied. 'That's the last time it was known to be in anyone's hands.'

'So, let me get this clear,' I said. 'A staff member went to collect the book from the desk in Duke Humfrey's library where Mr Lewis had been reading it, and it wasn't there – it had gone missing.'

'No, no, that wasn't it at all,' said Gooch, who was now looking around to see if there was another staff member who might come to his aid – as if the small cat was hoping a large alley cat who was a seasoned fighter might turn up to protect it.

Then what was it, I demanded? If the book had not actually disappeared from the reader's desk in the Duke Humfrey, why was the last reader there the suspect? What had actually happened? How had the book been found to be missing?

'The stacks,' said Gooch. 'The next time a reader asked for it, it was not in the stacks – well, not really in the stacks, as you'll see.'

'Then it had nothing to do with Jack at all!' Warnie thundered. 'It went missing from the stacks, not from a reader's desk!'

'I think, young man,' said Tolkien quietly but firmly, 'you should take us to the stacks and show us the place where the book was last seen. And who, by the way, reported it missing from the stacks?'

'That was young Mr Flack,' Gooch explained. 'Yes, come on, I'll show you the way, and then you'll understand why this is so peculiar.'

Gooch led us to the end of the reception area, and down a flight of steps. At the foot of the steps was a door that Gooch pushed open.

'Is this door normally locked?' I asked.

'Not while the library's open,' he said.

'Your security seems a little lax.'

'Our readers respect the library's rules – that's our security.'

Through the doorway we found ourselves in the endless miles of shelving of the central stack. Gooch told us to wait while he went to find young Mr Flack.

'Anyone could get in here,' said Tolkien sharply, as we waited. 'I had no idea the Bodleian took so little care of its valuable collection.'

The rows of shelving were dimly lit by naked light bulbs that glowed yellow. Gooch emerged from the gloom into one of the pools of yellow light. He was followed by a fellow who looked like fifty going on ninety. If this was 'young' Mr Flack, he'd been left out in the rain for far too long and had become shrunken and wrinkled. He could be called young only by comparison with that wizened old woman in Siberia who'd just made it into the *Guinness Book of Records* as the world's oldest person – but by comparison with no one else.

Much later, when I'd settled back into Oxford, I ran into young Mr Flack in the bar of The Mitre and asked him about the adjective. He explained that his father had also worked at the Bodleian, so that when he had begun, as a mere stripling, he became known as young Mr Flack – and the name stuck even as the years passed.

'Now,' said Gooch, 'tell these gentlemen what you found.'

'Better than that,' croaked young Mr Flack, 'I can show them.'

He dug into the pocket of his grey dust coat and pulled out a small volume. It was octavo in size and was bound in dark, old leather. He held it out, and Professor Tolkien took it and looked at the spine.

'But this is it,' said Tolkien in surprise. 'This is the edition of *Paradise Lost* that is supposed to be missing.'

'Look inside,' wheezed young Mr Flack. 'Open the covers.'

Tolkien gently opened the covers and to our astonishment there was no printed text, only a wad of blank pieces of paper. These blank pages were loose, so Tollers lifted them out. What remained was the cover, with clear signs that the original printed contents had been carefully removed with a razor blade.

'That's not carelessness – that's vandalism!' Warnie protested. 'How you could ever conceive that my brother . . .' He sounded as if he was building up to another explosion.

'No, no, major,' protested Gooch, looking more than ever like a frightened kitten – this time a kitten that was trying to persuade the leading bulldog that he was entirely innocent and the guilty cat must be somewhere else. 'All we ever said was that Mr Lewis was the last listed reader. We never imagined that he would cut out the pages.'

'So you say now, but the implication was perfectly clear,' Warnie snorted, barely mollified.

'This was how you found it on the shelf?' Tolkien asked.

Young Mr Flack nodded. 'Another reader requested it. I came to fetch it, and as I walked back to the stairs I opened it for inspection – a normal procedure – and this is what I found. Then the reader was told the book was not available and I told my boss, who told the Chief Librarian.'

'Who then sent an impertinent note to Jack asking for an explanation,' spluttered Warnie.

Tolkien continued to examine the wad of blank paper that had been substituted for the pages of *Paradise Lost*.

'All carefully cut to the exact size,' he said. 'This was no absent-minded don – this was a carefully planned theft. More than that – it's an act of cultural sabotage; a crime against our English heritage.'

EIGHT

~

'What I don't understand,' I said, 'is what anyone can do with the pages of a first edition if they don't have the cover. What good is one without the other?'

'Perhaps theft is not the motive,' said Tolkien gravely. We three were walking back across the Bodleian quad towards the main entrance.

'What other motive could there be?' Warnie sounded puzzled.

'There are dark forces,' Tolkien replied, pausing to light his pipe. This took several attempts in the breeze swirling around the enclosed quad. Then, in a deeply sad voice, he continued, 'There are people who hate all that is good and all that is healthy, beings who think only of power and possession, and who hate all they cannot control and cannot own. Such dark shadows plan only for destruction.'

'Huh, people like the Communists, you mean,' snorted Warnie, giving his best Colonel Blimp impersonation. 'And the horrid Nazis, come to that. They fit your description – destruction all the way. Power and possession are what obsess them.'

'Could they really hate our culture, our civilisation enough to want to perform acts of wanton malicious damage?' I asked as we resumed our slow stroll.

'That's not impossible,' said Tolkien seriously. Then a bright glint lit up his eye as he added, 'Mind you, there are sharp and clever thieves in the world and this strange act might just be by one of them – one who's thought of a different way to make a pocketful of money.'

'A way that involves stealing the middle out of a book rather than stealing the whole book? What would be the point?' I wasn't following Tolkien's drift.

'Perhaps the real intention of leaving the cover stuffed with blank paper,' said the professor, this time with a real twinkle in his eye, 'was to prevent the theft being discovered quickly? After all, the cover with its bogus filling was collected from the reader's desk in the Duke Humfrey and returned to the stack without discovery. The thief had a bit of bad luck – another reader asked for it too soon. Otherwise it might have been months, even a year or two, before the theft of the printed pages of Milton's first edition was discovered. More than enough time to turn the theft into cash – more than enough time. Yes, it might all revolve around time.'

I left Warnie and Tollers in the Bodleian archway, still deep in conversation about the peculiar method of theft employed in the Mystery of the Missing Milton and exchanging theories over what it could mean. I, meanwhile, headed down the Broad, past the Sheldonian, towards the Cornmarket. I had my hands in my pockets and my head bowed, deep in thought – the slashing out of pages from an old book had me intrigued. Which is why, just as I turned into the Cornmarket, I failed to notice that Penelope Robertson-Smyth had fallen into step and was walking beside me.

'Hello, slug,' she said cheerfully. 'Here you are again on the lettuce leaf of life. I didn't expect to see you this morning.'

I took this to be Penelope's idea of flirtatious banter. I explained where I had been, and that I was on my way back to Magdalen.

'Have you heard about the murder?' I asked.

She hadn't, so I filled her in on the ghastly demise of Aubrey Willesden.

'And,' I concluded, 'the decapitated head and the murder weapon are both still missing. Or, at least, they were the last time I checked. I believe the police are still searching. I spoke to the scout on Willesden's staircase this morning. He told me that both windows were closed and latched, and the door – and this is from my own personal knowledge – was both locked and bolted from the inside. And yet there, inside that locked room, was Willesden – well, most of Willesden, I suppose. But no murder weapon . . . and *no head*!'

This news I expected to take her breath away, and was surprised at how little Penelope – she of the divinely beautiful profile – was moved by the whole story. Mind you, she was a sturdy girl and very little was likely to take her breath away. This certainly didn't. She was calmly gazing around the Cornmarket as if looking for someone.

'Are you expecting someone?' I asked – being one who is never above stating the obvious.

'Rachel from St Hilda's is supposed to be meeting me here. That awful girl is always late.'

'But isn't it appalling about Willesden?'

'Hardly appalling, dear Tom. The man was a weasel and it was only a matter of time before somebody handed him his dinner pail. If I had been driving a car and he had stepped out onto the road, I would certainly have accelerated towards him. Wouldn't have hesitated. Now I don't have to bother.'

'But doesn't the method of the murder shock you?'

'It certainly surprises me. It never occurred to me that anyone in Oxford was so creative. And it's strange the police can find neither the murder weapon nor the head. But, of course, the police are not especially clever and any criminal with an average IQ would be able to out-think them.'

'Well, it's knocked me sideways, I can tell you that.'

'Of course it has, poor Tom. You are, after all, one of life's rabbits. Anything as melodramatic as this will always take the wind out of the sails of a rabbit.'

I left aside the question of whether rabbits ever went boating, and instead challenged her classification. Although nothing could shake my devotion to this girl, I was aware of a passing sense of annoyance.

'I certainly don't think of myself as a rabbit,' I protested.

'Of course not,' said Penelope with a hearty laugh. 'Rabbits never do. Rabbits never know they're rabbits. But they are. And that's what you are, Tom.'

That was when it struck me that she was using my first name. That was a level of intimacy she had never reached with me before. Perhaps despite all this rabbit business there was a growing fondness there. I think my resentment at being compared to the small mammals of the *Leporidae* family must have shown on my face because Penelope suddenly became quite tender and affectionate.

'There's no stigma attached to being a rabbit,' she said cheerfully. 'Every girl in her right mind is always on the lookout for a rabbit with a grain of sense. And you certainly do have a grain of sense. At least a grain. Possibly more. It simply means that you prefer a normal, wholesome life to gadding about like a . . . well, like a . . . a non-rabbit. Never try to change your zoological species, Tom, dear boy. It can't be done.'

Not just 'Tom' but 'dear boy' as well.

Thus encouraged, I asked, 'Can I buy you tea at the Randolph this afternoon?'

'Not today – we have a meeting in the Senior Common Room. But tomorrow I'm free. Shall we say three o'clock? Ah, there's Rachel. Must dash – I'll see you tomorrow at three at the Randolph.'

I continued down the Cornmarket in a cheerful and carefree frame of mind. I didn't much mind where I was going, or care either. Thus, I was almost at Carfax Tower when I realised someone was calling my name.

'Hi there! Morris! Can you spare a moment?' I looked over my shoulder and saw the eccentric David Bracken running to catch up with me. His trousers were cricket whites and were combined, oddly, with a college rowing blazer (which I doubted he was entitled to wear). And he was moving uncomfortably in his clothes, as if he was unfamiliar with them.

'You're quite a good chum with Mr Lewis and Professor Tolkien, aren't you?' he puffed, still slightly out of breath, as he caught up. There it was again: 'chum' was an odd word to use in that sentence. It was almost as if it was a word he had read but didn't know how to use.

'Well, I suppose I know Jack better than I know Tollers. He was my tutor when I was up, and he's helped me out of a tight spot once or twice since.'

'When you were "up"?' Bracken appeared to rack his brain, as if trying to find a bit of vocabulary he should have memorised. 'Ah, yes, when you were an undergraduate at the university.'

'Why do you ask?'

'I'm just wondering if you could possibly manage to introduce me to them?'

He was looking at me with big, soppy eyes – reminding me of a cocker spaniel I used to own.

'This means a lot to you, doesn't it?'

'A big deal,' he conceded. (There he was again – why didn't he say 'a great deal', if that's what he meant?)

'Is this part of your research into . . . what did you say it was? History?'

'Yes, back where I come from I am a postgraduate history student. I'm working on my thesis subject now.'

'What's the topic of your thesis?'

But this turned out to be something Bracken didn't want to talk about, so he rather clumsily grabbed the steering wheel and turned the conversational vehicle in another direction.

'Have Mr Lewis and Professor Tolkien taken any interest in this awful murder at Magdalen?'

I explained that the police had come to see Jack on the grounds that Willesden had been his pupil, and had taken an interest in the fact that the Inklings were the last people to see the young man alive.

'Apart, that is,' said Bracken, 'from his murderer.'

'Yes, of course. I assume his murderer must have seen him. You'd have to be pretty close to whack someone's head off – not just cut the throat but sever the spinal cord and take the whole thing off from the neck up. I assume you'd have to be within visual range to do that.'

'Do the police have any clues?'

'None they're sharing with us.'

'What about you? Do you have a theory?'

'Little green men from Mars, perhaps. The murder looks physically, technically impossible. So perhaps Willesden was attacked by forces with technology beyond ours.'

I was babbling, of course. Somehow Bracken's persistent cross-examination always made me unbalanced.

'Are Professor Tolkien or Mr Lewis involved in the investigation in any way?'

I could have told him about Jack's desire to follow the investigation closely, and help if he could – but Bracken was starting to irritate me so I just said no.

'When do you expect to be seeing them again?'

'What's today? Saturday? I'll certainly see them on Tuesday morning at the Eagle and Child . . .'

'Ah, yes, that's the informal meeting place of the Inklings, isn't it?'

'How on earth did you know that? And if I may ask you another question: where exactly are you from?'

'From one of the colonies. Small place. You would never have heard of it. Look, Tom – if I may call you Tom – would you ask if they'd allow me to come to the Eagle and Child on Tuesday morning?'

He sounded pathetic – as pathetic as my old spaniel begging me to play ball with him – so I said yes, I'd ask Jack if that would be okay and then I left quickly before he could start jumping all over me and licking my face in gratitude. Sadly, as things turned out, I completely forgot Bracken's request. But in my own defence, I did have rather a lot on my mind that week in Oxford.

As I entered the gates at Magdalen, Murray, the head porter, called out to me.

'Mr Morris, sir – there's a letter here for you. Well, a note really. As you can see it hasn't been through the postage. No stamp. Was delivered here by hand this morning just after you left.'

The envelope was addressed in an unfamiliar hand and I tore it open. There was a page of indecipherable scrawl, followed at the bottom by a more or less coherent and readable paragraph in which Mr George Rainbird – editor of the *Oxford Mail* – offered me the post of chief leader writer.

'Good news, sir?' said Murray, interpreting the grin on my face.

'Most definitely. If I wrote a reply, could you get one of your boys to deliver it today?'

'Certainly, sir, no problem at all.'

I entered the porter's lodge, took a sheet of paper and penned a hasty acceptance of the offer, stuffed it into an envelope which I addressed and handed to Murray.

'It'll go today, sir, I can promise you that.'

And I set off at once to break the good news to Jack.

NINE

~

On Sunday morning I was just leaving the Hall after a late breakfast when I spotted Jack emerging from the chapel on the other side of the quad. As he advanced down the cloisters a man in a grey suit walked rapidly after him – clearly trying to catch up with him. The man looked like a grey-haired, rather distinguished bank manager and was vaguely familiar. Soon the pursuer caught Jack and they were deep in conversation. As your faithful narrator, determined to keep you abreast of the action, I headed in their direction.

As I drew closer, I recognised the immaculately dressed visitor: it was Detective Inspector Gideon Crispin of Scotland Yard.

'Inspector,' I called as I strode over the stone paving towards them, 'a delight to see you again.' He returned my greeting and we shook hands.

'You won't be the least bit surprised, young Morris,' boomed Jack with a smile on his face, 'to discover that our old friend the dauntless detective is here to investigate our Headless Corpse.'

'Sir Richard Freeman, Chief Constable of Oxford,' Crispin explained, 'called in Scotland Yard as soon as the local team failed to find either the murder weapon or the head.' Then turning back to Jack he said, 'I was surprised – pleasantly surprised, I might add – to find you here in college on a weekend. I'd assumed that you'd be out at your suburban house . . . what's it called?'

'The Kilns,' Jack offered.

'That's right, The Kilns. I remember you telling me about it the last time we met. It's on the outskirts of Headington Quarry, you told me, near Risinghurst. So why aren't you there?'

A chuckle sounded behind us as Warnie arrived. 'It was the delightful Inspector Fleming – the local man – who asked us to stay close at hand.'

'Sorry about that,' said Crispin, scratching his head. 'He was probably feeling completely lost, thrashing about wondering what to do. A bit out of the ordinary, this murder of yours.'

'Not exactly *my* murder,' Jack laughed, 'but certainly well out of the ordinary.'

Warnie said grimly, 'I'd be surprised if there were many murders by decapitation in Britain. Our nation hasn't become quite that barbaric yet.'

'Given the nature of this killing,' said Jack, 'where do you begin? Since you're now taking charge of the investigation – or at least I presume you are – where do you pick up the threads?'

'I will start where I always start,' said the Scotland Yard man, 'with the character of the victim. I'm sure the local crime scene team have done a thorough job on the available physical evidence and I'll go over that in due course. But you've heard my theories about criminal investigation before: random killings are rare so it's very often the character and behaviour and relationships of the victim that put us on the right track. And that's what I thought we might chat about.'

'Come up to my rooms,' said Jack, 'for a pot of tea and we can talk things over.'

'Can I bring Merrivale with me?' asked Crispin. Jack said yes, of course, and Crispin waved to a man who was standing in the shadows of the archway under the Founder's Tower. In response to this beckoning gesture the familiar squat, solid figure of Sergeant Henry Merrivale stumped towards us, and then as a group of five we headed off to Jack's rooms in New Building.

Warnie played 'mother' and served the tea while the rest of us settled ourselves in the comfortable old furniture in Jack's large sitting room.

'Well, now,' said Crispin, taking a tentative sip from a cup of very hot tea, 'what can you tell me about young Mr Willesden?'

'Sadly, as I told the local man, Inspector Fleming, very little, I'm afraid.' As he spoke, Jack put down his teacup and lit his pipe. 'Although Willesden was my pupil, I saw nothing of him outside of tutorials and inside them we focussed our conversation entirely on medieval and renaissance English literature.'

'What else was he studying here at Oxford?'

'I believe he was reading history as well as English – early modern history, I think he told me.'

'Do you know who his history tutor was?'

'Yes, he once said that he was under Mallison – history fellow of this college.'

'Where might I find him?'

'Check with the porter, but I'm sure he has rooms in north quad – in fact, I think Willesden mentioned they were on the same staircase.'

'That's right,' I interrupted. 'I saw Mallison coming down to breakfast on the day I discovered Willesden's body. Absent-minded old duffer, he struck me as being.'

'Nevertheless, I'll talk to him,' said Crispin. 'He may know more about Willesden's private life than you, Mr Lewis. Now, Mr Morris, tell me about finding the body.'

So I told him the story. I won't retell it here since I trust your memory of chapter four is as fresh as mine. When I'd finished my gripping yarn – I do tell a good story – there was a long, thoughtful silence.

Warnie broke this to say, 'And we were probably the last people to see him alive . . . apart from his murderer, that is.'

'Fleming told me,' said Crispin, 'about the meeting of the Inklings on the night before the murder. But reading his account there seemed to be nothing helpful there.'

Everyone agreed this was so.

'Then you, Mr Morris, left with Mr Willesden and walked back to north quad with him?' I nodded. 'Did you form any opinion as to his character?'

'The man was a pill – he was a piece of cheese; he was an infectious disease. He deserved the Golden Pill With Bar award for distinguished unpleasantness.'

The Scotland Yard man asked me to explain the reason for my precise character analysis and by way of reply I reported the exchange we had shared that night. I have the ability to recall conversations verbatim, so I recited it word for word.

'I agree he sounds most unpleasant,' the inspector said at the end of my performance. 'But it gives us nothing that helps this investigation.'

'Certainly nothing,' said Warnie glumly, 'that justified slashing his head off with a whacking great sword.'

'Is that how you think it was done, Major?' said the usually silent Sergeant Merrivale from his chair in the corner (where he'd been quietly taking notes).

'Do I . . . ? Well, I really don't know, I suppose. I just had a sort of picture in my mind of some knight in armour swinging a massive sword. It must take a fair blow to entirely sever a chap's head.'

The conversation and the tea lasted for another half-hour – at the end of which we were as puzzled as before by the murder: both its method and its motive.

Then Crispin and Merrivale thanked us for our assistance and took their leave.

As Warnie cleared up the tea things Jack said, 'What impresses me is how focussed this Crispin chap is on his investigation. You and I, young Morris, have seen that characteristic in him before. He seems quiet and genial, but every ounce of his intelligence is focussed on a single goal.'

I agreed that this was a good description of Inspector Crispin, and I also agreed that this intense focus of his was clearly already in play in the Willesden case.

'I mention this,' said Jack, a smile breaking out on his face, 'because of your objection to the cross as a vile and violent symbol . . .'

'Which it is . . .'

'. . . when in reality it was purposeful and intentional. Jesus was just as focussed on the cross as the good inspector is ever focussed on an investigation.'

'You mean he knew it was coming? That it was unavoidable?'

'More than that,' Jack insisted. 'He chose that path.'

'A suicide?'

'Would you call Sidney Carton dying for Charles Darnay a suicide? Would you call a posthumous VC winner who died to save an injured man a suicide? Death can be the chosen path – chosen purposefully and intentionally – without being a suicide.'

Jack let this sink in and then he resumed, 'Jesus was held to the cross – that image that so disturbs you – not just by those six-inch rough, iron Roman nails, but much more by his own will: by his determination to obey his Father and achieve his goal and purpose.'

'Which was?'

'In his own words – to seek and to save the lost.'

'And this required his death?'

'If it did not, he would not have been so focussed on it. Though the final strokes of violence that deprived him of life came at the hands of others, yet it was his own act, calculated and determined, which armed those hands with their destructive power. Jesus himself said of his life, "No man taketh it from me, but I lay it down myself." In the middle of his public life he "turned his face towards Jerusalem" – as the Bible puts it – going to what he knew was going to be his death.'

'But does that make the cross an admirable symbol?' I challenged. 'Only if the death was an admirable death – a self-sacrifice for others, like those two examples you mentioned. Was it that?'

'His death was deliberately chosen, young Morris,' said Jack, his deep, firm voice rumbling at me with great clarity, each word given its full weight, 'because that was the only way he could effect the rescue he had come to achieve.'

'But admirable deaths, sacrificial deaths, are very rare things. The reason why your posthumous VC and Sidney Carton are so memorable is because they're so rare. And one of them is fictional! You still haven't persuaded me that the cross you Christians so cherish is a symbol of an admirable death. It still just looks to me like a symbol of death – full stop.'

'It was certainly an agonising death, but it was also the death of an innocent man in the service of others, and that makes it a powerful, forgiving death. Come on, let's go for a walk,' said Jack, rising from his chair. 'You know how much I like to walk and talk.'

'I'll join you shortly,' Warnie called as we made for the door.

And so our talk continued as we walked down the New Building path to the bridge over the Holywell Mill Stream to the water meadow beyond. Here we steadily, but fairly briskly, strolled around Addison's Walk – one of Jack's favourite walking routes. This was a broad, gravel path, completely overhung by trees, that circumnavigated the whole of the water meadow.

'You know, don't you, Morris,' said Jack pausing to relight his pipe, 'who I, and all Christians, say Jesus is?'

'You say he's the Creator God, don't you?'

'Precisely – the Mind behind the Universe invading the planet in the form of a human being at a particular moment in history.'

'The Big Brain behind the Big Bang, come in a bloke's body,' I suggested.

'If you wish to put it that way,' Jack said with a hearty laugh. 'But the point is that creating the heavens and the earth was, it appears, almost effortless for him. Certainly, that's the picture Scripture paints it – creation cost him no labour, no anguish. But to take away the sin of the world cost him his own life's blood.'

'Which means . . . ?'

'The focus of Jesus on his death. That, remember, is what we were talking about. Jesus came to die. That was his mission. That was the purpose of his coming.'

'But his teachings,' I protested, 'the example of his life?'

'Admirable. Vital, in fact. And a rich source for us to draw from. But his focus, his purpose, his intention, was his death. From fairly early in the piece Jesus explained to his first followers that his purpose was that he "must suffer many things, and be rejected of the elders, and of the chief priests, and scribes, and be killed, and after three days rise again". They, of course, couldn't cope with this idea – any more than you can, young

Morris. They wanted a great teacher, a healer, a leader – not a suffering servant. But this is what makes his death an admirable death: because it was a rescue mission to planet earth. Jesus said that he "came not to be ministered unto, but to minister, and to give his life a ransom for many". That's an admirable death – and the instrument that killed him becomes an admirable symbol.'

I said nothing in response, so Jack continued, 'It's in his death that he achieves his goal, or, rather, his Father's goal for him. In his death he is the Master. He is active, positive, supremely, totally in control of the situation.'

'So this execution implement the cross becomes . . . ?'

'The symbol of Christianity, because it's the symbol of his triumph.'

This sparked a thousand questions, a thousand challenges inside my head, but before I could voice any of them Jack said, 'Remember the Centurion – a Roman and a pagan – who saw Jesus die and found himself compelled to confess, "Truly this man was the Son of God." And for almost two thousand years now that same confession has been triumphantly won – over and over again – by this death, symbolised by this cross.'

TEN

~

At this point we had completed one full circuit of Addison's Walk, and as we returned to the path from the little bridge we saw Professor Tolkien walking towards us from the college grounds. We stopped and waited for him to catch up.

His coat was flapping open in the gentle breeze, revealing a startling scarlet waistcoat beneath.

'I went to your rooms to join you for afternoon tea and Warnie told me you were here,' said the professor as he fell into step beside us. 'We've had some great debates and discussions walking this path over the years, Jack, old friend.'

'*Hrum, hoom.*' Jack cleared his throat. 'We have indeed, Tollers, old chap – we have indeed,' he murmured in that distinctive voice of his – a rich voice, very like a deep woodwind instrument. 'I would still to this day be outside of the kingdom of God were it not for a conversation I had with you and Dyson right here on Addison's Walk.'

'How well I remember,' Tolkien responded with a smile. 'It must have been midnight when we began and we talked and argued and debated for at least three hours that night.'

'What about?' I asked in my innocence.

Jack chortled as he replied, 'About true myths.'

'Now come on, Jack, "true myth" is an oxymoron,' I protested. 'The whole point about myths is that they aren't true. The very word "myth" means a purely fictitious narrative. If it's a myth, it's made up – there's not a word of truth in it.'

'Ah, well, young Morris,' Tolkien intervened. 'There is another way of looking at myth.'

'What way?'

'Is it not possible, Morris, that a myth is a tale that in its very shape and structure, in its images and elements, conveys not mere "facts", but truth? Facts, after all, only give us information, raw data – what truth gives us is *meaning*. That's what a myth can convey: meaning – it can tell us what the mere facts mean. Why not think of a myth as a story that tells you an ancient truth, a deeper truth from before the dawn of time. Perhaps a myth delivers a truth that cannot be embodied in any other way?' Professor Tolkien said.

'Except in a story?' I asked.

'A story of symbolic power. A story that shows how the facts of our world fit together in a meaningful way,' Jack suggested. 'The great pagan myths may be "good dreams" sent to the ancients by God to convey – by their very shape and structure and images – deep truth beyond mere superficial facts.'

'And when the historical facts and the truth, the meaning, conveyed by myth coincide, ah, well, then . . . .' said Tolkien.

'. . . then,' said Jack, taking up his friend's point, 'then the deepest, most vital, most meaningful truth of all is revealed.'

'For instance?' I prodded.

'For instance,' Jack responded, 'a few years ago I was chatting with a fellow don, one of the most hard-bitten atheists I ever met, one night in my rooms. He was talking about the historical evidence for the New Testament and he said to me, "It's a rum thing, Jack, that old myth about the dying and rising God seems to have actually *happened* once!" To hear such words from a dyed-in-the-wool atheist – even late at night after a beer or two – really set me back and made me think again.'

'In fact, it led up to that late-night conversation of ours,' said Tolkien. 'But that's not what I came to talk about today. It's our Headless Corpse – the late Mr Willesden – I wanted to mention.'

Jack and I both waited to hear what he had to say. Tolkien kept us in suspense by stopping to light his pipe – having to turn his back to the breeze to accomplish this. In my impatience I prompted him by asking what it was he wanted to say about the murder.

'Just this,' he said at length. 'Another pupil of mine, a chap named Hanson, complained to me one day that he'd lost a lot of money to Willesden in a card game. It's the sort of remark a pupil will sometimes make when he's shuffling his papers and trying to delay reading his essay. And this Hanson chap was, I gathered, never very flush with funds, so losing a lot to someone rolling in money like Willesden rather hurt him.'

'You're surely not suggesting that as a motive for murder?' Jack asked.

'Wait – there's more,' Tolkien replied, holding up one hand to stop the flow of Jack's words. 'Sometime later, when we were looking at the Anglo-Saxon word "*searwian*", meaning "deceitful, cheating", he mentioned that he now believed Willesden to be a cheat. It seems that a number of undergraduates had lost money over cards to Willesden, so they took to watching his play very closely – and concluded that he was some sort of card sharp.'

'Dealing off the bottom of the deck or whatever?' I suggested.

'Certainly manipulating the cards in some way. Hanson and some others had become convinced that Willesden had the skill, the trick, and used it to empty their pockets.'

'*Hhmm*,' rumbled Jack. 'I suppose if he'd taken enough money from a needy student that might provoke revenge.'

'The problem is that beheading is such an extreme revenge,' I objected.

'Nevertheless,' boomed Jack firmly, 'I believe we should follow up Tollers' clue. What's this Hanson's first name, do you know?'

'Harold, I think,' replied the professor. 'Yes, I'm sure of it. Known as Harry.'

'Is he at Pembroke?'

'No, I believe he's at Exeter. He came to me to read Old English and Old Norse.'

'Then we should be able to track him down. Even if he didn't take bloody revenge on the card cheat, he might be able to point us to other undergraduates who suffered worse than he did, and who might be more violently inclined. Do you agree, Morris? Worth checking out?'

I agreed.

Then footsteps came padding up behind us, and we were joined by a rather puffed Warnie.

'Thought I'd find you still here,' he wheezed. 'Thought I'd join you.'

Then the four of us continued our companionable ramble around Addison's Walk, talking of all manner of things – as the other Lewis (Lewis Carroll, that is) says, "of shoes and ships and sealing wax, of cabbages and kings". Not literally, you understand, just that it was a wide-ranging chat, until Warnie said, 'I say, you fellows – I want to ask your opinions about this weird theft from the Bodleian.'

And that rather focussed our minds.

'I mean to say –' Warnie huffed and puffed as we walked '– it's outrageous, isn't it? Just because Jack is the last listed reader of the missing Milton the Bodleian chaps think it's all down to him. But it can't possibly be, can it? Not now we know how it was done.'

At this point it became clear that Warnie had not reported the results of our investigations at the Bodleian to Jack, so he had to backtrack several steps and explain.

'Most peculiar,' Jack agreed when he heard the story. 'To steal the contents rather than the whole book is something I've never heard of before. And to conceal the theft by packing blank paper in between the covers – well, clearly the hope was that weeks, or even months, would pass before the crime was discovered.'

'My thoughts exactly,' said Tolkien. 'This decidedly odd method is intended to delay the discovery that any theft had occurred.'

'Wait a moment!' I interrupted as a thought struck. 'This suggests that the Bodleian needs to conduct a stock-taking of just about everything on their shelves. How many thefts have been carried out along these lines before now – and have remained undiscovered?'

'A good thought, young Morris,' Jack agreed. 'Since you've been dealing with the Bodleian, Warnie, why don't you suggest a stock-take to them?'

'If you like, old chap,' his brother muttered, 'but I'm not sure they'll listen to me.'

'So let's assume,' I said, 'that this is a systematic stealing system that has been in place for a while. I still don't understand it! How can removed pages be valuable? Thieves steal for money. Can isolated pages, removed from the original binding, still be worth enough to steal?'

'Ah, now there I have an idea to offer,' Tolkien said. 'I've been giving this some thought and I wonder if the plan might not run along these lines . . .'

But before Tolkien could explain we almost collided with an absent-minded don walking in the opposite direction.

'I say, Wilkes!' protested Warnie. 'Watch where you're going!'

Wilkes was not just a Magdalen don, he was also a traffic hazard. There was enough of Wilkes to make two medium-sized dons. It was as if when Nature decided to make Wilkes it rolled up its sleeves to make a really good job of it – but got distracted and went too far.

'You chaps talking about our great mystery?' wheezed Wilkes.

'About two mysteries actually,' Warnie replied, 'both the Headless Corpse and the Missing Milton.'

'Never heard of the Missing Milton,' said Wilkes, 'but if you're after solving the mystery of how Willesden lost his head, I'm your man. You should be tapping into my brain.'

We, of course, asked why.

'I read all those yellow-back novels,' Wilkes said. 'All those thrillers and murder mysteries. I know how these things are done. I think I've read everything by that Edgar chappie . . . ah, Edgar . . .'

'Allen Poe?' I suggested.

'Wallace,' Wilkes added. 'Yes, that Edgar Wallace chappie. *The Clue of the Twisted Pin* and all that sort of thing. I'm full of that to the very brim.'

'In that case, Wilkes, old man,' boomed Jack heartily, 'tell us what's on your mind. In what direction should we, and the police, be looking for a solution?'

'It will be a gang,' hissed Wilkes in a kind of stage whisper. 'It's always a gang. Willesden will have been involved in a criminal gang. Probably led by a mad monk with a secret headquarters underneath a ruined abbey. It's always that sort of thing.'

We said nothing, so Wilkes continued, 'The leader of the gang will be known as "The Squealer" or "The Red Hand" or

"The Man In Black" or something of that sort. None of the gang will know his real identity, but they'll carry out his orders with ruthless efficiency.'

'Well,' Warnie muttered, 'I suppose "ruthless efficiency" more or less covers what happened to poor Willesden.'

'But surely, Wilkes, old chap,' Jack said with a smile on his face and light in his eyes, 'if a criminal gang had been operating around the college, we might have noticed?'

'Ah, they're much too cunning for that, Lewis. You take my word for it. It always takes the best brains at Scotland Yard at least three hundred pages to track down the gang leader, and even then they need a bit of luck.'

With that pronouncement Wilkes turned around and shuffled off.

'Now,' said Jack, as Wilkes rounded a corner and disappeared from sight, 'Tollers, you were just about to explain your theory of how this very odd theft from the Bodleian might work for the thief – how pages razored out of their cover might still be valuable.'

'Ah, yes,' said the professor, taking his pipe out of his mouth and gesturing with the stem as he spoke. 'It occurred to me that the plan could very well be to rebind the stolen pages in a suitably old cover – a binding of an appropriate age and size. And, of course, the only person who could supply such a rebinding would be an antiquarian bookseller.'

'But who would the customer be?' I asked. 'It can't be a museum or library or a serious collector – they'd recognise there was something wrong. So . . . who, then?'

'What about a rich American?' Tolkien suggested. 'An industrialist, let's say, who is not especially knowledgeable but who is starting to spend his wealth on collecting rare old books and works of art. If an antiquarian bookseller had on his shelves a relatively worthless book of the right period and the right size, and commissioned his thief to steal the pages of a valuable first edition – hiding the theft by returning the original cover with blank paper as filling – he might then bind the stolen pages into a jacket that looked real enough to fool an amateur and sell it for a song, a very expensive song . . . an entire opera, in fact.'

'Meanwhile,' Jack added, 'the very fact of the theft goes undetected – the thieves hope – for a considerable period of time.'

'That's a thought.' Warnie nodded. 'In fact, it's a very good thought. The transatlantic trade in collectables is apparently very big these days. I read about it in a Sunday paper. This is something worth investigating.'

ELEVEN

~

In due course we made our way back across the little bridge from the water meadow to the grounds of Magdalen.

'Morris,' said Jack, as Warnie and Professor Tolkien wandered off deep in conversation, 'why don't you and I follow up this student mentioned by Tollers – this Hanson chappie?'

I agreed, and, there being no time like the present, we made our way through the college gates and up the High Street. We turned right in the Turl and made our way to Exeter College. Here we found the porter in his lodge and asked for directions to the rooms of an undergraduate named Hanson. He told us which building and which staircase, and a few minutes later we were knocking on Hanson's door.

A young man with a shock of fair hair and a vague expression on his face opened the door. Jack, in his authoritative lecture-room voice, explained that we were trying to learn more about Willesden, the murder victim, and believed that he, Hanson, might be able to help us. Before the young undergraduate quite realised what was happening Jack and I were in his room, clearing away books, papers and untidy clothes to find somewhere to sit down.

Now, Jack asked, was it true that Willesden was a card cheat who took money from him and from other students?

Hanson nodded and then, stuttering at first but quickly getting into his stride as anger gave him fluency, told us his story.

He had run into Willesden in the public bar at The Mitre. They knew each other from the rowing club and so settled down with their beers at a corner table. That was when Willesden produced a deck of cards and said, 'Do you know how to play Persian Monarchs?'

Hanson said he'd never heard of Persian Monarchs.

'Quite simple,' Willesden explained. 'You bet a quid or ten bob or whatever you've got that you can cut a higher card than me, and if you do, you win, and if you don't, I win.'

Hanson said it sounded a lot like Blind Hooky.

'It *is* a lot like Blind Hooky,' Willesden agreed, 'except that it's called Persian Monarchs. My uncle, Lord Ickenham, taught me how to play. Top chap, my Uncle Fred – he often played Persian Monarchs, even with complete strangers. But you're quite correct, if you can play Blind Hooky, then you can play Persian Monarchs.'

And then, said Hanson, he proceeded to take him for every shilling he had on him.

'When I was down to my last sixpence, and couldn't afford to pay for the next round of drinks, he put the deck of cards back in his pocket.'

'Was that the last time you played?' I asked.

Hanson went pink with embarrassment. 'I was determined to get my money back,' he said. 'I thought I'd just had a run of bad luck. Not so much a run as a high-speed gallop of bad luck. But I was sure it couldn't last for ever. So I played Persian Monarchs with Willesden again. On the next occasion I won several times in a row. He let me win, obviously, then he cleaned me out again.'

'Did Willesden do this with anyone else?' Jack asked.

Hanson reeled off a list of names.

'Any of them angry enough to get violent with Willesden?' I asked.

'Some of the rugby chaps wanted to give him a good thumping . . . but . . . hang on . . . you're not suggesting that . . . no . . . no . . . none of the chaps would have actually . . . no . . . not that.'

'And how angry were *you* with Willesden?' Jack probed.

'Me? You think that I . . . ? No, no, really, Mr Lewis. It's true I ended up with only pennies in my pocket, but I blamed myself. I despised Willesden, but I blamed myself for falling for it. I could never have got violent with him. Certainly not *that* violent!'

'Did you ever think of lodging a complaint with the proctors and having Willesden sent down?'

'It had occurred to me. In fact, to tell you the truth, I was seriously considering that when the matter was taken out of my hands by his murder.'

'But you can't think of anyone angry enough to . . . ?'

'No, no,' insisted Hanson, interrupting Jack's question.

The conversation went on for another ten minutes, mainly by circling around and around this point of whether Willesden had upset anyone enough to get himself murdered. And Hanson remained adamant that this was not the case.

As we left Exeter College I realised it was almost time for me to meet Penelope at the Randolph and I hurried off.

Fortunately, I wasn't late. Penelope was just coming out of the Ashmolean and walking across the road to the Randolph as I came around the corner.

'What ho!' I said.

'What ho,' she responded.

'What ho.'

'What ho.'

This continued for a bit longer – a real meeting of minds – and then I ushered her inside to the Randolph's tea room. There we ordered a pot of Darjeeling and a cream tea.

Over the first cup and the first scone with strawberry jam and clotted cream she asked what I'd been up to.

'Jack and I are conducting our own investigation into the Willesden murder.'

'You boys!' she snorted.

I ignored the snort and asked her if she had known Willesden.

My question brought an unexpected silence. Perhaps it was just that she was applying herself assiduously to the tea and scones, but it took some time before I got an answer.

'Know him? Willesden, you mean? Know him myself?'

'Yes, did you know Willesden?' I repeated my question.

'Well, yes, a little.'

'How did you know him?'

'Just ran into him here and there. As one does, you know. Why do you ask?'

'Well, we're looking for suspects, and I thought if you knew him, then you might know someone he had had a falling out with.'

'Oh, is that what you're after?' Was it my imagination, or did she breathe a sigh of relief? 'In that case, you should check out Joe Muir.'

I asked who Joe Muir was when he was at home, and she said, 'A scholarship boy, from some mining town up north. A Marxist. Raving red revolutionary. Hates inherited wealth, and determined to bring the aristocracy to their knees. Very much "Come the revolution, comrade" is our Joe Muir.'

'And Willesden had a falling out with him?'

'They almost came to blows one night in the Lamb and Flag. They had to be pulled apart.'

I took my notebook out of my pocket and jotted down the man's name and his college – he was at St John's – promising to follow up this useful lead.

Then Penelope Robertson-Smyth steered the conversation back to the only topic that really mattered – namely Penelope Robertson-Smyth.

I got a detailed report of the meeting in the Senior Common Room at St Hilda's the previous afternoon, and what it meant for who was getting into whose ear about what and what the outcome might be.

The afternoon flew by and before I knew it, it was time to leave. I paid the hovering waiter and ushered Penelope out to the street. We walked down St Giles together and then she turned to head off towards the Bodleian to do some work.

We were just about to part when I suddenly remembered my good news and called after her.

'Oh, I say, I must tell you – I almost forgot – I'm coming back to Oxford.'

'You're already in Oxford, silly boy.'

'No, I mean I'm moving back to Oxford to live – to work here. I've got that job I told you about at the *Oxford Mail*.'

Sadly Penelope must have been distracted or something because her angelic face showed rather less interest than I had hoped to see. Ah, well, I told myself, the news will sink in later, and then she'll be delighted.

Back at Magdalen there was a note pinned to the door of my room from Warnie, asking me to meet him in Jack's rooms for the next stage in our investigation.

When I arrived I found Warnie in the small sitting room, which also served as his bedroom on weeknights. There he was hammering away on an ancient typewriter on the project he called 'the Lewis Papers' – which I understood to be a history of the Lewis family over the past few generations.

'Ah, Morris, my boy,' cried Warnie with delight. 'You give me an excuse to rest from my labours. I suggest,' he added, rising from the desk, 'that you and I follow up Tolkien's idea in the Case of the Missing Milton.'

I asked in what way, and he said we should do the rounds of Oxford antiquarian booksellers to see if we could smell anything fishy.

'What do we ask them? How do we prompt an aroma of dead fish to arise?'

'I've thought about that,' Warnie said. 'We'll ask if they could rebind an old book for us – not with new leather and a new binding, but if they could find an old binding of the appropriate age for the damaged book we have. We'll suggest the seventeenth century.'

'Clever,' I admitted. 'That might get an interesting reaction.'

And so we set out on our tour of Oxford antiquarian booksellers.

There turned out to be rather more of them than I had expected. The larger, long-standing establishments we both thought were above suspicion, but we still started there to see what sort of reaction our question might get. This was consistently negative: old covers without contents, and thus available for such a rebinding job, were very rare and they doubted they could help us.

What surprised me was the number of smaller dealers, some with stalls in the covered market, some operating in back streets and small lanes.

But even these were largely disappointing. Some were old codgers who appeared to be barely scraping a living, others were clearly dealing in second-hand modern popular books despite the world "antiquarian" in their title.

To be honest, I had given up all hope of this line of enquiry until our last port of call. This was a small shop in a narrow lane not far from the town hall.

We pushed open the dingy front door and walked down several steps into the dark shadows that filled the shop. The place was empty but the bell connected to the front door caused a voice to call out from an inner room, 'Coming. Coming. Just a moment.'

From a dark doorway behind the counter a small, middle-aged man appeared. He was so thin and spindly that he looked like an artist's preliminary sketch – most of the fleshy details being left out. The shop was as dark as a cave, and it was hard to see the stock, which filled the walls and every available surface. I found myself trying to negotiate piles of books that stood on the floor – and in the dim light that was difficult.

'I wonder if you can help us, old chap?' Warnie began. And then he spelled out our test question.

'Ah, a seventeenth-century binding, eh? To repair an old book, you say?'

There was a long silence as the proprietor leaned forward and squinted at our faces. Then he seemed to make up his mind.

'Yes, it's just possible I might be able to help you,' he said slowly. 'Mind you – it won't be cheap.'

'Price no object, old chap,' said Warnie with hearty enthusiasm. 'Price no object.'

'Well, in that case,' said the old codger, and I could swear that he was almost rubbing his hands together in anticipation. 'Do you have your damaged book with you? No? Well, I'll have a hunt among my stock, and I'll have a firm answer when you come back with the book you want rebound.'

A little later, standing out on the street, adjusting to the daylight after the dimly lit shop, I turned to look at the small sign on the front door.

'William Hare,' I read aloud. 'Antiquarian Books and Collectibles. I presume that old specimen was William Hare.'

'Not a name we'll forget in a hurry,' Warnie grunted. 'Hare – as in Burke and Hare. Come on, let's report our results to Jack.'

TWELVE

~

That night I dined at high table in the Hall at Magdalen as Jack's guest. It was, he told me, to celebrate the good news of my appointment to the staff of the *Oxford Mail*.

'Deer can't survive with their throat cut.'

There is only one place in the world where you can get this kind of intellectually stimulating conversation and original creative thinking, and that is at an Oxford college high table.

The speaker was an elderly don named Webster. When I say 'elderly', I must confess to being uncertain as to his actual age. He appeared to be either a robust man in his late nineties, or a chap in his early sixties who'd led a hard life.

'Deer can't survive with their throat cut.'

Up until that point our talk had been dealing with Einstein's Theory of Relativity, but we readily adjusted our minds to cope with this new topic.

'That was a month ago, Webster,' grumbled Mallison, who was sitting on my right hand.

'I believe the police investigated the matter,' said Jack, who was seated on my left, 'and they concluded it was local lads on a drunken night out who'd managed to get into our deer park.'

'But they never caught them, did they?' Webster said triumphantly.

'What happened?' I asked.

'Found a deer,' Webster wheezed quietly into his dinner plate, making it difficult to hear. 'One of the gardeners found it. Under one of the old oaks it was. Deep cut in its neck. Head almost off. Deer can't survive with their throat cut. The police should have caught the villains who did it. If they can't catch local deer killers, they'll never find out who killed Willesden.'

'There should be an IQ test for police officers wishing to join the detective branch,' Mallison suggested.

'Solving puzzling crimes may involve more than multiple synapses in the frontal lobe,' Jack suggested.

'Such as?' I asked.

'Imagination, above all else. The ability to imagine possibilities that have occurred to no one else. And the imagination to see into the mind and life of the victim – and from the victim into the mind and life of the killer.'

'So if we look into Willesden's mind, what do we find?' I asked.

'He was a killer,' Mallison said.

'Really?' I was astonished.

'Killed my daughter. Mind you, it was a road accident. No one's fault. These things happen. But perhaps it weighed on his mind? Coloured his personality?'

'I never got the impression very much weighed on Willesden's mind,' said Webster. 'Or what there was of it. But you tutored him in Modern History, Mallison, what did you make of his mind?'

'Efficient. But lacking, Lewis, in the quality you talked about – imagination. I tried to get him to picture the history he was studying, imagine himself in those circumstances, but his learning ended at facts, figures and quotations.'

'He was a cat,' said Wilkes from the end of the table, where he loomed like the overweight ghost at the feast.

'In what sense?' someone asked.

'The world is divided into dogs and cats – into dog people and cat people – into pack animals and solitary dwellers. Dogs seek companionship while cats have never quite got over having been worshipped as gods in Ancient Egypt, and thus tend to look down on all with whom they associate.'

This description of Willesden as a 'cat' certainly seemed to fit in with my conversation with the man on the last night of his earthly life.

'I have only just discovered,' Mallison said, 'that Wilkes' Christian name is Theodore. You don't look in the least like a Theodore, Wilkes. Don't you feel like a fraud being called Theodore when you don't look anything like a Theodore?'

'Names are not just for the moment,' said Wilkes haughtily, 'they are badges we wear for ever.'

This took the conversation in the direction of the Final Destination of the Soul and then on to whether pork fat was good or bad for the heart – would extend life or shorten it. Conversation at high table tended to be wide-ranging.

At length dinner came to an end. A senior student recited a Latin grace, and all at the high table rose to depart for the Senior Common Room and port and nuts.

Just as we left the Hall, Mallison appeared between Jack and myself and said, 'I have a much better port in my room – if you'd care to join me?'

And the port in his room was, indeed, as good as he promised: a vintage tawny port that had a deep richness to it.

'Now, isn't that better,' Mallison asked, 'than the invalid port they've been buying in bulk for the buttery lately?'

Jack and I both agreed it was, and Mallison poured each of us a second glass.

With my glass in my hand I stood up and walked around to look at Mallison's bookshelves. It's a habit of mine – I believe you can find out more about a man's mental furniture from his bookshelves than from any other source.

As you would expect there was volume after volume on history – mostly from the earliest period of history. Surprisingly, there were also shelves of popular thrillers. 'You share Wilkes' taste in light reading,' I said.

Then I came upon a shelf that contained the books Mallison himself had written: there were biographies of Maximilien Robespierre, Joseph-Ignace Guillotin and Marie Antoinette.

'It's clear what your special period of interest is,' I commented.

Jack chuckled and suggested that Mallison might burst into a chorus of the Marseillaise at the drop of a hat.

Mallison was himself amused and said with a smile, 'More likely at the drop of a *bonnet rouge.*'

'What's that?' I asked.

'A liberty cap,' Mallison explained, 'one of the symbols of the Jacobins. It's what France's national figure Marianne is shown wearing in most pictures.'

He passed around the port bottle once more, and I sank back into one of his comfortable armchairs.

'I was sorry to hear about your daughter,' I said. 'How did it happen? If you don't mind me asking?'

'I don't mind. It was a year ago now. I still miss her, but the pain has dulled,' said Mallison quietly. He no longer looked like an absent-minded, middle-aged don: now he was a lost and lonely middle-aged don staring into the distance and blinking furiously. 'She had a small car I'd bought her – a little Austin

Seven. A much bigger car ran into her, smashed the windscreen of the Austin Seven, and the flying glass killed her.'

'And Willesden was driving the larger car?'

'Yes. There was a hearing, of course, and the magistrate cleared him of any wrongdoing. So it was just an accident. These things happen. It doesn't make it any easier, of course,' he added, his voice dropping down to a mere murmur. 'Her mother died ten years ago. So it was just Judith and me. Now it's just me.'

He blinked his eyes and then shook his head, as if shaking away the memories.

Jack turned the conversation to more cheerful matters. Then, half an hour or so later, just as we were rising to leave, Mallison asked, 'Have the police talked to you about the murder investigation?'

Jack and I looked at each other, uncertain who Mallison was addressing.

'Either of you,' he clarified. 'Are they saying much about what they're doing, or what line of inquiry they're pursuing?'

'Only the standard background interviews so far,' Jack rumbled sonorously. 'My guess is they're still all at sea.'

'And although I'm a journalist by trade,' I said, 'I'm not a local journalist – at least, not yet – so I have no inside sources.'

'Just thought I'd ask,' Mallison muttered. 'Bad business for the college. Not good at all. Not good.'

A short time later Jack and I made our way down staircase three of the north quad building, from Mallison's top-floor rooms, into the rather chill evening air waiting for us outside. Turning through the archway, we walked slowly down the long path to the New Building, our hands in our pockets to keep them warm.

'Talking about the French Revolution,' said Jack, 'brings me back to Sidney Carton dying in the place of, or as a substitute for, Charles Darnay.'

'Which doesn't rescue your precious cross,' I told him, 'from being the ugly symbol of death that it is. Because that's what you're getting at, isn't it?'

'The death of Jesus on the cross *was* an agonising and ugly death,' Jack agreed. 'What makes it different, and what makes the symbol of the cross so powerful, is that – just like Carton's death for Darnay – Jesus died as a substitute.'

'For whom?'

'As a substitute for *my* sins, for a start,' Jack said, sounding remarkably cheerful for a man who was labelling himself a sinner. 'And not for mine only, but for the sins of the whole world, as St John says in one of his letters.'

'Is that legal?' I asked querulously. 'Is it legally proper for one person to substitute themselves for someone else – or for a lot of someone elses? How can a penalty against one person be shifted to another?'

A gleam entered Jack's eye and he plunged gleefully into the battle of ideas.

'Think of it this way,' he said. 'Let's say you owed a large debt to the bank, and you were taken to court and threatened with punishment if you failed to pay – and just when the bailiffs were about to be given orders to seize all your worldly goods, I walked into the court and paid your debts . . . would there be anything illegal or unjust about that?'

I had to think about this for a minute. Finally, I reluctantly agreed that such a thing would, most probably, be quite proper in the eyes of the law.

'But what if it wasn't me?' Jack continued.

'Wasn't you who what?'

'If it wasn't me – your entirely loveable old ex-tutor – who came rushing into the courtroom to rescue you by paying your debts. What if, instead, the judge himself stepped down from the bench, dipped into his own pocket and paid your debts? How would that stand in the eyes of the law?'

Probably much the same, I agreed. All the law would care about would be seeing the debt paid. Money, after all, is money. Where it came from wouldn't matter, as long as the debt was paid.

'Well, think of the cross in those terms – as the symbol of the judge himself stepping down from the bench and paying your debt and my debt. Does that make the cross a very different sort of symbol?'

'Hang on, hang on. This is not about money, it's about death – it's about an execution. How can your notion of sub-stitution work in that case?'

'It depends, surely, on the nature of the debt you owe,' Jack said. We had stopped our perambulations and were standing in the middle of the path with a soft, cool breeze blowing gently around us. Jack was in his element – for some reason he seemed to love cool weather. 'The Bible says that "the wages of sin is death",' he continued. 'So what if the debt you owe is a life – a death.'

'You mean there is something I've done that can only be paid for by death?'

'That's exactly what I mean.'

'Well, in that case,' I said, 'if I had done something so horrible that it called for my death – not that I ever have, of course – but if so, how could someone else come along and say, "I'll die his death". If it was me who did the something horrible, then surely it must be me who does the dying?'

Jack chuckled softly. As we moved on again, he said, 'Your brain is as sharp as ever, young Morris. I'm delighted to see that. But cast your mind back to the medieval texts we read together. You'll recall that under medieval law a king, or a nobleman, could be represented on the battlefield, or in the lists at a tournament, by his chosen champion. Especially so if the champion came forward of his own accord and said, "I will take your place, my lord. I will carry your banner. I will be your champion." Do you remember those kinds of instances?'

I said yes, I did.

'That's exactly what's happening on the cross. Jesus steps forward, willingly, of his own accord, fulfilling his Father's will for him, his Father's plan for him, and says, "I will be their champion – I will go onto the field of battle in their place." And on that "field of battle" he took the full weight of the penalty that should have fallen on you. And it killed him.'

My breath was forming a mist in front of my face. And I realised that, so hypnotised had I been by Jack's conversation, I was walking with him towards his room – in the New Building – rather than mine – in north quad.

'I think I'm going the wrong way,' I said, glancing around.

'That's when life changes,' Jack said with a sunny smile. 'When we realise we are going the wrong way – and turn around!'

THIRTEEN

~

The next morning I had a hearty – you might even say extremely large – breakfast consisting of several helpings of bacon, eggs and sausages and piles of hot, buttered toast. In truth, I was making up for the fact that I had slept badly. I had taken nearly two hours to fall asleep. It was my conversation with Jack that kept going around and around inside my head and refused to let me drop off. I made a mental note never to argue with Jack late at night.

In fact, I ate so much that morning I felt I was waddling – or perhaps wallowing like a flat-bottomed boat in a large swell at sea – as I walked through the north quad archway and headed towards the New Building.

I came out of the arch into morning sunshine that was being generously scattered around the place under a dome of blue sky. There were just a few white clouds drifting in decorative patterns. The morning was cool but sunny and still, without a breath of air. It was as if the weather was keeping its options open depending on what sort of mood it found itself in later in the day.

Standing still and enjoying the fresh air for a moment, I saw one of the older gardeners step back from a flower bed, pull off his gardening gloves and throw them down on the ground with a look of disgust on his face. He was a disgruntled gardener. I'm tempted to say that I'd never seen a gardener look less gruntled (except that 'gruntled' and 'disgruntled' mean exactly the same thing).

I recognised him from my days as a member of the college, so I said, 'You look unhappy, Alf.'

'Who's that? Ah, it's you, Mr Morris. Nice to see you again, sir. Well, sir, I am positive cranky and that's the truth.'

I took a step towards the garden and asked him to explain.

He puffed and groaned like an ancient steam locomotive building up boiler pressure. Then, like a steam whistle being released, he burst out with his complaint.

'Someone's chopped the roots off my rose bushes,' he growled. 'Now why would anyone do a daft thing like that? Eh? Why?'

'Your rose bushes are famous, Alf, so I can't believe anyone would attack them.'

'There's those as don't appreciate beautiful things, Mr Morris, and that's the truth.'

'But surely none of the young men in the college would attack your legendary roses? Everyone admires them, Alf – everyone.'

'It's nice of you to say such kind words, Mr Morris. But, no, I don't believe it *was* our young men here who done it.'

'Then who?'

'It were town not gown. That's what I think. There've been some yahoos in town lately – young chaps who are on the production line out at the motor works at Cowley. There've been one or two fights between town and gown – when they've had a skinful on a Saturday night. Nothing big, mind you. Unpleasant, just the same. Aye, it's them that's done this.'

He frowned in angry silence for a moment, and then he added, 'And did you hear about the deer over the grove yonder?'

'I was told about it last night at high table. I gather someone actually killed one of the deer.'

'They did. That they did. And the police never found who done it, neither. Well, not satisfied with the deer they've come and had a go at my roses. See here, you have a look.'

He scraped away a layer of dirt with his spade and showed me where the roots of some old, long-established rose bushes had been cut straight through. Alf's face contorted in agony as he inspected the damage. He looked like a man who'd just ripped a piece of sticking plaster off the hairy part of his leg.

'It's vandalism, Alf, that's what it is,' I said. 'Just plain vandalism. Will you report it?'

'Well, I'll tell Mr Murray. If he wants to tell the police about what they've done, that's up to him.'

'Will the rose bushes recover?'

'If I look after them proper, and I will. So, yes, they'll recover, but not soon enough to give us a really good display through spring and summer.'

A few minutes later when I arrived at Jack's rooms I told Jack and Warnie about the vandalism of the rose bushes. Warnie clucked his tongue sympathetically and then offered to put the kettle on.

A moment later there was a tap on the door and Professor Tolkien walked in.

'Tollers, delightful to see you, old chap,' cried Warnie. 'I'm just putting the kettle on, will you join us?'

Tolkien said yes and Warnie asked him the purpose of his visit.

'Not social,' said the professor. 'There are matters to do with English Department politics I need to discuss with Jack.'

As we waited for the kettle to boil, I repeated my story about the vandalism of Alf's famous Magdalen roses.

'The mysteries multiply,' said Tolkien. 'Both large and small, we seem to be surrounded by mysteries. Speaking of which, have we heard anything from your friend Inspector Crispin?'

'Not yet,' Jack said. 'No doubt he'll drop in for a chat when he's ready to review the case. Have you heard anything new?'

'On my way through I stopped to chat with the scout on staircase three in north quad,' Tolkien responded. 'I am just as intrigued as anyone else. He's been questioned repeatedly by the police, he tells me, and he remains adamant that the door was locked and bolted on the inside. He's also quite certain that both sash windows were latched. So how the head and the weapon were removed from the room remains the biggest mystery of all.'

'Speaking of mysteries,' said Warnie, bring a tea tray over to the big table in the middle of the room. 'Young Morris and I have continued our investigation into the mystery of the Missing Milton. I'm determined to keep going on this until I clear Jack's name.'

Over tea Warnie told the story of our – largely fruitless – trudge around the antiquarian booksellers of Oxford, ending up with the possibility that Mr William Hare might give us a doorway to discovering what really happened.

'Could there have been some motive other than money for the theft of the Milton pages?' I asked.

'Possibly,' said Jack with a cunning smile. 'Perhaps, for example, someone who objected to Milton's theology.'

I asked what there was to object to.

'By the end of his life Milton was holding views that most middle-of-the-road, reasonable Christians would find offensive.'

'Did he?' asked Tolkien. 'I knew he started life as a Puritan of some sort, and thus vigorously anti-Catholic.'

'So he certainly offended your branch of the Christian family,' Jack agreed. 'But he moved on to become almost anti-Puritan and certainly anti-orthodox in what he denied.'

Tolkien asked, what did he deny? Jack replied, 'The divinity of Christ. He denied that Christ was the loving maker and ruler of the universe come in human form. Now, the Christian faith is a big tent, but such a view as that puts him right outside the big tent altogether – possibly on the other side of the fairground.'

Tolkien agreed that Catholics as well as Protestants would find such views offensive.

Jack drank his tea and smoked his pipe in silence for a minute.

'But the answer to your question, Morris, is no,' he said at length. 'I firmly believe a theft such as this must have been motivated by money – by simple greed – and nothing else. People who are offended by Milton, or dislike Milton's theology, write articles for journals, they don't vandalise libraries.'

'Speaking of which,' said Warnie, 'while I have you and Tollers together I have a question for you both. Of all the students you know who are reading English at the moment, can either of you think of one who had enough interest in Milton, and enough knowledge of Milton, to know what to steal . . . if he was so motivated?'

Tolkien looked at Jack, and Jack looked back at the professor and smiled. Their eyes lit up.

'We're both thinking of the same name, I believe,' Tolkien said. 'There's an undergraduate named Guilford who, throughout Hilary Term, kept asking questions about Milton.'

'And Bennett told me,' Jack added, 'that at one stage he was even asking questions about early editions of Milton. Now, he may just have been interested in the possibility of Milton correcting the text between the first and the second editions; however . . .'

'Sounds like our man!' cried Warnie with delight. 'What's his other name, this Guilford?'

'Nicolas,' Tolkien replied. 'Nicolas Guilford.'

'Young Morris,' Warnie said with enthusiasm, 'you and I are going to interview Mr Nicolas Guilford in order to find out whatever we may find out.'

I think he might have leapt up to start then and there if we hadn't been interrupted by a knock on the door.

Our visitor was Inspector Gideon Crispin.

He was offered a cup of tea and settled at the table and then he was peppered with questions:

Had the head been found yet?

Had the weapon been found?

Did he have any suspects?

Was the room definitely locked from the inside when the body was found?

Crispin held up his hand to stem the flood.

'The answer to those questions, in order,' he said, 'is no, no, no, and yes. We're spreading the search out wider – I've left Sergeant Merrivale in charge of that – and we're being extremely thorough. This is just routine police work, so this is the sort of thing we're good at. But so far: no head and no weapon. As for the room – I've inspected that myself and the splintered wood of the door frame is conclusive evidence that the room was locked from the inside. As for the windows – they're ordinary sash windows, which latch when they close, and both were closed and latched when the body was discovered. On top of which, they are not especially large windows, so it would be difficult to get a body in or a large weapon out. I'm not saying impossible – just difficult.'

We all drank our tea in silence for a minute while we absorbed this.

'Then,' Crispin resumed, 'there's the time of the murder. The police pathologist says Willesden appears to have died in the early hours of the morning. The headless body was dressed in pyjamas and the bed was crumpled.'

'So after I spoke with him,' I said, 'he retired to bed and then ... what? Got up in the early hours of the morning in order to be murdered by some mysterious method as yet unknown?'

'Not a bad summary, Mr Morris,' agreed the Scotland Yard man.

'Did anyone see or hear anything in those silent, early hours of the morning?' Jack asked.

'We're covering that, Mr Lewis,' Crispin said reassuringly. 'I've had the local uniformed officers go door to door around the quad. Because it's break, quite a few rooms are empty, and of the rest no one had their sleep disturbed – no one saw or heard anything. Even one don who was up all night preparing a paper for a conference says he didn't hear a sound.'

'A not only mysterious but also silent murder,' I remarked.

'It seems so,' Crispin agreed. 'And of course once the gates are locked there is no one on duty. All the college servants were also in bed. However ...'

And with this he pulled out of his pocket a brown envelope, unfolded it, opened it up and shook its contents onto Jack's table.

'What on earth is that?' asked Tolkien.

Warnie picked it up and examined it. 'It's a small iron bolt tied to a length of fishing line,' he said.

'Exactly, sir.'

Jack asked where it had been found.

'In the garden bed immediately underneath Mr Willesden's window. And because of that location we wonder if it might have had something to do with the murder. At the moment, however, we can't imagine what that might be.'

'Of course, it could have been there for quite a while,' I suggested.

'The gardeners say not. They've been working in that area for the past week. So this object, whatever it is, has turned up at around the time of the murder. I admit we're baffled. Does this suggest anything to Mr Lewis?'

Jack laughed heartily and said, 'Thank you for your vote of confidence in my omniscience. But this odd thing suggests nothing at all to me at the moment.'

'Why don't you go on thinking about it for me, Mr Lewis,' urged Inspector Crispin. 'A flash of inspiration might come.'

FOURTEEN

~

It was a little later that morning when I was walking through the covered market that I spotted the Perfect Profile coming towards me.

Because, like most men, I am hopeless at packing a bag, I had run out of socks, and I was there to buy a couple of pairs – and hoping to find some stylish cotton socks with clocks. I thought a bit of sartorial style might impress Penelope – and suddenly, in the midst of shopping, there she was.

At almost the same moment that I spotted her, Penelope Robertson-Smyth spotted me.

'What ho, reptile!' she said affectionately.

'What ho, worm!' I replied lovingly. To which I added, to make the greeting complete, 'What ho, what ho, what ho.'

'What have you been up to?' asked the Vision of Loveliness.

'You mean apart from getting a job here in Oxford so you and I can see each other more often? Apart from, I suppose you mean, investigating the Mystery of the Missing Milton and taking an interest in the Mystery of the Headless Corpse and discovering the Mystery of the Vandalised Roses – apart from all those, you mean? Well, that's what I've been up to.'

'Not much, then.'

'And what about you – what have you been up to?'

'Oh, the usual. Now, tell me,' said Penelope, grabbing the conversation and sending it spinning wildly off the road, 'what do you think of neo-Vorticist poetry?'

'Just the usual *vers libre* rubbish,' I said, snapping off a nifty one-liner.

Suddenly her voice, and her face, turned arctic as she uttered one word: 'Really?' Somehow she managed to make that one word sound like the outbreak of blizzard conditions in the Klondike.

This abrupt change in the weather pattern alerted me to a wrong move on my part, so I started pedalling backwards as fast as I could.

'That is to say . . .' I said, trying to work out where to go to next. 'That is to say . . . well . . . *vers libre* is *vers libre*, don't you know? And the Vorticist branch . . . that is to say the neo-Vorticist branch . . . is actually . . . the most . . .' But I ran out of words before I'd got my foot out of the pothole I'd fallen into or, indeed, out of my mouth.

She sent me a tingling look that shot straight through my spleen and embedded itself somewhere in my spine.

'*I write* neo-Vorticist poetry!' said Penelope coldly, thus making the deep freeze complete. At that moment the air between us was about minus four-hundred degrees kelvin.

'Oh . . . oh . . . oh . . .' I stuttered.

'Several new pieces of mine have just been published in a small literary magazine in London,' said the ice queen, declining to thaw at all.

'I'd love to see a copy,' I responded, adding my warmest smile.

'So you could throw it in the rubbish bin, I suppose? Along with every other piece of *vers libre* poetry?'

My warm smile having failed to make the mercury start spluttering upwards in the thermometer, I decided to try another approach.

'Of course, when I read English as an undergraduate,' I said as humbly as I could, trying to out-humble Uriah Heep, 'I never really got past the eighteenth century. The course actually stopped in the early nineteenth century. So I've never really had a chance to study what the moderns are up to. Perhaps,' I added hopefully, 'you would like to complete my education?'

At this the ice cracked a little and a small, cunning smile appeared on Penelope's face.

'What a deprived upbringing you've had,' she said, and she almost sounded sympathetic.

'Did you say "deprived" or "depraved"?' I asked.

Ignoring my feeble attempt at humour she continued, 'I think I need to take you in hand. Yes, you need to be firmly taken in hand and properly introduced to the world of modern literature. Starting with *Spindrift* by my friend Florence Craye and followed by a small volume of neo-Vorticist verse published in a limited edition by one of the smaller presses – which just happens to contain half a dozen of my pieces.'

'Yes, yes, by all means, take me in hand. I'm sure I'd find that very . . . very enriching.'

At that moment I think she saw me as the subject for an interesting experiment.

'We could meet in my rooms with a volume of modern verse and a bottle of red wine,' said Penelope, looking at me as if I was a specimen at the bottom of a glass jar in a laboratory.

What she proposed sounded just delightful. To sit sipping red wine with Penelope in her room I would even put up with modern poetry.

She agreed that this would be the next step in my development towards becoming a human being, but declined to set a date for the time being.

However, we parted on a more-or-less friendly note and I went off to buy socks with clocks.

Five minutes later, having purchased some extremely stylish socks certain to impress Penelope, I wandered out of the covered market in the general direction of the Cornmarket to buy a newspaper and find a telephone booth where I could call George Rainbird and settle the exact terms of my employment and my starting date.

I had bought my paper and made my phone call when I saw Jack and Professor Tolkien, and scampering after them, like a small terrier bouncing along behind its master, was the rather odd David Bracken. In fact, I'm not sure his tongue wasn't hanging out.

As I approached the group, I discovered that Bracken was asking them endless questions and that both Jack and Tolkien were being patient and indulgent with him.

I heard Bracken asking, 'So exactly how did you come up with the idea for Hobbits, professor?'

There was no notebook visibly present, but Bracken sounded exactly like one of my journalistic colleagues conducting an interview.

'I don't really know,' said Tolkien vaguely but patiently. 'They just sprang into my head. I remember I was marking exam papers at the time, and one candidate had left the last page of his answers blank. Well, I ask you – a blank sheet of paper? That's impossible to resist, isn't it? So I dipped my pen into my inkwell and wrote, "In a hole in the ground there lived a Hobbit." Until that moment Hobbits didn't exist. So, where did they spring from? You tell me, for I haven't the faintest idea.'

'It's the great mystery of how the human imagination works,' said Jack. 'You should read Coleridge on the imagination.'

'Good morning, Jack, morning, professor,' I said, interrupting Bracken's line of questioning. 'Morning, Bracken – I see you've managed to meet these two distinguished dons, even without my introduction.'

Bracken went bright pink and said, 'Well, I introduced myself really. Bit of a cheek, I know, but there you are.'

'Not at all, old chap, not at all,' said Jack heartily. 'Now, as I said – Coleridge on the imagination, that's where you should go. It's the consideration of objects of the mind. But where those objects come from remains mysterious.'

'There are theories about the subconscious,' said Tolkien, 'but I believe imagination is part of what makes us human. We were made by a Creator, and we were made in his image. Now, stop and think about that, Mr Bracken: when a Creator makes beings in his own image, what will be one of their defining characteristics? Naturally they will also be creators – just like their maker, whom they resemble. They will be, if you like, sub-creators – fashioning new patterns from the whole of creation around them, and reassembling parts of the creation into new forms never known before. But exactly how that happens, I don't really know. They just "flash upon that inward eye" – not remembered daffodils, but new forms reassembled by the human who is a sub-creator.'

'Chesterton writes about something similar,' Jack said. 'In the opening chapters of *The Everlasting Man* he speaks of human creativity as being definitive evidence that humans are made in the image of the Creator who made them.'

All of this I could see was going down in Bracken's invisible notebook, so I said good morning to the trio and kept walking.

As I strode down the High Street towards the college I dwelt on the oddness of Bracken and tried to make some sense of it.

Did his strange behaviour reflect the character of whatever colonial university he came from?

Swinging in through the gates of Magdalen, I saw Murray the head porter standing there – a formal smile on his face and his bowler hat on his head.

'Ah, Murray,' I greeted him, 'did Alf tell you about his roses?'

'Good morning, Mr Morris. Yes, he did indeed, sir.'

'Are you going to report it to the police?'

'I think not, sir. What would be the point? Upsetting though it is, vandalism is not the sort of thing the police are likely to put much in the way of resources into just at the moment, are they, sir?'

'You mean with an impossible murder on their plate? No, I suppose you're right.'

We chatted about the damage done to Alf's famous roses for several more minutes, and then I came out of the porter's lodge, walked under the Muniment Tower and into the cloister quad.

It was only when I was climbing staircase two that the subject of David Bracken sprang back into my mind. I recalled that his room was also on this staircase, on the landing below mine.

Now, I thought to myself, if he's still in the Cornmarket cross-examining Jack and Tolkien, and if his door should be unlocked, what is there to stop me from having a little look inside his room? What is there to stop me from trying to find something that might help me to understand his odd character and weird behaviour?

Nothing! That's the reply I gave to myself. There was nothing to stop me from doing a little investigating into the strange David Bracken. And, I told myself – searching for some justification for my curiosity – if we have a strange person living in college when strange things are happening, perhaps there's a connection? Perhaps he had something to do with our murder?

Or even with our other mysteries: the Missing Milton and the Vandalised Roses?

By now I had thoroughly convinced myself that he was worth investigating.

I tried the door. It wasn't locked. Doors were often left unlocked in college, so I wasn't surprised. I pushed the door a little harder and it swung wide open. I stepped inside.

It was a typical undergraduate's room with one bed, one desk, and against the side wall a surprisingly large wardrobe. The room was empty, as I had expected. I took a pace forward and looked around.

It was surprisingly neat. Everything was in its place. There were no loose sheets of notepaper covered in writing – something that might have given me a clue to the mysterious Mr Bracken. And – rather more surprisingly – there were not many books.

Among the few books lying on the desk I recognised a first edition of Jack's first book, *The Pilgrim's Regress*. I picked this up and thumbed through it. It was heavily underlined and the margins were filled with notations – all in the same neat, small handwriting (Bracken's, I assumed).

I was just considering sliding open the desk drawers or opening up the suitcase that stood at the end of the bed when I got the shock of my life.

The wardrobe door opened and David Bracken stepped out!

'Ah, Morris,' he said, looking as startled as I felt. His mouth flapped open like a mullet in a fish shop window that's not too sure how it got there, and is looking around for that nice cool Atlantic water it was swimming in only a short time before.

'Ah, yes, Bracken, just dropped in to . . . to apologise . . . for not having introduced you to Jack and Tolkien when I'd promised to . . . or more or less promised to,' I stumbled.

Bracken continued to look as awkward and uncomfortable as me.

'Not at all, dear boy, not at all,' he said when he managed to recover enough to speak. 'They were very amiable when I introduced myself.'

'Good. Good. That's fine, then. Well, in that case I'll just take off . . . head up to my room.'

I turned to go, and then a thought struck me. 'I was just a little surprised to see you step out of the wardrobe. Quite took me aback, that did.'

'Just looking for my dinner suit, dear boy,' Bracken replied, having more or less recovered his sangfroid. 'Yes, the thing went missing so I couldn't come to dinner in the Hall last night. But I've found it now. It was hiding away in the back of the wardrobe. So all is well.'

'Indeed. Well, see you tonight at dinner.' And with those words I made my welcome escape and hurried up the next flight of stairs to my own room.

But as, with a sigh of relief, I entered my room and closed the door behind me, this thought struck me: what on earth was this Bracken character doing *inside* his wardrobe? I mean to say, most of us can find any item of lost clothing in the usual way – just standing on the floor and rummaging through the contents of the wardrobe. Who steps *inside* the bally thing just to find a dinner suit? And then closes the door behind him! Who does that?

The more I thought about Bracken, the less I understood.

FIFTEEN

~

Naturally, I wanted to discuss David Bracken's 'oddness' with Jack. So after lunch I headed towards his rooms.

'In the wardrobe,' I said. 'He was actually *in* the wardrobe. With the door closed!'

Warnie chuckled and said, 'I've come across some rum coves in my time in the army, but that's a new one on me.'

'Extraordinary I call it,' I said, 'dashed odd. Very, very odd.'

'An excellent word, young Morris,' said Jack. 'A simple, clear, one-syllable word. A month or so ago I overheard two of my pupils trying to describe eccentric behaviour. One of them labelled such behaviour as "funny". The other asked, "Do you mean *funny ha-ha* or *funny peculiar?*" Now, that is a revolting expression. To replace "odd" with "funny peculiar" is a clear case of verbicide! You'd expect that to come only from someone for whom English was a second language, but these two pupils both came from good English schools.'

'Quite right, Jack,' snorted Warnie, 'quite right. It's a horrible expression, "funny peculiar", and apart from anything else it's six syllables, while "odd" is only one.'

'And "odd" has been a part of our language for centuries – we don't need to replace it now with something clumsier and less euphonious,' Jack added.

'As a matter of curiosity,' I asked, 'where does "odd" come from?'

'From a Middle English word behind which, as I learned from Tollers, lies an Old Norse expression.'

'Did "odd" always mean what we mean by it now? Did it always mean "eccentric"?' I asked.

'In Chaucer's day it referred to numbers,' Jack said.

'Ah, yes, of course,' I exclaimed, 'as in odd and even numbers.'

'Exactly. To begin with it meant the third man – the extra person – the one who ended up with the casting vote if the vote was split evenly between the rest. From this it came to mean the solitary person, a bit separated, left over from the rest. And you can see how that leads to the transferred sense of eccentric.'

'Well, that's what Bracken is,' I said, returning to the subject, 'definitely eccentric or odd.'

'Did he offer an explanation?' Warnie asked.

'He said he was looking for his dinner suit.'

Jack threw back his head and hooted with laughter: 'Ho, ho, ho! An odd explanation for odd behaviour. It would almost have been disappointing if he'd had a sensible explanation.'

'I'm trying to think of one,' said Warnie, scratching his head. 'How about this – looking for a dropped cufflink at the back of the wardrobe and the door swung closed behind him.'

'I'm sure if he'd thought of it, he would have said it,' Jack chuckled. 'Instead of which he remains the very embodiment of oddness.'

'And while we're on the subject of oddities,' I said, 'you have so far failed to persuade me that the cross – an implement of vicious death – is not a very odd symbol for you Christians to adopt as your most prominent and common symbol.'

'But again,' Jack said, 'odd is exactly the right word. Because the death of Jesus on the cross was, in a way, a very odd thing to happen. It was not what anyone expected. It was not the way those devout early followers of Jesus – Peter, John, Andrew and the rest – expected God to behave.'

I asked him to explain, so Jack went on, 'As good, devout Jews they knew God had promised an "anointed one" – in Hebrew a "messiah", in Greek a "christos" – because such a one *was* promised and prophesied and foreshadowed throughout their Bible (which we know today as the Old Testament). And when Jesus of Nazareth arrived on the scene they were convinced he was this long-promised "anointed one". So they knew who he was, but they didn't understand what he'd come to do.'

'Surely he'd come to do whatever this long-promised anointed one was supposed to come and do?' I said, feeling puzzled.

'Which was to win a victory for God's people. But for a long time God's people had been defined in ethnic and political terms – so they expected a *political* victory. What Jesus understood, and tried to get them to understand, was that his real task was a very different sort of victory. That's what was so odd. He was expected to deliver a political triumph, while his intention all along – his real task – was to die.'

'What sort of a victory is that?'

'A victory over death, darkness and evil.'

'But your cross – an implement of execution – doesn't look much like a victory!' I protested. 'It looks like a memorial to yet another martyr's tragic early death. Nothing very victorious in that.'

'If,' rumbled Jack, leaning forward across the table to make his point and enunciating each word clearly, 'his death was as my substitute – if he died my death, and suffered my punishment, and purchased my forgiveness – that looks to me like a great victory. And if he died not only for me but for millions of others as well, that is a victory on a gigantic scale. And if he then went on to conquer death itself on my behalf – that's a victory on a cosmic scale.'

Jack stopped to relight his pipe, which had gone out, and then he continued, 'That was the unexpected, surprising victory Jesus won. That's why, when the local Roman ruler – the great earthly power of that day – seized him he said, "My kingdom is not of this world." I think he left the local Roman governor slack-jawed with amazement. He'd been told this Nazarene was a political rabble-rouser, and yet this man was claiming a cosmic kingdom, not an earthly one, and knew he had to die to win it for his people.'

'I would never have thought of calling that "odd", but you're quite right, Jack,' muttered Warnie, 'to his first followers it must have looked mighty odd. He was this powerful orator who could move the masses, heal the sick and raise the dead, and as soon as a bunch of Roman soldiers turns up he stops his followers resisting and lets the military march him away. They must have been dumbfounded, that little band that saw him led away by armed men.'

'They little understood at the time that in walking to his death he was walking to his great victory. Of course, within days the light had dawned and they *did* understand. One of the old Puritan theologians wrote a book about the cross called *The Death of Death in the Death of Christ*. A good title, for that's exactly what he achieved. That was his very "odd" victory.'

Every time this subject came up, I very quickly started feeling overwhelmed with information, and I knew I needed time to absorb this, process it and work how to respond. That meant it was time for me to steer the conversation in other directions.

'I've run into a friend,' I said, 'someone I knew when we were both undergraduates. She's a junior don at St Hilda's these days, and it seems she knew Willesden a little. Anyway, she said if we're looking for people Willesden fell out with, we should start with Joe Muir. He's a Bolshevik, it seems, hates inherited wealth, and found the snobbish and privileged Aubrey Willesden more than he could stomach. I'm told they almost came to blows one night in the Lamb and Flag.'

'Really,' said Warnie, his eyebrows shooting halfway up his forehead. 'We've always found it to be a most civilised pub, haven't we, Jack?'

'Indeed. In which college is this Muir to be found?'

I said St John's, upon which Jack grabbed his battered old felt hat and said let's go and talk to him.

Joe Muir was not in his rooms in St John's, but his neighbour, on the same landing, told us that Muir had gone to the Lamb and Flag.

Exiting the college onto St Giles, we walked into the pub and saw a young man, drinking alone, at the back of the bar parlour. He was wearing a cloth cap, smoking a Gauloise, had a pint of beer in front of him and was reading a copy of the *Socialist Worker*.

'My infallible instincts as a journalist,' I said to Jack, 'tell me that's our Mr Muir. Don't ask me how I do it, I'm just amazing.'

I bought a pint each for myself and Jack, then we walked over and sat down, uninvited, at his table.

'Oh, hello,' he said, looking up from his paper. 'Who are you two?'

'My name is Lewis,' said Jack. 'I'm a don at this university. Magdalen College.'

'Yes, I've heard of you.' Then he turned and looked at me.

I just shrugged and said, 'I'm with him.'

'We're here to ask you about Willesden – Aubrey Willesden,' Jack said. 'We're told you were not very fond of him.'

'Willesden is proof – if proof were needed – that life is like stew: the scum rises.'

'Was,' Jack corrected. 'Willesden was . . . whatever you wish to say he was. But not any more. He's dead.'

'Yes, I had heard. Of course, I should have used the past tense of the verb "to be". I shouldn't confuse the tenses of my verbs when I'm talking to an English don.'

At this point I stepped into the conversation to remind Muir that Willesden had been brutally murdered.

'You see the tears in my eyes?' he asked caustically. 'Oh, no, of course you don't. There aren't any. One less parasite, that's all his death means to me.'

'So explain to me,' said Jack, in that uniquely authoritative voice of his, 'just why you and Willesden were such mortal enemies.'

'One day the scales just fell from my eyes, that's all. The industrial towns up north are filled with struggling families who survive on bread and potatoes and cups of tea. And yet this Willesden eats caviar, drinks champagne and gets a Rolls Royce ride through life. There's something wrong with that picture. That's when I suddenly realised what these Bolshevik blokes were driving at. If Stalin came wandering into this pub right now – not that he's likely to, I suppose, but if he did – I'd be the first to leap up and shake his hand. These Communists have spotted – and now I've spotted, too – that what's wrong with the world is that the cash is all in the wrong hands. What's needed is a bit of fairly rugged redistribution. I told Willesden so, too.'

'How did he take that?' I asked.

'He didn't seem to fancy it much. In fact, he quite took offence when I pointed out that all the money has been collared by a bunch of rotten bounders, while the good and deserving blokes are left standing on the outside looking in. Merit, I told him, counts for nothing where money's concerned. Look who's got it, I said, that's the proof. And I admit I was pointing at him when I said it.'

'Did he offer a counter-argument?' Jack asked.

'Not an argument as such,' said Muir. 'He just took a poke at me. In those terms he offered quite a forceful argument, although I believe I gave as well as I got.'

'I was told,' I said, 'that you almost came to blows.'

'Whoever told you that was definitely not an eyewitness,' Muir said with a sour laugh. 'There was no "almost" about it!'

I asked him what the result was, and he said they were both banned from the Lamb and Flag for a week and fair-minded onlookers were inclined to call the match a draw.

'And now,' Jack rumbled, in his most serious voice, 'Mr Willesden has been brutally murdered – as my friend Morris here said. You can understand why your name should appear on any list of suspects.'

'That's right! That's what always happens! A toff is murdered, so the police look for a bloke with a working-class background to blame. The police are just the paid servants of the rich. Well, let them come and put their handcuffs on me – I don't care. I'll make an impassioned speech from the dock about the oppression of the workers that'll make the hairs stand up on the back of your neck.'

'I take it,' Jack said gently, 'this will come just after you plead guilty?'

'Plead guilty?' Muir was outraged. 'Why would I do that? I didn't kill Willesden. According to the *Oxford Mail*, he was killed in the early hours of the morning. Well, I was here in my rooms at St John's. And the gates were locked.'

'Every student knows a way over the walls of every college,' I said quietly.

'Now, don't try that on me. I'm not guilty. I didn't kill Willesden. I shall write an article for the *Socialist Worker* about the persecution of the working class.'

Jack chuckled and said with a broad smile, 'You're a student at Oxford University – you're hardly working class.'

Muir looked a bit uncomfortable. 'Well, perhaps not now. Not at this very minute. But I was. Once. And I'm being persecuted. By you. Now leave me alone.'

SIXTEEN

~

Leaving Joe Muir to his morose, solitary drinking, we headed down St Giles past the Martyrs' Memorial.

As we passed the church of St Mary Magdalen, I glanced up at the modest stone cross on the chancel. I was about to resume my debate with Jack but I didn't get the chance. Before I could say a word we were hailed by a distinctive voice. I looked down from the church and saw, standing at the corner of Magdalen Street and the Broad, Detective Inspector Gideon Crispin of Scotland Yard.

'I was told I'd find you here,' he said as he strode towards us. 'I called at your rooms and Major Lewis said you were visiting someone at St John's.'

The inspector stopped to catch his breath, and then said, 'We've found the head.'

This dramatic announcement brought us to halt.

'If it's not too distressing for you, Mr Lewis,' Crispin continued, 'I'm asking you to come and have a look. At least at where and in what circumstances it was found. Not at the head itself, if you don't wish to – it's fairly grisly.'

'It can't be any more grisly than some of things I saw in the trenches in the Great War. Lead on.'

'Whereabouts was it found?' I asked, falling into step with the Scotland Yard man, me on one side and Jack on the other.

'In the Cherwell,' he replied. 'On the far side of the river – on the Angel Meadow bank. It was just under Magdalen Bridge, caught up in the stanchions of the bridge. Since all searches around the college property had proved so fruitless I had some uniformed officers with grappling hooks scour the waters of both the Holywell Mill Stream and the Cherwell. And after a day's searching – they found it.'

We had to walk very briskly to keep up with Crispin – so much so that walking and talking at the same time became difficult. So Jack and I kept our questions until we reached the scene.

Arriving at Magdalen Bridge we found a crowd of gawping onlookers hanging over the bridge looking at the policemen gathered on the far side.

The first thing Crispin did when we arrived at the scene of the discovery was to grab a uniformed constable and order him to disperse the crowd.

Then the other police officers stepped aside to allow Crispin – and us – to pass through to view the grim remains.

What we saw, lying on the damp grass by the water's edge, was a cricket kit bag. The bag was unfastened and was gaping open. But all we could see inside the bag was a rather muddy-looking old towel.

'The head is wrapped in that towel,' Inspector Crispin said. 'There are some stones in the bottom of the cricket bag, obviously intended to weigh it down. Any thoughts, Mr Lewis?'

'Only the obvious ones, I'm afraid, inspector. Clearly it's not far from the Magdalen cloisters to this spot, so the killer wrapped the head in a towel, and transported it in the cricket bag to the nearest point at which he could dispose of it. But you'd worked all that out for yourself.'

'Is it possible to know whose cricket bag it is?' Crispin asked.

Jack turned to me and said, 'You're the sportsman, Morris – can cricket bags be distinguished from one another?'

'Highly doubtful,' I said. 'Some chaps I've played with mark their names on the canvas of the bags with India ink – so you could look for that.'

'My men have looked,' Crispin said, shaking his head sadly. 'Nothing. No markings of any kind.'

'Then I must say that every cricket bag is pretty much like every other cricket bag. I doubt very much that you'll be able to identify the owner of this one.'

Just then an officious little man pushed his way through the crowd.

'I'm Dr Cedric Mulliner – Oxfordshire and Thames Valley official police surgeon. Inspector Fleming sent a message for me to come here. Who's in charge?'

'I am. Detective Inspector Crispin from Scotland Yard. I'd like you to take a look at the contents of this cricket bag.'

'Which are . . . ?' the doctor asked.

'A human head. My men have wrapped it back up in the towel in which they found it. They tell me it's now exactly as it was when they pulled it from the river.'

Dr Mulliner just nodded, and crouched down, placing his black doctor's bag on the grass beside him. He pulled back the opening of the cricket bag as wide as it would go and looked carefully at the contents. Then he put both hands inside and pulled out the grisly package it contained. He turned this over gently and then said, 'You won't get much off the towel, I'm very much afraid. Very plain, very common. You'll find towels exactly like this in just about every college.'

Then, taking one edge of the towel he gently drew it back.

What was underneath was an awful mess. It was covered in streaks of black mud and strands of water weeds from its time submerged, but it was still clearly a human head. The skin was deathly white and puckered from its time underwater. The hair was wet and plastered down and the eyes closed. But I still recognised it as Willesden.

The doctor turned the head over gently several times. He inspected the back of the head, and then the severed neck.

'What can you tell me, doctor?' Crispin asked.

'He's dead,' snapped the doctor. 'Anything else will have to wait until I get this back to pathology.'

'You still have the body?' the inspector asked.

'Yes, it's held in refrigeration. Has this head been formally identified?'

Jack and I both said that we could recognise Willesden from the battered remains.

'Any obvious injuries?' Crispin asked.

'Other than the severing of the neck, you mean?' the doctor responded. He gave the impression that being sarcastic with the police was his usual mode of operation. 'A first, brief, superficial examination shows no blows or slash marks other than the one that severed his neck,' he continued.

'How much force would it have taken?' Jack asked.

'Considerable force, sir,' Mulliner replied. 'A young, healthy man, with strong bones and good musculature – it would require a sharp cutting blade wielded with considerable force.'

At this point someone loomed up just behind me. I turned around and saw it was Warnie.

'Dreadful business, dreadful,' he muttered into his moustache.

As the doctor stood up he turned to Inspector Crispin and asked, 'Do you know when the murder was committed?'

'It appears to have been in the early hours of Friday morning.'

'That would be consistent with what we see here,' Mulliner said. 'My first guess is that the head has been in the water since very shortly after the murder. But I'll be able to tell you more once I've got it on the slab and examined it. Can I take it with me?'

'We're done here,' said the Scotland Yard man.

'Then if you can spare a constable to carry the bag, I'll take it straight back to the laboratory, and try to get you a preliminary report by the end of the day.'

Crispin thanked the doctor, who then left, accompanied by a constable who carried the cricket bag, to which the head had been returned. The uniformed man held the bag at arm's length and was clearly relieved to dump it in the boot of the doctor's car.

'Are you certain about the cricket bag, Mr Morris?' asked Crispin as the doctor drove away. 'Is identification really unlikely?'

'I think so,' I said. 'More than once I've seen one chap pick up another chap's kit bag after a game because they all look so much alike. It's worth checking, of course, but I wouldn't hold out much hope.'

Jack, Warnie and I left Crispin ordering his men to step up their search of the whole surrounding area in close detail as we headed back across the bridge towards Magdalen.

'A meaningless death,' I said as I stuffed my hands in my pockets. For some reason this whole business was making me feel a bit down among the wines and spirits. Understandable, I suppose.

'We journalists,' I continued, 'report on ghastly crimes, grisly murders and the rest, all the time. The only meaning it has is to fill the front pages with a sensational story people can talk about in shocked tones over their breakfast cup of tea and slice of toast and marmalade. Then the story disappears from the front page and it's forgotten. A life is over, the world moves on, and it all means nothing. Very sad.'

'A death doesn't have to be meaningless,' Jack said. 'A death can achieve something more than the end of a life. You haven't forgotten the death of the soldier who laid down his life to save another – to save the life of his brother?'

'No, of course, I hadn't forgotten. Well, perhaps for a moment I forgot, so I take back the word "meaningless". It's not exactly the word I want.'

'What you want,' said Jack, a broad grin on his face and the light of battle in his eyes, 'is to understand the meaning of a particular death – a death remembered and symbolised by that old Roman instrument of execution, the cross.'

'Yes, that's what I'm really pursuing. I want to see that death defended as being so incredibly meaningful that it justifies using an instrument of torture and death as the symbol of the Christian faith.'

'I quoted to you a little while ago those words of Jesus when he said that he "came . . . to give his life a ransom for many". He said those words as part of his explanation to his first followers that his real task in life was to die – so he had to explain why his death was necessary, and what his death would mean.'

'And his explanation was that it was a "ransom" of some sort?'

'Precisely. So how do you understand the word ransom, young Morris?'

'As a sort of purchase price, I suppose. Chicago gangsters kidnap a wealthy businessman and hold him to ransom. They demand a bucket-load of dollars – in unmarked bills of small denominations – to be delivered to a certain place at a certain time. They usually add that the police must not be informed.'

Jack laughed and said, 'You've seen too many of those Warner Brothers gangster films at the picture palace.'

'Perhaps I have,' I said with a slightly embarrassed smile. 'But I know how a ransom works. If the family make the drop-off, the kidnapped businessman is returned safe and sound. That's why I said a "ransom" is like a price paid.'

'That's the death of Jesus – a ransom, a price paid. The most immeasurably valuable price ever paid: valuable because the price was his death, and valuable because what was purchased was human souls.'

'No, no, no,' I insisted. 'My human soul has never been kidnapped and held to ransom. And I find it hard to believe that any human soul – even so noble a soul as yours, Jack – has ever been kidnapped and held to ransom.'

'How can I make this clear?' Jack muttered to himself. Then an idea occurred to him and he brightened up. 'Picture lost dogs held in a dog pound. They have run away from their owners – they are lost or strayed. No one has come to claim them, and they are scheduled to be "put down", in the polite language of the dog pound. Then along comes a stranger who pays the price to purchase those dogs.'

'But I'm not a dog in a dog pound,' I protested.

'Are you so sure?' Jack asked quizzically. 'In a large dog pound there are always some dogs that throw themselves against the wire fences, protest their incarceration, and long for freedom. But there are also dogs that just lie down peacefully in the middle of the dog pound, enjoying the free food and water and the company of so many other dogs. This second group don't even seem to realise that they don't have the freedom they might have. But they are still scheduled to be put down in a week's time. They need purchasing, they need "ransoming", even if they don't realise it.'

'And that's the kind of "purchase price", the kind of "ransom" that you see symbolised in the cross?'

'In the ancient world a ransom was, just like today, the price paid for release. It applied widely to the release of prisoners of war or of slaves. The Old Testament adds another use. In certain circumstances a man under sentence of death might be released on payment of a ransom. These things give us the use of the word "ransom" in antiquity. There's always a plight into which a man has fallen – captivity, or slavery, or condemnation. Then there's the payment of the price that brings about the release, and that price is always called the "ransom".'

SEVENTEEN

~

The following morning, the Tuesday, I again breakfasted late, having sat up late the night before puzzling over the mystery of how Willesden's body had been found in his locked room, while his head had been found in the Cherwell, in a cricket kit bag, half a mile away. I chewed over the problem until the early hours. In the morning when I awoke the puzzle looked just as tough and unchewable as it had the night before.

Hence, as I say, I went down to breakfast late. As I was walking out of the Hall, I ran into Murray, the head porter. He was standing in the cloister looking lost. Not something Murray was known for. He sometimes looked like a king surveying his kingdom, but not lost. Except on this particular morning.

'You haven't seen Mr Bracken by any chance, have you, sir?' he asked as I approached.

'Not today, I haven't – have you mislaid him?'

'It's just that his scout is worried. Mr Bracken asked his scout to call him early this morning – which he did, with a cup of tea – but Mr Bracken wasn't there. I'm told his bed has been slept in, but there's no sign of Mr Bracken.'

'He's just somewhere else in the college, that's all,' I said.

'But we've searched, Mr Morris, we've searched. He's not in the Hall and the staff tell me he hasn't been down for breakfast.

He's not in the Senior Common Room, he's not in the Denning Library or the Old Library. He hasn't visited the Bursar or the Grammar Hall. I even knocked on the door of the President's Lodgings and asked the maid who answered the door. In short, we just can't find him. And this letter arrived for him – it's marked urgent, special delivery. But we can't find him to deliver it.' Murray held up a brown manila envelope as he said these words.

'And you've looked everywhere?'

'Every blessed place in this college, sir. And if it hadn't been for what happened to Mr Willesden, we might just assume he's around somewhere and we've missed him. But after Mr Willesden . . . well, sir . . . we don't like to take chances.'

'Could he have left college last night? Stayed somewhere else overnight?'

'He was seen in his room, sir, after the gates were locked. And Mr Bracken never struck me as the type to go climbing walls.'

'I agree. Not a wall climber, I would have said. So will you break down his door?'

'No need, sir – it's not locked.'

'So, you've checked inside?'

'The scout did early this morning, and I did just a while ago. There's no sign of him.'

'Would you like me to have a look?'

'Would you, sir? I would be grateful. It's just that after Mr Willesden we have a duty of care, you see, sir.'

So I went back to staircase two – the staircase I shared with Bracken.

On Bracken's landing I tried his door. I knocked, then I opened it. It swung inwards, revealing a deserted room. It looked much the same as it had the last time I was there.

Remembering that last occasion I went to the large, heavy oak wardrobe and threw open the doors. No sign of Bracken. Then I pushed back the hanging shirts, coats and trousers. Definitely no Bracken.

For a few minutes I prowled around the room, and then decided to go and consult Jack.

'You mean completely missing?' Warnie asked when I explained the situation to them.

'Completely,' I said.

'You remember Bracken, don't you, Jack? He's that chap who's been pestering you and Professor Tolkien with questions.'

'I most certainly remember the man,' Jack said. 'In particular I remember him as the man you said stepped out of a wardrobe.'

'Well, this time I checked the wardrobe and he wasn't hiding there.'

'I suppose after Willesden,' Warnie said reluctantly, 'we should check this out. What do you think, Jack? Strange things are happening in this college.'

'Come along, then,' said Jack, 'let's the three of us conduct a search of this Bracken's room.'

And that's what we did.

In Bracken's room Warnie, in his methodical military way, poked and prodded and lifted and shifted until there wasn't an inch of the room he hadn't carefully searched. Jack's interest focussed on the sheets of writing paper (there were only a few) and the books. He flipped these open and shook them to see if they contained slips of paper, and then leafed slowly through them looking for Bracken's notes.

Jack seemed amused, but also surprised, by the amount of detailed interest Bracken appeared to have taken in his own book, *The Pilgrim's Regress*.

I stood in the middle of the room and watched my friends at work. Then I once again threw open the doors of the large, old wardrobe and pushed aside the hanging clothes to reveal that no one was hiding there.

'There's nothing more we can do here,' Jack announced.

He was quite right, of course, and he and Warnie headed off down the stairs. I lingered behind, reluctant to abandon all hope.

The door of the wardrobe was still standing open. As Jack and Warnie's footsteps receded on the staircase I once again began pushing aside clothing and tapping on the back wall of the wardrobe. I don't know what I expected to find – a hidden compartment? I don't really know to this day what I was expecting.

What happened, as it turned out, was totally unexpected.

I had put one foot on the floor of the wardrobe and I was leaning forward, pushing against the back wall when I, somehow, fell. Everything seemed to give way and I toppled forwards. It happened so suddenly I had no time to respond and put out my hands to break my fall. The result was that I landed heavily.

And I think I must have bumped my head. I certainly lost consciousness for a moment or two. When my senses returned everything had changed.

Still feeling a bit woozy, I looked around. I was no longer inside Bracken's wardrobe. Or inside his room. In fact, I couldn't tell where I was.

I was in a large, well-lit room. It was brightly lit by rows of small lights set into the ceiling. The walls were white and were tiled from floor to ceiling. The floor was covered by grey carpet, or some sort of soft material that felt a bit like carpet. The ceiling was painted white. It didn't look like any room in Oxford I'd ever seen or heard of.

I pushed myself up onto my knees, and then staggered to my feet. Everything seemed to spin around and I almost lost my balance. The fall must have been heavier than I realised. I was definitely light-headed and disoriented.

Taking a few uncertain steps forward, I turned around to survey my strange environment. That's when I got my biggest shock – the walls were solid: tiled white and solid, on all four sides.

Where was the wardrobe? And if all four walls were solid, how had I got in? The far wall had a bench that ran the full length of the wall. Apart from that there was no furniture of any kind. The bench seemed to be filled with technical equipment of some kind – dials, and knobs, and switches and levers – all set into the surface of the bench. It all looked incomprehensibly complex to me. I looked them over closely but dared not touch anything.

That was when I became aware of the sound. There was a steady low hum – I would have called it an electrical hum – that filled the air.

I must have walked around that strange room half a dozen times looking for a way out. At length I gave up and sat down on the floor – there being no chairs – and asked myself all the obvious questions: where was I? How did I get here? And how was I to get out again?

Within two minutes inaction became unbearable, so I rose to my feet and resumed my restless circumnavigation of the room. That was when I became aware of a pale grey metal panel set in the white tiled wall opposite the bench containing all that equipment.

It was the only part of any wall that was not white tiling. I placed the palm of my hand gently against it. It was warm. Not hot, just warm. I tried pressing and it yielded a little, so I tried again and this time I pressed hard against that panel.

The next thing I knew I was surrounded by overcoats and suits and was stepping out of the large wardrobe in Bracken's room.

Feeling just as dazed as before – but glad to be back – I looked around. This was quite definitely Bracken's room, and it looked exactly as it did when I 'left' it (if that's what I did). Jack and Warnie were both long gone – I could no longer hear the sound of their footsteps on the stairs.

Turning, I looked at the wardrobe, with its door still standing open. I considered re-examining it. Then I decided against it. Given how frightening I had found my recent experience – or hallucination or whatever it was – I was in no hurry to repeat it.

Instead, I left Bracken's room in a hurry, intent on catching up with Jack and Warnie.

They must have hurried because the path to the New Building was deserted. I almost sprinted up Jack's staircase and stumbled into his room just about out of breath.

Jack, Warnie and Professor Tolkien were sitting around Jack's large, well-worn table with a teapot and teacups scattered between them.

As I struggled to catch my breath Jack looked up and said, 'Where have you been for the past hour, young Morris? We thought you were right behind us?'

'But I was,' I protested. 'And what do you mean by "the past hour"? I was only in the room for a few minutes.'

'What room?' Tolkien asked. 'What are you three talking about?'

I sank down into a chair and asked for a cup of tea – a strong cup of tea with three heaped sugars.

Then I told them what had happened.

At the end of my tale a hush fell on the room and all three of them looked at me anxiously.

'You've had a turn, old chap,' Warnie muttered sympathetically. 'I knew a chap in my old regiment. He had to leave the army on medical grounds. He started having some sort of turns. Might have been epilepsy. Not sure.'

I threw my hands in the air and said with disgust, 'I might have been hallucinating. I suppose I was. What I saw – or thought I saw – was nothing like any room in Oxford I've ever seen . . . or heard of . . .'

Anxiety came washing over me. What sort of a journalist would I be if I started imagining things? Or hallucinating? Or having 'turns', to use Warnie's expression?

Then I snapped out of it. 'No, no, that's impossible,' I insisted. 'I walked around that room. I ran my fingers over the white tiles on the walls. I heard the equipment humming. I pressed against that metal plate and felt it give under my hand. Somehow – don't ask me how – I "fell" into a hidden room, and then, I suppose, fell out again. I didn't imagine it. Or make it up. You do believe me, don't you?'

'I've always found you entirely trustworthy and truthful,' Jack said.

Tolkien muttered, 'There are more things in heaven and earth, Horatio, than are dreamt of in your philosophy. Jack, I think we should check this out.'

'You're quite right, Tollers, quite right. Come on,' he said, grabbing his battered old grey felt hat. 'Let's explore the impossible in Mr Bracken's room.'

A few minutes later our motley group was standing at Bracken's door.

Rather than barge in, I knocked.

There was an answering call from within. 'Come in – it's not locked.'

I pushed open the door and we all walked in.

Bracken was lying, fully clothed, on top of his bed, which had now been made, reading a book. He seemed surprised to see such a large delegation enter the room – a journalist, a retired Major and two dons. He raised his eyebrows in surprise but said nothing.

'We've come . . .' I began, and then felt very uncertain as to where I should go next. So I took the easy option. 'We've come to tell you that Murray has a letter for you. It's marked urgent and special delivery.'

'Thank you,' said Bracken. 'Although I'm a little surprised that it took four of you.'

'To tell you the truth, Mr Bracken,' said Jack, 'we and others have been looking for you all morning.'

'I've been here,' he said. 'Apart from the time I was having my morning bath, I've been here.'

We knew that couldn't possibly be true, so I felt emboldened to tackle the man.

'Look here, Bracken, something decidedly odd has happened to me,' I began, and I went on to narrate my whole adventure.

He listened in silence. He didn't look in the least bit surprised – and that, in itself, surprised me.

When I finished he said, 'Morris, old chap, I don't know what's happened to you, but whatever it was it didn't happen here, and it didn't involve me, and it most certainly didn't involve my wardrobe.'

'Do you mind if I check it out?' I asked.

'Be my guest,' Bracken said, his arm sweeping in a gesture of invitation towards his wardrobe.

I walked over and opened the door. There were the hanging clothes. There was the solid oak back of the wardrobe. I stepped closer, pushed the clothes aside, and tapped the back wall of the wardrobe, then I leaned in and pressed against it.

Nothing happened. I certainly didn't fall through it into a hidden room.

I stepped back into the college room feeling puzzled, and a little frightened.

'Satisfied?' Bracken asked, looking, I thought, a little smug.

Jack apologised for our intrusion and we all left – me feeling like a dog slinking away with its tail between its legs.

EIGHTEEN

~

It was Tuesday morning, so the Inklings were due to meet at the Eagle and Child. Once we had descended from staircase two and were back out in the open air, Jack patted me on the shoulder by way of encouragement and said, 'Come along, old chap, what you need is a drink.' I certainly felt like a drink in the sense that my insides closely resembled a cocktail vigorously shaken by a muscular barman.

Given this cue, all four of us headed out of the college gates, down the High Street, into the Turl, and thence down St Giles and into the welcoming, dimly lit, oak-panelled interior of the Inklings' favourite pub.

We sidestepped our way through the public bar at the front to find that Coghill and Fox were already there, waiting for us. Warnie went to the bar to order pints all round as Jack, Professor Tolkien and I took our seats in the back parlour.

'When is Barfield joining us for another session?' Coghill asked.

'From what he tells me in his latest letter,' Jack replied, taking off his shapeless felt hat and stuffing it into a pocket, 'not for some time. His legal practice is rather busy at the moment.'

Warnie approached, carefully balancing a tray containing four pints – Coghill and Fox having barely begun sipping theirs.

'Jack, you're friendly with this Scotland Yard man, this Inspector Crispin, aren't you?' Adam Fox asked.

'We have met before,' Jack admitted as he slowly filled his pipe, 'and I find him to be an admirably sensible man.'

'So what is he telling you, then?' Nevill Coghill asked. 'Do they have a suspect? Or a list of suspects? Do they know how the murder was committed? Or how the head was removed from a locked room?'

'Crispin is playing his cards close to his chest,' Jack replied, 'which is, of course, quite right and proper. So I have no special inside information.'

'Mind you, Crispin did ask Jack to have a look at the head when they recovered it,' Warnie added, clearly proud of the respect in which the Scotland Yard man held his brother.

'Were you now? You were asked to go and have a look?' Fox was clearly impressed. 'All I know is what I read in the *Oxford Mail* this morning. Now, don't tell me what the head was like, I don't want the grisly details, but answer me this: how can the body be in a locked room in Magdalen, and the head in a bag in the Cherwell half a mile away? Any theories, anyone?'

'In Middle Earth it might be the work of a wizard,' said Tolkien. 'Or of one of the evil beings who'd come under the spell of the dark forces of Morgoth. Perhaps a servant of Morgoth, such as the Necromancer. But without such a being at hand I remain as baffled as everyone else.'

'Mind you,' huffed Warnie in his bluff way as he lit a cigarette, 'there is some sort of wizardry afoot. Strange things are happening in Oxford. Morris, why don't you tell these chaps about your experience? Listen to this – it's an amazing story . . .'

It was the last thing I wanted to do, but I felt obliged not to let Warnie down – so I told them the whole story. I told them about the strange experience of passing through Bracken's wardrobe into something else – either a hidden room or a powerful hallucination. And then, when invited by Bracken to check out the wardrobe, I had found it solid and impenetrable – showing, it seems, that I could not have had the experience I remembered having.

'I'd vote for hallucination,' Coghill said, when I finished. 'Don't take any offence, Morris, old chap. It's just that you are, by profession, a journalist, and as such you have an over-active imagination.'

'But what might trigger off such a bizarre, and very precise, hallucination? Surely it couldn't just spring out of nowhere?' Fox asked.

'Why not?' Tolkien asked. 'Ideas, images, people, spring out of "nowhere" onto a blank sheet of paper when a storyteller sits down to create a story – or to "sub-create" a story in the pattern of the great Creator. So, who knows what deep well of creativity is lurking inside the mind of our friend Morris?'

'True, true,' Adam Fox admitted, 'but this seems to be of a different order. His conscious, active imagination seems not to have been involved.'

'Quite right,' Jack said firmly. 'My friend Morris is not a fanciful man. He's a rather down-to-earth, nuts-and-bolts man. I've certainly had pupils from whom such a story might have been a student prank or a moment of drunken madness – but not Morris. So what we have here is a "trilemma". In other words, there are only three options: his story is an invention, a mental aberration or the truth. Morris does not invent foolish jokes and he is mentally well balanced – so the only remaining possibility is that his story is true.'

I was about to thank Jack for his vote of confidence, but Adam Fox leapt in before me to say, 'Coghill, you're our Chaucer expert – did Chaucer ever write about someone being transported to the realm of faerie? Because that's what Morris' reported experience most resembles – stepping into a magic circle, being transported to another realm.'

We never got to hear Coghill's answer, because Tolkien took up this theme enthusiastically. 'It does sound rather as though Morris stepped over a threshold to another realm. And as dismissive,' he said, 'as our present, excessively materialistic society is, there is no solid ground for discarding totally the concept of other realms.'

Jack joined in to suggest that if, as he and the rest of the company believed, there is a spiritual realm, it would be, by its very nature, beyond physical, material measurement and, therefore, beyond the reach of even the most subtle scientific instruments.

'And anyway,' said Warnie, 'there are all these chappies inventing scientific romances these days. Mr H. G. Wells and the rest. They seem to think that even in a scientific age it may be possible to be transported to other planets, or other realms, or other dimensions.'

'But! But!' protested Coghill. 'How do we account for the fact that Morris couldn't repeat his experience?'

'If this was a story by Wells or one of his crowd,' Warnie responded, 'there'd be a switch or a valve or some other piece of technology to explain it.'

I lost track of the conversation for a bit as I fell into a reverie, wondering if Jack was implying that I might have had some sort of religious experience when he talked about other realms in spiritual terms. He wasn't – but I only worked this out later. When I emerged from my reflections I discovered that fresh pints had been ordered and the conversation had swung back to the murder of the odious Willesden.

'Well, it wasn't wizardry,' Adam Fox was saying. 'At least not the kind of wizardry Tollers writes about. But there is another sort of wizardry: the wicked ingenuity that a human mind can concoct. In this case, surely Willesden's head was removed from his body, his room was locked, and his head transported some distance by means of extremely clever, but extremely wicked, human ingenuity.'

'Of course, this elevates Willesden to a plane he never occupied during his lifetime,' Jack said, with one of his characteristic grins spreading across his face.

Tolkien asked how, and Jack said, 'From now on Willesden will be known as "the head" of Magdalen.'

This produced loud groans as well as laughs and a demand that Jack pay for the next round.

'He told me he was going to enter the diplomatic service,' I told the Inklings. 'His father was organising things. His only interest in Oxford was in getting a good enough degree to set him off on a flying start. After that he was determined to rise. And given his ruthless ambition I'm sure he would have ended up as an ambassador somewhere.'

'A young man determined to get ahead,' Fox said.

'Instead of which he lost one,' Coghill suggested – provoking another round of groaning chuckles.

'How is your debate with Jack going?' Professor Tolkien asked. 'I mean your objection to the Christian symbol of the cross on the grounds that no great movement should be based on a worship of death – that's what you and Jack are debating about, isn't it?'

Hearing our discussion trotted out for all the Inklings to consider, I very quickly found myself in a minority of one. All joined with Jack in seeing my objections to the Christian symbol of the cross as missing, as Fox said, 'the whole point of the whole thing'. This produced murmurs of approval all round, and I was told it was my turn to buy a round.

'How much longer will you be in Oxford?' Adam Fox asked when I got back to the table.

Only another couple of days, I explained, as I had to go back and work out my time on the *Bath Chronicle* before taking up my new post on the *Oxford Mail*.

'What a pity,' Fox said. 'Shame you can't stay another couple of weeks. If you were here at Easter, I would drag you along to church and I think much of what Jack has been saying would become abundantly clear. I think the pieces might come together for you.'

I turned to Tolkien and said, 'Professor, let me ask you the same question I asked Jack when this whole battle began – when I look at the cross as a symbol, I see it as symbolising torture and execution, like the broad sword or the blade or whatever it was that slaughtered Willesden. Why doesn't it look like that to you?'

'Because,' Tolkien replied, speaking in his usual quiet, rapid way, 'symbols can be transformed. When a pirate vessel runs up a skull and crossbones flag it's a challenge – it's the pirate captain and his crew offering violence to the merchant ship they are closing in on. It's a challenge to their chosen victim to surrender. But that same symbol – the skull and crossbones – on a bottle in the garden shed is a warning. It's a signal designed to alert me to the fact the contents are poison. And unlike the pirate situation it helps me – reminds me to wear gloves when using the stuff to poison wasps in the garden. Symbols can be transformed.'

Adam Fox leapt in at this point to say, 'Jesus did exactly that to bread and wine. He transformed them from ordinary food and drink into symbols of his suffering on that cross and what that suffering means for us.'

'So what has the cross been transformed into?' I asked. 'Professor, when you look at the cross you don't see torture and execution, so what *do* you see?'

Tolkien sipped on his beer while he thought about this, and then said, 'I see divine love and human need. Fallen human nature nailed Jesus to the cross and he died because he loved fallen human beings, and by his death he lifts them up to their feet and takes them home to his Father. The arms of the cross are spread out to show us the breadth of divine love and depth of human need.'

'Whoa, slow down there. This is all getting a bit theological for me,' I said.

Now, I love a good debate with every fibre of my being. Get me into a debate and the blood flows – my red corpuscles think it's time for a picnic, they wake any other red corpuscles that happen to be dozing and tell them to get moving and do their bit. But however much I love a debate, I draw the line at theology. I think I'm too old to take up theology. Tolkien, on the other hand, I could imagine lapping up St Augustine from the age of about eight – he probably couldn't get enough of the stuff.

My bacon was saved by Warnie, who, in his bluff sergeant-majorly way announced that it was lunchtime and he was going to the bar to order a pie and peas and what did the rest want?

'If you'll excuse me,' I said, rising from the table, 'I'm off to have lunch with a friend.'

So with a barrage of jokes behind me about how surprising it was to discover that I actually had a friend, I left the cavern of the Eagle and Child and stepped, blinking, into the bright sunlight of St Giles.

NINETEEN

~

The truth was that I had no appointment for lunch, but I had been thinking all morning that I might try to catch up with Penelope and invite her to join me. With that in mind I retraced my steps through Oxford, back down the High Street and over Magdalen Bridge to where St Hilda's stood in Cowley Place.

With St Clement's Street behind me and the St Hilda's archway leading to the porter's lodge in front of me, I suddenly felt nervous. I wasn't at all sure how I stood with Penelope. On top of which, standing between me and any contact with Penelope was the head porter of St Hilda's – a terrifying termagant known as Miss Mobbs.

Miss Mobbs was generally assumed to be about a hundred and fifty years old and to be a reincarnation of either Ivan the Terrible or Genghis Khan or, possibly, both.

I found her at the window of the porter's lodge at her ease, stroking Murky, the college cat.

'Good afternoon, Miss Mobbs,' I said, as I resisted the impulse to tug a forelock. 'I'm here to call on Miss Penelope Robertson-Smyth.'

'Is she expecting you?'

'My visit is intended to be a pleasant surprise.'

Miss Mobbs picked up Murky the cat and turned it around on her lap to face me – in case she wished to consult the cat's opinion in weighing me up.

'Do I know you?'

'I am a member of this university, but I'm now a journalist – about to join the staff of the *Oxford Mail*. Morris is the name – Tom Morris.'

As I spoke, I reached through the window and gently scratched Murky's neck. The cat began to purr as loudly as a badly tuned motorcycle, indicating, I think, a high level of approval.

'Gladys,' bellowed Miss Mobbs.

In response to this summons a girl in a maid's uniform appeared.

'Run around to the Senior Common Room and tell Miss Robertson-Smyth that Mr Morris has called for her and is waiting at the lodge.'

In response to this command the girl trotted away.

As we waited, Miss Mobbs and I discovered we had little to talk about.

'Nice weather for March,' I ventured.

Miss Mobbs nodded but said nothing. Somehow she managed to convey the impression that any opinion from a mere male carried no weight and was not to be taken seriously.

After an awkward ten minutes Penelope appeared.

'You still making a pest of yourself all over Oxford?' she said by way of cheerful greeting.

'Mostly in the parts of Oxford where you are,' I said with a grin.

'The curse has come upon me, cried the Lady of Shallot – and the name of the curse is Tom Morris,' she replied affectionately.

'Would you like to come to lunch with me?'

'Love to. Just give me five minutes.'

As a result, just twenty minutes later she reappeared having changed her dress and brushed her hair.

'Let's go to The Rose,' she said, naming a tea shop we had frequented as undergraduates. 'Their sandwiches are scrummy.'

However, during those intervening twenty minutes I'd had an interesting exchange with one of Penelope's colleagues – one of the younger dons at St Hilda's named Ruth Plumber. A few years earlier, during my undergraduate days, she'd attended the whole of Jack's series of lectures on medieval literature and we'd fallen into conversation a number of times.

'Tom, isn't it?' she had said with surprise, as she bowled in through the archway.

'Yes, Tom Morris – I'm amazed you remember.'

'You calling on someone here?'

I told her that I'd come to invite Penelope to lunch, and then we talked about my present employment, which seemed to lead, almost inevitably, to the murder that was dominating the newspapers and so much of the gossip in Oxford.

'What did you think of Willesden?' I asked. 'Did you know him?'

'Only slightly, but like everyone else who ever encountered the man I . . . well . . . *de mortuis nihil nisi bonum* and all that . . . but he was a pimple.'

'I'm yet to hear anyone speak well of him,' I admitted.

'If you really want to know about Willesden,' said Ruth, 'the person you should ask is your friend Penelope. She knew him better than most of us. And she ended up hating him. Well, I must be going – toodle-pip.'

And it was a little after this that Penelope turned up and we headed back across Magdalen Bridge in the direction of The Rose. All the time my brain was buzzing with this new information. Penelope knew Willesden better than she had led me to believe, and knew him well enough to hate him.

A quarter of an hour later we were seated in The Rose with a pot of the best Darjeeling in front of us and a plate of mixed sandwiches cut into delicate quarters.

So far the conversation had been a running monologue in which Penelope had recounted her adventures with the Poetry Club at St Hilda's. She had, it seemed, become its leading light. As a don and a published poet this was inevitable, she explained. What was unclear was whether she saw the club in purely literary terms or as a power base within college politics.

I had just bitten into a small sandwich that turned out to be a nice vintage cheddar with gherkin when Penelope changed the subject.

'Anything new on the murder?' she asked.

'You've heard that the head has been recovered?'

'I'm fully up to date. Any suspects?'

'I've heard nothing officially,' I said, 'but I gather Willesden was pretty universally disliked.'

'That has the ring of truth about it.'

'And while I was waiting for you at the porter's lodge I ran into Ruth Plumber. She mentioned,' I said, choosing my words carefully and pausing to take another bite of sandwich, 'that you knew Willesden quite well at one stage.'

Penelope said nothing to this, but flashed me a look that would have made a charging rhinoceros pause and think it had come up against something fairly tough.

The silence lingered uncomfortably for a bit, so I said, 'Ruth actually said that you ended up hating Willesden. A bit strong, I thought.'

'Lots of students, and quite a few dons, hated Willesden,' said Penelope, quietly but firmly. That beautiful profile was starting to look as if it was carved out of marble – very cold, white marble.

I thought it best to say nothing, so I poured another cup of tea and waited to see if she'd continue. She did.

'Willesden was a smug, sneering, arrogant, self-important wart – so naturally enough he was deeply disliked by every decent human being.' My darling Penelope was sounding rather more like a serpent than a dove. 'In fact, I believe even cats and dogs avoided his company – at least those with any taste did.' Clearly dove-mode had been parked in a cupboard and serpent-mode was in full flight.

'So how well did you know him?' I asked, trying to make my tone sound as gentle and diplomatic as possible.

She didn't answer immediately so I reached out to touch her hand, and asked again. Penelope withdrew her hand and turned a basilisk eye upon me. I was shocked to notice a gleam of moisture in that eye – moisture that at any moment threatened to become a tear.

'If you must know, we went out a few times.'

'A few times?'

'Just here and there. And I went with him for a weekend at his family's country house.'

'So you met Sir James Willesden and Lady Willesden and . . .'

'. . . and the rest of that odious clan.'

'And after that?'

'After that he dropped me like a hot potato. Told me he was shopping for a wife who could play hostess at diplomatic events, and his father had scratched my name off the list of possibles.'

'Absurd! What possible reason . . . ?'

'I was too intelligent, I was told, too well-educated. I was too keen to participate in debates that should be left to the menfolk.'

The memory seemed to come flooding back to her at that point – and it was a bitter memory. With a catch in her voice she said, 'So Aubrey Willesden, who cared for nothing in this life except Aubrey Willesden, gave me the bird.'

At this point a definite tear began to roll down one cheek. 'And you should never have asked me,' she said with a sob in her voice. 'You should never have dragged that up. You're a beast.'

She pushed back her chair and staggered to her feet. 'You're a total, absolute beast.'

With those words she turned and marched angrily out of The Rose.

I sat there feeling stunned for a while, then I paid the bill and stepped out onto the High Street. The world seemed to tilt wildly and swim around as if I had suddenly developed an inner ear infection.

When it came back into focus I saw Jack striding towards me, raising his hand in greeting.

'You look a bit glum, young Morris,' he said in his most determined-to-cheer-you-up manner. 'Tell me all about it.'

So I did. My meetings with Penelope, her amazing profile, what I thought was a growing friendship, and then this recent explosion.

'She called me a beast,' I said.

'Think nothing of it,' Jack suggested.

'You don't think she meant it?'

'She was probably just making conversation.'

'Just looking for something to say, you mean?'

'Precisely. What you need,' Jack said, 'is something to do to take your mind off it. And I have the very thing. Why don't you and I pay a visit to Nicolas Guilford – the pupil both Tollers and I remember as having an excessive interest in Milton, and in early editions of Milton.'

I agreed that being active would be good for me, so we set off.

'I thought Warnie was conducting this investigation into the Mystery of the Missing Milton,' I said.

'But you need some activity, to take your mind off recent events. Hence,' said Jack, 'you and I will interview Guilford and report our results to Warnie.'

It turned out that Guilford had rooms in the Longwall quad at Magdalen. When we knocked on his door we found him at home. Jack made the introductions and we entered a room that looked like the product of either hurricane-force winds or else an extremely random filing system.

As we stepped through the doorway, Guilford was scooping up some objects – I couldn't see what – and shovelling them under the heap of untidy clothes on the bed. His actions were, I thought, those of a guilty man. Guilty of what, I hadn't the faintest idea, but guilty of something.

'We've come to talk to you about Milton,' Jack said.

'I don't know any Milton. Which college is he at?' Guilford mumbled, succeeding in looking and sounding even more nervous and more deeply guilty.

Jack and I glanced at each other, and then Jack said, 'Well, let's ask you instead about the Bodleian.'

'What about the Bodleian? Are they saying I'm not supposed to work there, are they? Well, it's not against the rules. It's only part-time work in the stacks. Just to give me a bit of pocket money. I'm not as well off as the toffs, you know.' All of this poured out in an awkward, nervous jumble of words.

Our conversation with Guilford went around and around in concentric – or possibly eccentric – circles for ten minutes. We learned nothing more from him in that time, so we excused ourselves and left.

As we headed back towards Jack's rooms, I said, 'Well, he's the thief. There's no doubt about it. I have no idea how, or why, but he's the thief.'

'That much our friend Guilford made abundantly clear,' Jack agreed. 'And a not very intelligent thief, at that. We must pass this on to Warnie, who will, undoubtedly, follow it up enthusiastically.'

'And I'd bet London to a brick that the Milton theft wasn't the first.'

'I'm sure you're right, Morris. Whatever that young man is involved in, he's dug in so deeply as to be extremely nervous – in fact, quite frightened.'

We walked on in thoughtful silence for a bit, and then I said, 'For all I know, there might be a connection between Guilford's programme of thieving and the death of Willesden. I can't see how at the moment – but if, let's say, Willesden found out what Guilford was up to . . .'

'. . . and whoever else is involved with him,' Jack added. 'He can't be involved in whatever thieving is being done on his own. At the very least, he needs someone to repackage what he steals and someone to sell it to. He clearly hasn't the brains to be running any sort of complex operation on his own.'

'A fence,' I said. 'A receiver of stolen goods is called, in police jargon, a fence.'

'I'll take your word for that. Whoever these other people are, they might be hardened professional criminals.'

'Exactly the type,' I suggested, 'to commit murder to cover their tracks.'

'Making it possible that there's a link between our two mysteries – the Missing Milton and the Headless Corpse.'

TWENTY

~

Back in Jack's rooms we shared our discoveries with Warnie, who was very excited.

'Here's a thought, Morris, my friend,' he said, 'if we can put this young Nicolas Guilford toad together with the grimy William Hare, the dubious bookman, we will have tied up two members of the gang.'

I suggested that the presence of a criminal gang operating in Oxford threw a new light on the murder of Aubrey Willesden.

'It's certainly criminal gangs that commit murder to keep their secrets secret,' Warnie said, enthusiastically taking up the idea. 'Those crime novels you see on the shelf over there are mine – Jack would rather read H. Rider Haggard than Sapper any day of the week. But you do learn things from those books – and the danger of falling foul of one of those criminal gangs is something I've learned.'

'If,' I said, picking up the theme, 'Willesden had stumbled across this racket, he's not the sort of person – from what I've learned about him – who would keep quiet about it. Willesden seems to have had the sort of self-importance that made him feel invulnerable. He would have thought he was as bulletproof as any ironclad. So my guess is that he wouldn't have hesitated to boast in pubs about what he'd found out.'

'That could have got him killed,' Warnie agreed.

Just then there was a knock at the door and Detective Inspector Crispin of Scotland Yard entered.

'I hope I'm not interrupting anything,' he said.

'You're welcome at any time, inspector,' Jack assured him. 'What news do you bring?'

'Fairly momentous news, in fact – it appears likely that we've found the weapon.'

Warnie ushered the Scotland Yard man in and settled him on one of Jack's rather old and tatty armchairs, then we gathered to hear the news.

'After finding the head in the Cherwell yesterday, I kept our uniformed officers searching with grappling hooks. And this morning it paid off when they pulled out of the river a strange-looking object that might well be – can't be certain at this stage – the weapon that killed young Mr Willesden.'

Asked about the purpose of his visit to us, Crispin looked at Jack and replied, 'I want to keep you fully informed, Mr Lewis, on the progress of the case. At some point you'll have enough information to have an inspired idea of what happened and how it happened.'

'You say you're not certain,' Jack said, 'that this thing you've found really is the murder weapon?'

'That's right. But it looks to me like something savage enough to take a man's head off. So, I was rather hoping you'd come down to Oxford Police Station to take a look at it.'

'Certainly. Delighted,' said Warnie, grabbing his old tweed hat and walking stick – making the assumption that we were all included in the invitation.

'Actually,' Warnie added, 'before we do, there's something that we should tell you.'

Warnie sat back down on the Chesterfield and told Inspector Crispin the whole story of the Mystery of the Missing Milton – from the first suspicions that fell on Jack to our recent discoveries involving Nicolas Guilford and the antiquarian bookseller William Hare.

Crispin took all this in, and thought about it for a moment. It was almost possible to hear the gear wheels swinging smoothly into operation in his brain.

'We'll follow this up,' he promised. 'Now, shall we head off to the police station and take a look at our find?'

As we walked down St Aldates past Pembroke College, I spotted Tolkien talking to the head porter of the college.

'Professor,' I called out, 'come and join us.' Then I realised that this was not my party and it was not my role to invite guests, so I turned to Inspector Crispin and asked, 'If that's all right with you?'

The policeman chuckled and said, 'The more Oxford brains I can engage in this mystery the better. By all means bring your friend along.'

As Tolkien joined us, Jack explained that we were being asked to take a look at the weapon – or possible weapon – that may have beheaded Willesden.

Plunging into the police station, Inspector Crispin led us past the front desk, through an office where a couple of uniformed constables were slowly tapping out their reports on typewriters to a back room.

'It's in here,' he said, 'in the evidence room.'

On a table in a high-ceilinged, well-lit room was a square-looking object wrapped up in oil cloth. Crispin carefully unwrapped it and then asked, 'Now, do you agree with me that this could well be the murder weapon?'

What we saw was a square of wood – dark and water-stained. Attached to the bottom of this piece of timber was a long blade, set at an angle.

As we stood, looking in silence at this strange object, Inspector Crispin said, 'The blade is steel, and is extremely sharp. The timber is some sort of hardwood – I suspect it's beech.'

Another silence followed this explanation.

'Have you ever seen any weapon like this before, inspector?' Jack asked.

'Never,' the Scotland Yard man replied. 'I've had a long and varied – and quite colourful – career in crime, but I've never come across anything like this before.'

'I was certain the murder weapon was a sword,' Professor Tolkien said. 'Perhaps my head is filled with too many swash-buckling adventures, but I kept picturing a sword – perhaps something as large and heavy as a Scottish claymore.'

'It could still turn out to be something like that,' Crispin admitted. 'But take a look at this contraption and tell me what you think.'

Warnie had pulled off his soft tweed hat and was scratching his head.

'It reminds me of something,' he said. 'I can't think quite what. It'll come to me in a moment.'

'Something from your army days?' I asked.

'Possibly. Just give me a moment to think about it.'

'Let me show you the other side,' Crispin said, as he turned the object over.

The reverse side was much the same as the front, except for two additions. On the bottom edge of the wooden square, just above the blade, was a bar of grey metal, and on the top edge a thick bar or slat of wood.

'The grey metal you see is lead,' Crispin explained. 'It appears to have been carefully moulded and fitted to the board just at the top edge of the blade. The blade itself is very strong – eighth-inch steel, hand sharpened, I would say, with a file to give it a razor's edge.'

'It would be a difficult weapon to swing or wield or attack with,' I commented. 'Perhaps this is not the murder weapon after all – perhaps this is just a discarded tool from some sort of factory.'

Crispin asked what sort of factory, and I said I couldn't possibly guess. 'It could be a factory involved in any manufacturing process that requires heavy cutting or slicing.'

'Have you tested the blade for blood?' Jack asked.

'We have,' Crispin replied, 'and despite its lengthy immersion the lab managed to detect minute amounts of blood in the crevices. These are being tested at the moment.'

I stuck to my factory theory by saying, 'Could it be from an abattoir?'

Crispin agreed that it could be, and that the strange object might be yet another blind alley.

'But how would an attacker use it?' Tolkien asked. 'How would anyone grasp it in order to employ it as a weapon?'

'It looks to me, Tollers,' Jack said, 'more like a mechanical weapon than a hand-held weapon.'

'That's it!' Warnie cried. 'I've got it.'

Inspector Crispin's face lit up. He was clearly hoping that his unofficial Oxford 'team' would come up with ideas that might not occur to an ordinary policeman.

'It's the blade from a guillotine!' said Warnie. 'Well, you chaps know my interest in French history. I've been researching seventeenth- rather than eighteenth-century French history – nevertheless, I've done enough reading to be fairly confident this is a blade from a guillotine.'

'That would certainly explain the manner of Willesden's death,' Jack said.

We all turned to Inspector Crispin for his response to Warnie's idea. But before he could speak the door of the evidence room opened and a young constable entered. He handed Crispin an envelope and left again. Crispin hurriedly tore open the envelope, read the sheet of paper within, then turned to us.

'The minute amounts of blood on the blade,' he said, 'were human blood, not animal blood. So I'm afraid that's your abattoir theory out of the window, Mr Morris. And this report contains one more vital fact: the blood was the same blood group as the victim.'

'Well, that's it, then,' Jack agreed. 'This was indeed the murder weapon.'

'And if Warnie's right,' said Tolkien, 'young Mr Willesden was guillotined to death.'

'You have to keep your men dragging the river, inspector,' Warnie insisted. 'This is just the blade; the rest of the machine must be somewhere. If the killer disposed of the head and the blade in the river, he probably put the rest of the guillotine machinery in there as well – perhaps broken up into pieces.'

'What would the rest of the machinery look like?' Crispin asked.

'Well, this thing here,' Warnie replied, gesturing at the object on the table, 'would have slid down a frame. It would have to be a fairly solid, stout wooden frame. To get up enough speed it would have been perhaps fifteen feet tall – possibly taller. During the French Revolution the frame down which the blade slid was sometimes up to twenty feet tall.'

'A large object, then?' the policeman asked.

'Quite so,' Warnie agreed. 'But as I said, it may have been broken up by now.'

'I see a problem,' said Tolkien. 'While I don't question your expertise on French history, Warnie, I can't see how it can apply in this case. We've been puzzled all along by the fact that Willesden's body was found inside his room – in a locked room, we're told – and his head, and the weapon that removed his head, found half a mile away in the Cherwell. So how was the murder committed? The sort of weapon you're describing, Warnie, would not fit in a college room. The ceilings are quite high, but not that high.'

'Perhaps it was a smaller guillotine,' Warnie muttered, looking a bit deflated.

'Perhaps that's what the lead was for,' I suggested. 'That lead bar on the back of the timber fixture. Perhaps that weight was there so the blade could have a shorter drop and still be effective.'

'What would be involved in setting up an elaborate piece of machinery like that inside a college room?' Crispin asked.

I laughed cynically – my journalist's laugh, I call it. 'It's a lot of timber to get up the steps of staircase three. Then once you've got it there, it would require a lot of noisy woodwork to assemble it.'

'And the biggest problem of all,' said Jack, 'is spiriting the whole apparatus out of the room once Willesden has been killed.'

Warnie was now looking very glum. 'Perhaps it wasn't a guillotine after all that did the chap in. Perhaps this guillotine-looking implement had nothing to do with it.'

'But it did,' Crispin reminded us. 'Human blood, of the same blood group as Willesden, has been found on the blade.'

'Well, he certainly wasn't shaving with it,' Warnie said with a grumpy laugh.

'Since the blood suggests that he was indeed guillotined,' Tolkien said, 'perhaps he was guillotined outside his room, not inside. That obviates all that impossible assembly of a guillotine inside a college room.'

'It's possible, I suppose,' Crispin admitted. 'Could it be that the victim was lured from his room, guillotined somewhere nearby – possibly on the lawn outside his window – and then his body returned to his room?'

'But the room was locked,' Tolkien objected.

'That's the double problem we're faced with,' Jack said. 'It's the problem of either getting the guillotine machinery into – and then out of – the college room, or else getting the victim out and then his lifeless body back in while leaving the door locked and bolted and the windows latched on the inside.'

'I give up,' said Warnie, throwing his hands in the air in despair. 'It's beyond me.'

'So which was it, Mr Lewis?' asked Inspector Crispin, turning to Jack. 'Was Willesden killed inside his room or outside?'

As I turned to look at Jack his face lit up. There was suddenly a spark glinting in those intelligent eyes.

'That's the question, isn't it?' he said with a definite smile on his face. 'Inside? Or outside? Or both?'

Crispin had seen what I saw. 'You know how this crime was committed, don't you, Mr Lewis?' he said.

'No, I don't know,' Jack protested, 'at least not for certain. But I do have an inkling.'

TWENTY-ONE

~

Outside the police station we were about to go our separate ways when Professor Tolkien said, 'Just a moment, my fellow Inklings – I have a suggestion.'

Jack, who had remained stubbornly silent since dropping his teasing suggestion earlier, said, 'Speak on, Tollers, old chap.'

'I propose that we four head back to the scene of the crime,' he suggested. 'Jack, you can talk your head porter, Murray, into lending you the key to Willesden's room. And perhaps if four pairs of eyes go over the crime scene in a fresh way, we might get a hint as to how this awful murder was committed.'

So it was that ten minutes later we walked up staircase three in the north quad block at Magdalen College, where Jack turned the key in the door of what had once been Willesden's room.

The splintered timber had been repaired around where the bolt had entered the door frame, but apart from that it was pretty much the same as it had always been.

It was a standard student's room – bed, desk, a tallboy for clothes, bookcase, two armchairs, one with a reading lamp. There was nothing unusual or out of place. It resembled the room I was staying in on staircase two, or the one David Bracken had on the floor below me (except, of course, for the massive old wardrobe in Bracken's room).

Warnie closely examined the door frame and the repair to the bolt.

'It's pretty clear this door was locked and bolted,' he said, 'with Willesden's body lying inside.'

'I can testify to that,' I said. 'I was here when Murray turned the key in the lock and the door still wouldn't open. We had to get two hefty young gardeners to break it down.'

Jack looked through the books and papers that still lay scattered over Willesden's desk.

'His family still hasn't come to take away his things, I see,' said Jack.

'Possibly they're waiting until the body is released for burial,' Tolkien suggested. 'Which raises the question: when will the coroner hold an inquest into Willesden's death? I take it there will have to be an inquest?'

'Undoubtedly, old chap, undoubtedly,' Warnie said. 'But there's been no word yet as to the timing. Perhaps the police are asking the coroner to hold on for a bit – waiting until they understand more. The police don't enjoy looking like complete ninnies in the coroner's court.'

I walked over to the two sash windows that, side by side, looked out over the lawn that separated the cloister quad from the New Building. I unlatched one of the windows, slid it up, and leaned out. I found myself looking down on Alf, kneeling in the flower bed just a matter of feet below, working on his rose garden.

'Morning, Alf,' I said, and he looked up, startled.

'Who's that? Who's there? Oh, ah, it's you, Mr Morris.'

'What are you doing, Alf?'

'Just digging some blood and bone in around my damaged roses. Make 'em as good as new soon enough.'

I wished Alf good luck with his roses, and turned around from the window to the room. But the moment I let go of the window it came sliding down with a bang, and made me jump.

'The sash is broken in the window,' said Warnie knowingly. 'Often happens with sash windows.'

'There are a lot of broken sash windows in our colleges – takes ages to get them fixed,' Tolkien said.

'Makes them a bit dangerous, doesn't it?' I asked.

'Not at all, not at all, old chap,' said Warnie, walking across to where I stood. 'I know this type of window – they're common all over Magdalen. If you slide it up with your right hand, you can push the latch with your fingers and it'll hold the window in place.'

He demonstrated what he meant, and it worked.

I estimated the height of the windowsills from the ground – about ten feet, I would have guessed.

'I can't see how anyone can have got into the room or out of it through the windows,' I said. 'I could squirm through if I tried, but it's a tight fit.'

'Willesden was, I suspect, a little slimmer than you, Morris,' Tolkien said with a smile. 'Not that you're over-weight – just a bit more solid than I remember you as an undergraduate.'

Jack came over to my side and looked at the height of the window above the ground.

'Hard to get up from the garden bed,' he remarked, 'without a ladder. But somebody who was already here could probably jump that distance safely enough. I must ask Crispin if any footprints were found in the garden bed.'

Professor Tolkien joined us and looked at the garden below and the lawn beyond.

'These windows were definitely latched at the time of the murder?' he asked.

I told him that I had seen for myself that they were closed on the morning of the murder – and it's not possible for these windows to be fully down without the latch clicking into place.

'That seems to settle that,' Tolkien said.

I reached up my right hand, released the catch and let gravity slide the window down, where it latched in a closed position.

Jack slid open the drawers in the tallboy and found a half-empty bottle of brandy underneath the socks. Warnie reached over and picked it up.

'Jolly good brandy, this,' he muttered. 'Why hide it under socks?'

'I wonder if our Mr Willesden was less self-assured than he appeared to be?' Professor Tolkien asked.

'Bit of a secret drinker, you mean?' Warnie responded.

'If so, he would not be the first student with such a problem,' said Jack as he paced slowly and thoughtfully around the room. 'And this is just how you saw the room on the day of the murder?' he asked. 'Nothing different? Nothing changed?'

In response to that challenge I closed my eyes to picture the dreadful scene that day, then opened them again and looked around.

'The rug is gone,' I said. 'There was a rug, right here, in the middle of the floor – where the body lay. It was soaked with blood.'

'Which explains why it was removed, old boy,' huffed Warnie.

'But everything else is in place?' Jack persisted.

'Yes, everything,' I said. 'I'm sure of it.'

'Then we've learned all we can here, and we should return this key to Murray before he comes to a slow boil worrying over whether he should have let us have it in the first place.'

We returned the key to the head porter, and then set out for Jack's rooms in the New Building.

Tolkien took his leave from us, expressing disappointment that the scene of the crime had revealed so little, in order to head back to Pembroke College. But before he went he said to Jack, 'Turn your mind to something else – let your subconscious take over wrestling with this puzzle. You may be surprised at what it'll come up with.'

He paused and then said with an elvish grin, 'I know – you and Morris should go back to your debate over Morris' objections to Easter, or whatever it is. And while you're doing that your subconscious can get creative.'

With a smile and wave of his hand he walked away.

Back in the rooms in New Building, Jack and I settled into armchairs, while Warnie retired to his room. After a few minutes I could hear him tap, tap, tapping away on his old typewriter.

Jack lit his pipe and puffed at it for a moment and then said, 'Our headless corpse remains deeply mysterious, young Morris.'

'Now, you heard what Professor Tolkien said,' I responded with a grin. 'Leave that to your subconscious. Let's talk about that other even more mysterious death instead.' Jack raised his eyebrows so I continued, 'The death of Jesus remains a total mystery to me. You keep saying the cross is a noble symbol, because his was a noble death – a sacrificial death on behalf of others. To me, those are just words. I can't see how it makes any sense.'

Jack puffed in silence for a moment and then said, 'I'll give you one sentence of Scripture, and we'll see if we can tease some clues out of that to solve this particular mystery.' Another puff, puff and a cloud of blue smoke began to drift around his head, then, 'St Paul says in one of his letters, "The wages of sin is death; but the gift of God is eternal life through Jesus Christ our Lord." Now that, young Morris, is your clue.'

I laughed out loud at Jack's subtle clue. 'I'm not really very good at cryptic crosswords. You'll have to explain, please. Or at least get me started.'

'Very well. The problem most people have in making sense of that statement is that most people don't understand death.'

'I was the one who found Willesden's body,' I said. 'I think I understand death perfectly well.'

'Give me a definition, please.'

'The final cessation of life. The end of all living functions. How will that do?'

'Well enough. But can we do better? Consider this: what is it that makes death, death – so to speak? What *causes* the end of living functions, the cessation of life?'

'I'm sure you have an answer . . .'

'Separation. I want you to consider death as being separation.'

'Willesden's head was certainly separated from his body,' I said with a mirthless, cynical laugh.

'So in his case death involved physical separation. Even in non-violent death it's possible to put it in much the same terms. A heart attack, for instance, separates the brain from the blood flow it needs to function. Any key physical separation of that sort is death.'

'Fair enough.'

'But go one step further: death is also social separation.' Waving a hand in the direction of the unseen Warnie typing in the next room Jack said, 'Our father died in nineteen twenty-nine. That became for us a final separation in this world. Never again could we holiday in Belfast and see him and talk to him. Death is that kind of separation between human beings.'

'Again, fair enough.'

'We even use that sense metaphorically. If your old circle of friends "cuts you dead", as we say, they separate themselves from you and from all dealings with you. Separation is death – in that case "social death". But we can go further still. Those of us who believe in the soul would say that the moment of death is the moment when the soul is separated from the body. The moment when all electrical impulses cease in the brain is the moment when the soul leaves – is separated from – the body. Even those who reject the notion of the soul might be prepared to describe death as the separation of the body from that which animates it – the mind or the *élan vital*.'

'I suppose that's also fair enough.'

'And then there's spiritual death.'

'Spiritual death?'

'Separation from God. We were made to function connected to God. When the connection is broken, we are spiritually dead – we are separated from God: because separation *is* death! The spiritual vitality that comes from a connection to our Creator is lost when that connection is lost. Separation from God is spiritual death.'

'I'm not sure I'm still with you,' I warned Jack, 'but I'll keep listening.'

'In that sentence I quoted, the expression "the wages of sin is death" is a warning of spiritual death – a warning of separation from God. It's a warning of being eternally cut off from God and from the life, and light, and love and meaning and purpose of the universe – and cut off, separated, for ever.'

'You make it sound like hell.'

'Because that's what it is. I've heard foolish people say they'd prefer to spend the afterlife in hell because "that's where all the fun people will be". Perhaps, but they won't be having any fun. The best earthly equivalent of that sort of permanent separation, isolation, from God – and from all that is good and worthwhile – is the solitary confinement cell in a prison. While the Bible consistently portrays heaven as being a gathering of God's people – with each other in the presence of God – hell is the very opposite. In fact, there is a pattern in the Bible that when God blesses he gathers and when he curses he scatters. Separation is death. An eternity of separation, of solitary confinement, is a grim picture.'

'But what on earth can I – or anyone, for that matter – have done to deserve such an endless punishment?'

'Chosen it.'

'But who would choose that? No, that can't be right.'

'Remember that phrase "the wages of sin is death" – "wages" tells us that sin is something that we have *earned* by what we have done. But what exactly have we done to *earn* those wages? What have we done to have *earned* the separation that is death? Well, I'll give you a two-word definition of sin.'

'Let me give you one – unmarried sex.'

'Nothing so trivial, young Morris. The word sin means "ignoring God" – that's the two-word definition: ignoring God.'

He paused and puffed while I took this in, then continued, 'If you were to walk down the Cornmarket asking people what role God plays in their lives, the answer you'd get from most of them – if they were honest – would be "none". It's what we human beings do: we live our lives, our way, without God. We choose to separate ourselves from God. We choose separation. We just ignore God. If we persist in our separation until the moment of physical death, God treats us like adults, takes our choice seriously, and gives us the total, permanent, ultimate separation that we have been driving towards for the whole of our lives.'

'That makes the offence and the punishment . . .'

'Exactly. In *The Mikado*, W. S. Gilbert says that the punishment should fit the crime. Well, in God's court of final judgement the punishment *is* the crime – they are one and the same thing. The crime is choosing separation from God, and the punishment is separation from God – that complete separation, that total isolation, from God, continued for ever.'

'Hold on a moment – I thought you were giving me a clue to the mysterious death of Jesus.'

'I have. That understanding of death as separation is the clue.'

I opened my mouth to speak but thought better of it, so Jack resumed: 'On the cross Jesus took the death, the punishment you deserve. As he died, his most revealing statement is what is called the "cry of dereliction" – the moment when he cried out, "My God, my God, why hast thou forsaken me?" Can you hear what's happening there? In that very moment, Jesus is going through that final, total, ultimate separation from God that you and I deserve but he did not. That's *our* ultimate separation, *our* total isolation, from God that he is suffering *for us*. If you and I were ever in that place – ever that cut off from God – we would be there for ever. But because Jesus was and is the Son of the Living God, he came triumphantly through that separation – through that death and hell.'

My head was hurting and my temples were pounding, but I was following Jack closely enough to ask, 'Well, if death is separation, what is life?'

'The very opposite. If death is *separation* then life is *connection*: "the wages of sin is death; but the gift of God is eternal life through Jesus Christ our Lord." By suffering our final *separation* from God Jesus can then give us, as a free gift, a *re-connection* with God – a *connection* so powerful nothing can break it . . . not even physical death.'

I was silent for a long time so Jack said, 'That is the mystery of the death of Jesus – he was dealing with death, and purchasing life, for us. Dealing with our self-chosen *separation* from God, and purchasing a new *connection* for us – a welcome back into God's family.'

TWENTY-TWO

~

The next day, the Wednesday, I was lying on my bed reading a magazine article that Jack had lent me. It was written by Austin Farrer – the chaplain of Trinity College and a friend of Jack's. I was startled from my deep thought by a loud knocking on the door. Welcoming the excuse to toss the magazine aside, I hurried to the door and threw it open.

'Morning, old chap,' said Warnie cheerfully. 'Let's you and I go to the Bodleian and sort out what they're doing to Jack's reputation for good and all.'

As we strolled through the streets of Oxford, we chatted about both the Mystery of the Headless Corpse and the Mystery of the Missing Milton.

About the former, Warnie commented, 'All I can say is that I hope the Scotland Yard chappies are making some progress, because we aren't.'

'I wouldn't be so sure about that,' I said. 'Ever since that strange blade was recovered from the Cherwell . . .'

'. . . the guillotine blade, you mean?'

'Yes. Ever since then, I've had a feeling that Jack's on to something.'

'Huh, may very well be, old chap, may very well be. My brother has a brain the size of the Albert Hall. He'll work something out, I'm sure he will. This other business, though . . . the Chief Librarian of the Bodleian writing to Jack asking what he knows about the missing Milton . . . well, Jack's just not taking it seriously. That means it's up to us, Morris, old boy. We need to clear Jack's name.'

'And your theory?'

'This Nicolas Guilford you and Jack talked to,' Warnie said. 'He's clearly as guilty as Ivan the Terrible and Vlad the Impaler put together. I'd like to see the Bodleian chappies switch their attention to him and exonerate Jack.'

We were still chatting as we crossed the Old Schools Quad at the Bodleian and approached the reception desk.

'You're still in Oxford, I see,' said the young man behind the desk. It was Gooch again – he of the glassy eye and the slowish brain.

'Well observed, Gooch,' I said cheerfully. 'Time has not dimmed your sharp intelligence or your acute observational powers. Major Lewis and I are here to take our investigations a step further.'

'Ah, I see, you're still going on about that missing Milton?' Gooch sighed wearily. 'Well, as it happens, you're in luck. Bootle is back.'

'That sounds like the title of a West End musical – *Bootle Is Back*, starring Ivor Novello. Or have I misunderstood you? Is there some poor human being labouring under the name of Bootle?'

Gooch rolled his eyes as if searching for inspiration from the vaulted spaces of the Bodleian. 'Bootle,' he said patiently, addressing me as if I needed to be humoured so that I wasn't provoked to violence, 'is Cedric Bootle. He's a young staff member of the library. He was on duty in the Duke Humfrey on the day the Milton first edition was last signed out to a reader.'

'Yes, to my brother. So, where can we find this Bootle?' Warnie asked.

'He's in the Duke Humfrey this morning. Follow me.' Gooch led us towards the staircase in the far corner. As we tramped upwards he said over his shoulder, 'Bootle has been off sick for more than a week now.'

I asked him what the problem was. Gooch replied, 'No idea – it might have been measles or tropical malaria or possibly leprosy. All I know is, it kept him in the Radcliffe Infirmary for days.'

We entered the oak-panelled outer area of the Duke Humfrey and saw, seated at the duty librarian's desk, a spotty young man. He looked up as we entered.

'You feeling better now, Bootle?' asked Gooch. But he didn't stay for an answer. 'This is Morris and this is Major Lewis; they're enquiring into that missing first edition of *Paradise Lost*. Tell them anything you can.'

With those words Gooch turned on his heels and skipped off down the stairs.

Bootle rose to his feet to face us. He was a pale, thin young man with a carrot-coloured crop of hair and a face about as expressive as a slab of concrete.

Warnie began the interrogation by reminding Bootle of the day and date when the Milton was last signed out, and the fact that the reader who signed it out was Jack.

'Yes,' said Bootle, 'I know Mr Lewis. He often works here.'

'Do you remember that day?' I asked.

'That day?' he repeated, as if the words were strange to him.

'Yes, that day. The day Mr Lewis had the first edition Milton on his reader's desk in there.' I gestured towards the body of the Duke Humfrey library as I spoke.

'Oh, *that* day,' Bootle said, swallowing so hard that his Adam's apple danced a small jig up and down his throat. 'That day. Yes . . . yes . . . I remember.'

'Well, these wretched library authorities,' growled Warnie, 'have had the temerity to write to my brother asking does he remember returning the Milton and was it in good order when he did so? The hide of them!'

Bootle's glance flickered backwards and forwards between me and Warnie as if he was watching a tennis match.

'Do you remember,' I said, speaking slowly, 'picking up the Milton from Mr Lewis' desk when he had finished?'

'I do, actually,' Bootle replied, his voice squeaking adenoidally. 'It was a quiet day. Not many readers here that day. I only had a few books to collect from the desks that afternoon, and that small book, that first edition Milton . . . yes, I remember picking it up and taking it back to the cart, to be wheeled down to the stacks.'

'The accusation being made,' I explained, 'is that the pages of the Milton were cut out with a razor blade, and pieces of blank paper of the correct size inserted to hide the theft. In fact, it's more than an accusation, because we've seen the vandalised book, or what remains of it . . .'

'Not that day,' Bootle interrupted.

'What was not that day?' Warnie demanded.

'The vandalism,' squeaked Bootle. 'When Mr Lewis left, the book, the first edition of *Paradise Lost*, was on the desk lying open. That's how I found it. Lying open. There was nothing wrong with it. No pages had been cut out. So if anyone is saying that I . . .'

'Snap!' cried Warnie triumphantly. 'Don't you worry, old son, no one's accusing you of anything. But if you can give evidence that the Milton left the Duke Humfrey intact, well then . . . well, whatever happened to it happened elsewhere.'

Back in the Old Schools Quad Warnie had a grin on his face as wide as Tower Bridge.

'That gets Jack off the hook entirely,' he said, rubbing his hands together in glee. 'I shall write to the Chief Librarian, on Jack's behalf, directing him to the testimony of Cedric Bootle, and suggesting that an apology to Jack might be in order.'

'So that's the end of our investigation?' I asked.

'I suppose so.' Warnie was clearly reluctant to give up. 'However, we might just follow up the Nicolas Guilford angle. If he worked in the stacks, as he said, then I'll bet buttons to bootlaces that he vandalised the book when he was alone in the stacks. That must happen sometimes. Being alone down there, I mean. We should see if we can find a link between him and William Hare, the dubious bookseller. Always nice to tie up the loose ends. Well, I'm off to get a drink to celebrate. You coming?'

'No, I don't think I will, Warnie,' I replied. 'I've just spotted an old friend I'd like to talk to.'

'Cheerio, then.' And with those words Warnie sauntered off. The person I had spotted, on the far side of the quad, was Penelope. With her was a small boy in a khaki uniform.

With considerable diffidence I sidled up towards her.

'Morning,' I said. She turned as if startled.

'Oh, it's you.'

'I hope you've forgiven me for yesterday?'

'For what? Oh, that! Don't worry your small brain about that, you silly worm. It's not of the least importance. This little lizard here beside me is my nephew, Bertie. I'm just taking him for tea – would you care to join us?'

'Would I? I mean, yes, I would.' I was, it appeared, back in the good books of the lovely Penelope.

'Good morning, young man,' I said to the nephew. 'My name is Morris – Tom Morris.'

'Oh, yes, I should have introduced you. Bertie, this man is one of the intellectual inferiors I studied with when I was young and foolish.'

'Good morning, sir,' the young squirt replied politely.

'You're in the Boy Scouts, I see,' I offered, by way of extending the hand of friendship.

'No, sir.'

'No?'

'No. I'm a Cub Scout. I'll be a Boy Scout when I'm older.'

'And are you enjoying Cub Scouts?'

'Very much, thank you, sir. I can tie seven different types of knots. Would you like me to show you? I could show you on your shoelaces, if you wish.'

'That's very kind of you, Bertie, but I think I might leave my shoelaces laced up just as they are, thank you all the same.'

We had by now left the Bodleian quad and were heading down Catte Street towards the High Street and The Rose teashop.

'Do you know why this is called Catte Street, sir?' asked Bertie.

'No, I'm afraid I don't, young man.'

'Well, I do. Would you like to know?'

'Nothing would please me more,' I lied.

'In the Middle Ages it was called Mousecatchers' Lane – and I think it was changed to Catte Street because cats catch mice.'

'What nonsense, Bertie,' Penelope snapped. 'You do talk terrible nonsense. It was renamed Catherine Street and Catte is short for Catherine.'

'But I thought . . .' Bertie began to protest. But Penelope ignored him and turned to me. 'He's my sister Rosemary's boy. He's going to Magdalen School so I pick him up some days and put him on the bus to North Oxford.'

I knew that Magdalen College School was next door to St Hilda's, so that made sense.

At The Rose teashop Bertie ordered 'the largest cream and jam bun you have, please' and a glass of milk. Perhaps put off by Bertie's massive, sugary bun, Penelope and I limited ourselves to ordering a pot of tea.

Conversation was desultory for a few minutes. Bertie was totally occupied by a bun about the size of the Sydney Harbour Bridge and Penelope was staring out of the window, apparently totally distracted.

'What's on your mind?' I asked as I poured the tea. 'Not our last conversation, I hope?'

'What? Oh, no, not that,' she replied, dragging her attention back to her fellow diners at The Rose. 'Last thing on my mind.'

'Well, something seems to be troubling you.'

She leant forward confidentially and said quietly, 'It's St Hilda's Poetry Club.'

'What about St Hilda's Poetry Club?'

'I think the other faction is planning a coup,' she said dramatically.

'I had no idea poets led such colourful and violent lives.'

Penelope said nothing and sipped her tea for a while.

'However,' she said, putting her cup back into the saucer, 'I'll fix the plotters in due course. I have a trick or two up my sleeve. But that's enough about me – what about you? How's the investigation into your severed head progressing?'

'I think Jack might have some idea of how it was done. He dropped a hint that an idea is forming in that massive brain of his.'

'Jack? Oh, you mean Lewis. Well, yes, he is quite clever, I suppose.' That was extremely high praise coming from Penelope.

'And what about suspects?' she asked. 'You know that Scotland Yard man, I believe – so do they have any suspects as yet?'

'From what Inspector Crispin has told us so far, they've not been able to narrow down the list of suspects at all. Everyone who had anything to do with Willesden is still a suspect.'

'Everyone?' she threw back her head and laughed. 'Why, that would mean I was a suspect. What a hoot!'

My mistake was to answer her quite seriously, 'Well, yes, I suppose you must still be on their list. You see, that's the way police investigations . . .'

But she was not interested in explanations. She had gone pale and stiffened with anger.

'Come along, Bertie, we're leaving,' she said coldly.

'But I haven't finished my bun!'

'You can bring it with you,' Penelope said as she rose from the table and dragged up Bertie by his free hand – the one that wasn't sticky with bun.

'As for you,' she added, fixing me with a steely gaze, 'having the unmitigated gall to suggest that I might be a suspect in this murder case . . .' For a moment the eloquent Penelope seemed lost for words. Then she found the ones she wanted. 'You are a mindless buffoon.'

With those words she turned to flounce out.

'You don't mind paying, do you, Mr Morris?' she said over her shoulder as she disappeared.

I decided there must be an ancient medieval curse on The Rose teashop – every time I came here, I had a falling out with Penelope.

It was with a heavy heart that I went to the counter to pay my shilling, and with an even heavier heart that I trudged back to Magdalen, muttering to myself, 'Mindless buffoon? Mindless buffoon? Really? Mindless buffoon?'

TWENTY-THREE

~

Feeling miserable, and dragging my feet – a shattered wreck of the cheerful Tom Morris I had once been – I ambled aimlessly from The Rose down the High Street. Anyone chancing to glance at me would have no difficulty telling the difference between my face and a ray of sunshine. It was a warm spring afternoon, but if any small bird had tried whistling cheerfully at that moment I would have filed an official complaint.

How could that beautiful profile be combined with a nature that took offence at any slightly careless utterance I might make? Had I been wrong to say the police had not whittled down their list of suspects? Surely not! I'd just told her the truth, that's all.

Head down, hands in pockets, I kicked at paving stones.

But instead of heading back to my own room, I directed my feet once more towards Jack's rooms – looking for solace, a little comfort and some wise counsel.

I knocked on the door and entered to find Jack and Professor Tolkien deep in conversation. Jack welcomed me and waved me into a chair as the two of them continued to talk English Department politics.

I paid little attention. I heard the word 'syllabus' buzzing about once or twice and then I tuned out.

My mind drifted away to the many puzzles I was wrestling with. One of them – the puzzle of the Missing Milton – was looking fairly resolved. The puzzle of how Willesden lost his head was the opposite – anything but resolved. The puzzle of why Jack (and Christians in general, I suppose) make so much of the cross – a symbol of death – remained a puzzle I was still working on. And the puzzle of how Penelope really felt about me had me wanting to bang my head against a wall or start biting the carpet.

After a little while Tolkien began scooping up the papers that lay on the table in front of him as he said, 'I need to head back to Pembroke, I have a student in half an hour.'

As he walked towards the door, Tolkien turned around and, looking me directly in the eye, he smiled warmly and said, 'Jack's told me a little more about this Great War you two are fighting over the symbol of the cross, and I have a quotation for you. These words were in the Epistle read at Mass last Sunday.'

He closed his eyes as he concentrated to quote exactly: 'The words were, "God was in Christ, reconciling the world unto himself." Think on those words, young Morris. See you later, Jack.'

And with that he was gone.

His departure gave me the opportunity to unburden myself to Jack about the tragic, heartbreaking novelette that was the love life of Tom Morris. The story so far: our hero has tried to win the heroine, but is being hampered by his habit of putting his foot in his mouth.

'I don't know what she really thinks of me, that's the problem,' I complained.

'You wish to look inside a young woman's mind, do you?' Jack asked with a chuckle.

'But look at what she said to me, Jack. She called me a "mindless buffoon". They're hardly words of affection, surely?'

'In some women, they very well might be,' Jack said. 'Although I claim no particular knowledge in such matters.'

'But *mindless buffoon*?'

Jack chortled loudly and said, 'But you *are* a mindless buffoon. That's a reasonable description, is it not?'

And I couldn't really argue with that. Any fair-minded person would probably say Penelope's words just amounted to an accurate bit of observation and description. Just a bit of sound reporting, that's all.

Not wishing to pursue that line of thought any further, I returned to our 'Great War', as Tolkien called it.

'Those words of Tolkien's,' I said, 'about God being in Christ, reconciling the world to himself – if they are meant to make sense of the cross, they only confuse me further.'

'Your problem being?' Jack asked as he lit his pipe.

'Being the issue of the Trinity, I suppose,' I said, struggling to put my thoughts into words. 'You tell me that Jesus went to the cross in obedience to God the Father. And that at the height of his suffering he was separated from God the Father – in our place, as we deserve to be, but he did not. At the same time Tolkien says that God the Father was somehow at work in what Jesus did on the cross.'

I got up and paced about as I said, 'I struggle with this conception of God you Christians have. If God is this "three-persons-in-one", then how can one of those persons be working through the suffering of another? Or how can one of them – God the Son – be cut off from another – God the Father? Especially at a time when he was doing the will of God the Father? You see how hard this is to grasp, don't you?'

'Of course I do,' Jack replied, 'and that is exactly what you'd expect. If God is God and we are not, then God's inner being must, ultimately, be vastly beyond human comprehension. Fortunately for us, God has chosen to reveal a great deal of himself to us. And part of what he reveals is that his inner nature consists of relationship: the eternal relationship that binds together Father, Son and Spirit – the Father who loves the Son, the Son who serves the Father, and the Holy Spirit who is commissioned and despatched by both the Father and the Son.'

Jack told me to sit down, so that he could talk to me properly. I stopped my restless pacing and sat down as he said, 'All three persons of the One Being were involved in the cross – the rescue mission planned by the Father, sacrificially carried out by the Son, and applied to our lives by the Spirit.'

Jack paused and raised his eyebrows, as if to ask me how I was coping with all of this. I nodded, so he continued: 'This concept of the Trinity is unique to Christianity. No one could have made up such a thing. We have the concept only because God has revealed it to us.'

'But it's a nonsense concept,' I protested. 'Logically, you must admit, this whole notion of the Trinity makes no rational sense at all. Either God is one – as the ancient Jews insisted – or else God is three persons, Father, Son and Holy Spirit. Three? Or one? Which is it to be? You can't have it both ways, Jack.'

Jack paused to relight his pipe, and as the match flared up I saw a brilliant glint in his eye – clearly something had occurred to him.

'You're quite right that it's difficult. And over the ages many have tried to solve that difficulty in wrong ways – some by saying that Jesus was not God and others by espousing a kind of tri-theism: three Gods not one. But we are stuck with what the Bible actually says. And it insists that this is not an either-or, it's a both-and.'

'You mean *both* three *and* one at one and the same time?' I asked.

In response, Jack picked up an old envelope that lay on the table, and turned it over to the blank side. He pushed it towards me as he fetched a pencil and handed it over.

'Now, Morris, I want you to try a little thought experiment – are you game?'

I said that I was as I picked up the pencil and pulled the scrap of paper closer.

'First, young Morris, draw a straight line,' Jack said. So on the back of the envelope I drew this.

'There you are: one straight line. Now what?' I asked.

'Excellent,' said Jack, 'now draw a second line that starts at one end of your straight line and goes up at an angle.' Following Jack's instructions I drew this:

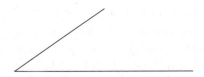

'Now two straight lines: is that it?' I asked.

'One more step,' Jack replied. 'Now join the ends of your two straight lines with a third straight line.'

So I did what he said.

'There's your third straight line,' I said. 'Now, come on, Jack, tell me what the point is.'

'The point is a question,' Jack said. 'Tell me, Morris, what have you drawn – three straight lines? Or one triangle? Which is it?'

'Well . . .' I began, and then I saw my problem. 'Very well, I'll be honest – it's both. I've drawn *both* three straight lines *and* one triangle at the same time.'

'As an illustration it's not really adequate, but it gives you a glimpse of what I'm driving at.'

He puffed in silence for a moment, and then said, 'No example of "three-in-one-ness" invented by mortal minds can ever really capture the complexity of God's nature, but this is perhaps as close as we, at our merely human level, can get to seeing that a being, or an object, can be *both* three *and* one at the same time.'

I thought for a bit, and then asked, 'But the Jews started off as monotheists, didn't they? It was central to their thinking that God, the Creator, was One. How come they missed this business, this three-in-one business, from the beginning?'

'Perhaps it all depends on how your triangle looks,' suggested Jack with a twinkle in his eye. Then he reached over, picked up the pencil and shaded in the outline triangle to make it solid.

'The three straight lines that make the outline of the triangle are still there,' he said, 'but on this view all you notice is the one-ness, and the three-ness is, perhaps, less obvious.'

Jack puffed silently on his pipe for a long moment while I looked down at the little sketch, then he resumed: 'And bear in mind that God's self-revelation was progressive – he revealed what people were able to take in. Then added a bit more as that was absorbed; and so on, over time. Rather like a curtain slowly rising on a stage set. Once Jesus Christ walks onto the stage of human history the curtain is all the way up and all is revealed.'

'And this helps us understand the cross, does it?'

'For you, I think it does, young Morris. For you are intelligent and you have an enquiring mind. A child could understand what lies at the heart of the cross – a good person choosing to die in place of a bad person. You could put that sort of thing into a children's story fairly easily and it would be perfectly clear. But you want to understand more about the nature of the cross and what it means – especially the transaction that happens on the cross between the three persons of God.'

'I agree,' I said. 'I do want to understand more.'

'In response I'm telling you two things here. First, that there *is* more that you and I can understand about what Christ achieved on the cross, and how he achieved it, than the child can grasp – and that's what we're working on. But in the second place, we must accept that we have limited, mortal minds and we will never understand *everything* about that transaction between the Father and the Son on that first Good Friday – that astonishing, powerful, sacrificial death that brings us hope and life.'

At that moment the door burst open and Warnie staggered in. He had been running and was out of breath.

'I just met . . .' he gasped, then he stopped to fill his lungs with air as his eyes bubbled. '. . . I just met Crispin . . .'

'Here, sit down, old chap,' Jack said. 'Put your feet up for a moment. A minute's delay will make no difference to your news.'

I fetched Warnie a glass of water, which he gulped down greedily.

'Now,' Jack said to his brother, 'what's all this about?'

'It's about Nicolas Guilford,' Warnie wheezed.

'That odious, and clearly guilty, piece of slime Jack and I encountered yesterday? The man we're pretty sure was the book thief? That Nicolas Guilford?'

'That's right, Morris – that's the chap,' said Warnie, then he stopped to take another sip of water.

'Well,' he resumed, more in command of himself, 'I was coming back to college from the White Horse where I'd had a pint or two – to celebrate our solution to the problem of the Missing Milton. Did Morris tell you about that, Jack?'

I'd been so immersed in my own problems that I had forgotten to pass on the good news, so I did so now.

'There's a staff member at the Bodleian, a weed named Bootle, who remembers collecting the first edition of *Paradise Lost* after you'd been working with it, Jack. He remembers that it was intact – no pages razored out. So his testimony puts you in the clear. And from your desk in the Duke Humfrey library the book went back to the stack where – as you know – this Nicolas Guilford worked. That's the background. So what's your news, Warnie?'

'I was walking back from the White Horse,' Warnie said, 'and as I reached the High Street I almost bumped into Inspector Crispin, who was moving along at a great rate of knots. I asked where he was going and he said down to the Cherwell – and would I please fetch you, Jack, and ask you to meet him there. He said it was urgent, so I trotted here as quickly as I could.'

'And did he give any reason for this urgent request?'

'Because of this Nicolas Guilford, that's why,' gasped Warnie, who was still catching his breath.

'But what about Nicolas Guilford?' I asked.

Warnie fixed me with a gimlet eye and said, 'He's dead. That's what about him.'

TWENTY-FOUR

~

Detective Inspector Gideon Crispin and his police team were gathered on the Angel Meadow side of the Cherwell, only ten yards or so from where Willesden's head had been found in its cricket bag.

Jack was never one to push himself forward and so we waited in the middle of Magdalen Bridge, watching the police group working on the far side, until Crispin spotted us and waved us over to join him.

The small group of uniformed policemen parted like the Red Sea as we approached. We came to a halt facing Inspector Crispin and Sergeant Merrivale. At their feet was a body – soaking wet, covered with water weeds and smeared with river mud. The pale, still face looking up at us was undoubtedly that of Nicolas Guilford.

'The body was discovered by some chaps in a punt,' Sergeant Merrivale explained. 'It was caught in the roots of that willow – otherwise it might have drifted for miles, and it might have been days before it was found.'

'Did he drown?' Warnie asked.

'The police surgeon is on his way,' Crispin replied. 'But to my eye there appears to have been a savage blow to the back of the head.'

'And we found stones in his pockets,' Merrivale added, 'no doubt intended to weight the body down. I was just saying to the inspector that my guess is there were originally a lot more stones, some of which have come out in the buffeting the body got from the current, which is why it floated to the surface.'

'Makes sense,' Warnie muttered.

'Do you see a connection between this death and the Willesden mystery?' Jack asked.

'The local chap, Inspector Fleming, assumed there must be,' said the Scotland Yard man, 'that's why he asked us to take a look. And they do have one thing in common.'

'The dumping site?' Jack suggested.

'Exactly, Mr Lewis,' Crispin agreed. 'The head was dumped less than ten yards upstream from here. The strange wooden blade contraption was found about twenty yards downstream. And now here is this body right here, smack in the middle. Assuming that blade drifted, as seems likely, then all three may have been dumped at almost exactly the same spot – just underneath Magdalen Bridge. One dumping spot suggests one killer.'

'Out of my way there, out of my way,' came an officious, bumptious voice from behind us. I turned around to see little Dr Mulliner, the police surgeon, bustling over the grass towards us carrying his black leather medical bag.

'We meet again, Crispin,' he said. 'Do you bring murders with you? Or do murders simply cluster around you, drawn like iron filings to a magnet?' Not waiting for an answer he said, 'Stand back, let me see what we've got.'

He examined the body and poked and prodded, then he turned it over and, seeing the wound on the back of the head, began gently pushing at the skull with his fingers.

'Was he drowned?' asked Sergeant Merrivale.

'The answer to that depends on whether he has water in his lungs or not, and that answer depends on what I find when I get him on the table. Do we know who he is?'

'He's been identified,' Crispin said, 'as Nicolas Guilford, a student of the university. What do you make of the blow to the back of his head? Could that have killed him?'

'Could have,' Dr Mulliner admitted – a little reluctantly, since he never liked to concede that a policeman was ever right about anything. 'At the very least it would have rendered him unconscious.'

'There is some evidence that the body had been weighted down,' said the inspector.

'In that case,' Dr Mulliner said, 'his attacker was either trying to dispose of a dead body, or else trying to kill a still living, although unconscious, one. I'll be able to tell you which when I open him up. Can I remove the body now?'

Inspector Crispin told him that he could, and Mulliner recruited two uniformed constables to lift the body onto a stretcher and carry it to the waiting vehicle. As the black van drove away, Jack asked, 'So, the question has to be: is there really a connection? And if there is, what is that connection?'

'You've hit the nail precisely on the head, Mr Lewis,' Crispin said, stroking his chin thoughtfully. 'We need to look for a connection between Willesden and Guilford – a connection that might have led both of them to their respective deaths.'

As he spoke he led the way up the grassy slope to the road.

'How about a criminal connection?' I asked.

'Do you think there might be one?' the Scotland Yard man asked.

'Well, as you know Warnie and I have been investigating the theft of valuable books from the Bodleian. At least, we started with one book – and that's still the only one we know about for sure. But if our theories are correct, there is, or has been, some sort of conspiracy involving more than one person to thieve from the Bodleian.

'Furthermore,' I added, 'we are now fairly certain that the person doing the thieving from the Bodleian was the late Nicolas Guilford. He certainly worked, part-time, in the stacks at the library, so he had opportunity, and he turned on a performance that advertised his guilt when Jack and I went to interview him.'

Crispin agreed: 'Let's assume for the moment that there was an organised plan along the lines you've suggested – how would it get people killed?'

'The thing is, inspector,' said Warnie, puffing out his moustache, 'we have no idea how wide this thing goes. It might, for all we know, be the work of a gang.'

'And once you get a criminal gang involved,' I interrupted, 'surely violence may well follow? Perhaps they've killed to protect their secrets? Perhaps they've killed members of their own gang for reasons we're yet to discover?'

Crispin looked doubtful, but he did say, 'It's possible – I suppose – that the unusual method of murder employed to kill young Mr Willesden was meant to be a dramatic warning to other members of the gang, a warning designed to frighten them into silence, or terrify them into obedience.'

By this time we were all walking slowly over Magdalen Bridge. Detective Inspector Crispin asked, 'What do you think, Mr Lewis? Do you think these deaths may be linked?'

'It would be surprising if they were not,' Jack replied. 'Surprising, but not impossible. Both are violent deaths of students; in both cases the criminal appears to have used, as you pointed out, the same dumping point. All of these mysterious and puzzling happenings are most probably part of the same complicated web. But the web may be complicated in ways we do not yet see.'

Crispin was rejoined, at this point, by his sergeant, and the two of them made their farewells and headed back towards the police station in St Aldates. Jack, Warnie and I continued a little further and then came to a halt in front of the entrance to Magdalen.

'Jack, you either know something or suspect something,' I said. 'Something you're not telling us.'

Jack's face broke into a broad smile. 'I like a notion to be fully finished before I share it, young Morris,' he said.

'All right, no need to share the whole theory, just give me a hint,' I said. 'That's all I'm asking for – a clue.'

'A clue, you say?' Jack responded. 'Very well, then – here is your clue. Over the years some of my students have been adroit and some have been sinister. Statistically, most have been adroit and only a minority sinister. You, Morris, were and are adroit. Willesden was sinister. There is your clue – make of it what you will.'

With a chuckle Jack left me and went in through the college gates, with Warnie at his side. I was feeling restless, and frustrated by Jack's cryptic clue, so I kept walking towards the town.

I continued up the High, past The Rose, past the university church, past Brasenose and Lincoln, past the covered market, and kept going until I reached the Cornmarket and found myself in Carfax Square.

And there, in the shadow of Carfax Tower, was the radiant Penelope. She was deep in conversation with an older woman. Dare I approach her? Could I simply apologise for offending her and thus get our relationship back on to a cordial footing?

As I stood irresolute the two finished their conversation and the older woman walked away.

'What ho,' I said in as jolly a tone as I could manage as I walked up to Penelope. 'A friend of yours?' I asked, gesturing at the back of the older woman who was now disappearing in the crowd in the Cornmarket.

'Head of classics at St Hilda's,' said Penelope. 'I think she's coming over to our side. She used to be a stick in the mud, but I think she's coming over to the side of the progressives.'

'Look – about you calling me a mindless buffoon,' I said.

'Well, you *are* a mindless buffoon,' Penelope responded with a giggle.

'Well . . . yes . . . that's what Jack said . . . and the point is . . . that I took no offence, and I hope that what I said to you didn't cause any offence, if you know what I mean.'

'Of course I know what you mean.' Penelope laughed heartily. 'Water off a duck's back, old bean. Water off a duck's back.'

'Oh. Righto, then. Well, that's a good thing.'

'What's the latest on the investigation?'

'Another body has been found.'

'Who is it this time? Someone as odious as Willesden, I hope?'

'His name is Guilford – Nicolas Guilford.'

'Don't think I've come across him. Was he a treacherous worm like Willesden? Well, I suppose he must have been if he got himself killed. Who are you and your fellow sleuths going to interview next?'

'Well, I did have one idea,' I said, as I fell into step beside her, walking briskly down the High. 'I thought maybe we should go and interview Professor Mallison. I know the police have already done that, but he did have the room above Willesden, and even if he saw and heard nothing on the night, he might know something useful about Willesden's comings and goings, don't you know.'

'Uncle Alec? Yes, I suppose he might know something. But he's such an absent-minded old dear he wouldn't even know that he did know – if you know what I mean.'

'Uncle Alec?' I asked. 'I didn't know Professor Mallison was your uncle?'

'Oh, yes. Mother's older brother. And the poor dear never has got over the death of Judith in that terrible car accident.'

'His daughter? Yes, I heard about that. Killed by flying glass from the windscreen, I was told.'

Penelope actually shuddered. Then she said in a quiet voice, 'Sliced through Judith's throat, I heard. Almost all the way through. Terrible, terrible. And then there was the business of the ghost. That just brought everything back. Made everything worse.'

'Ghost? What ghost?' I almost stammered.

'You mean you haven't heard? You poor, pathetic detective, you! In recent weeks – coming up to the first anniversary of her death – Judith's ghost has appeared on the lawn at Magdalen . . . almost under Uncle Alec's window. Brrr, doesn't the very thought of it make you shudder?'

At this point I went a bit slack-jawed with astonishment. Penelope believing in ghostly appearances? Penelope – she of the cold nerves and sharp mind? Surely not?

'Who told you about this?' I asked. 'About the ghost, I mean?'

'Uncle Alec. He saw it himself, poor old soul – it got him all of a dither, it did. Of course, it was such delicious, shivery gossip that I told everyone I knew. And the consensus was that if anyone was going to walk at night, it would be someone who died a violent death – like poor, dear Judith. Oh, look, there's Gwendolyn. I have to talk to her.'

With those words she rushed off, and I was left utterly gobsmacked in the middle of the pavement.

'Well, well,' I said to myself, there being no one else to talk to at that moment. 'Well, Tom, old chap,' I said, 'what do you make of that?' And by way of reply I told myself that I now felt more thoroughly confused than ever – confused at a higher and more elevated plane than before, but just as thoroughly confused.

TWENTY-FIVE

~

It was one of those moments when I needed to hurry back to Jack's rooms to confer – and that's what I did.

On the path from the cloister quad at Magdalen to the New Building I caught up with Professor Tolkien – also on his way to visit Jack, no doubt to conspire further over English Department politics.

'How are you, young Morris?' he asked in his gentle and genial way.

'Vastly confused,' I replied.

He asked me to explain, and his concern was so clearly genuine I thought here was a man I could pour my heart out to.

'Well,' I began, and then I faltered. 'I'm not sure where to begin.'

'In that case, old chap, I suggest you begin with a cup of tea in Jack's rooms, sit down, sort out what's on your mind and then lead us all gently into sharing your confusion.'

Which is, more or less, what happened over the next twenty minutes.

Once I was seated in the largest and shabbiest of the armchairs with a large cup of tea, expertly brewed by Warnie, in my hand and Jack, Tolkien and Warnie all looking at me expectantly, I began.

'There's a young woman . . .' I started and then I faded to silence.

'There often is,' Tolkien said encouragingly. Then he hesitated, as if doubtful about saying any more, but seeing the anxiety etched on my face, he chose to open his heart to me: 'In my case, her name was Edith. I was kept waiting a long time before I could marry her – but it was worth the wait. In your case, the young woman's name is . . . ?'

'Penelope,' I said quietly.

'Pretty name,' Warnie murmured.

'It turns out that she's the niece of Professor Mallison, although I've only just discovered that. She's at St Hilda's. I've had several . . . well, meetings with her, I suppose, in the few days I've been back in Oxford . . .'

I hesitated again and then resumed: 'I'd been turning over in my mind the idea of us re-interviewing Mallison. After all, he's on staircase three of north quad, above Willesden, so there might be something he's observed regarding Willesden's behaviour that would help the investigation. And I don't just mean at the time of the death. I was thinking about the way Willesden was behaving in the days and weeks leading up to his death. Anyway, I told Penelope I had this idea and she told me he was her uncle.'

'Does this relationship add anything to what we already know?' Jack asked.

'It's important only because of what he told her, and she then told everyone else.' Having said those words, I froze again. I was reluctant to speak the word 'ghost' aloud in front of such an intelligent group of friends. The Inklings, I was sure, would not believe in ghosts!

'Well, come along, Morris,' Jack said with a laugh. 'Having got us so far you shouldn't keep us hanging in suspenders, as they say. What did Mallison tell his niece, your friend?'

'That the ghost –' (there, I'd said the word) '– of his daughter, Judith, had been seen here in Magdalen – more or less in the vicinity of where the murder was committed.'

'You're not suggesting a ghostly, occult solution to our Headless Corpse Mystery, are you?' Warnie asked in a disbelieving tone.

'No, no, of course not. Nothing of that sort. But because of the coincidence in the timing, and the role Willesden played in Judith's death, I wondered if there could possibly be some sort of connection.'

'Judith was killed in a car accident, wasn't she?' Jack asked.

'Yes, and Willesden was driving the other car. Apparently, from what Mallison himself said, the magistrate's court cleared Willesden of any wrongdoing. Still, Judith's death was particularly horrible – sliced into by flying glass from the shattered windscreen. And Oxford was buzzing, I gather from Penelope, with the story of her ghost appearing at around the time Willesden died. Leaving aside all occult nonsense, could there be a connection?'

'It's hard to see how,' Warnie muttered, puffing out his moustache.

'In the first place,' Jack said, 'the dead do not hang around haunting the living – even the living they are particularly annoyed with, as Judith Mallison might conceivably be annoyed with young Willesden. Death is followed immediately by judgement, and that by rewards or punishments. Tollers will back me up on that.'

'Quite true, Jack – quite true,' said the professor. 'I find it easier to believe in alien or unusual beings than in hauntings by the ghosts of the dearly departed.'

'Secondly,' Jack said, 'even if such disembodied ghosts did exist, they would pose no threat – no physical threat. If they are as amorphous, as ghostly, as folk tales and legends tell, then they can't pick up a weapon and launch a physical attack.'

We drank our tea and pursued this subject for a little longer, and then I steered the conversation onto another course.

'As well as my Mallison idea,' I said, 'I had another thought – Bracken, David Bracken.'

'What about him?' Tolkien asked.

'Don't you find him odd? Strange in his behaviour, in the way he speaks sometimes, in his persistent questioning?'

'Well, he's not from around here,' said Tolkien, 'that's perfectly clear. And social conventions, and speech patterns, may be quite different in whatever colonial state he comes from.'

'And that's another thing,' I said. 'He's extremely vague about exactly where he *does* come from. He never gives a straight answer to that sort of question.'

Professor Tolkien leaned back in his chair, lit his pipe, and said thoughtfully, 'You may be onto something there, Morris. What do you think, Jack?'

'Mr Bracken certain appears to be an oddity. As you say, Tollers, there may be a perfectly reasonable, cultural explanation for that. But why don't we go and talk to him? If we discover Morris' suspicions about Bracken are a dead end, we can cross him off the list. If not, well . . .'

'I shan't come, if you don't mind,' Warnie said. 'I'm in the middle of typing out some stuff that I'd like to get finished.'

So it was that a few minutes later just three of us were heading towards staircase two – Jack, Professor Tolkien and myself. As we approached we saw Bracken darting into the staircase. We hurried after him.

On Bracken's landing his door was closed but he hadn't sported his oak, so I stepped up to the door and knocked. There was no answer, so I knocked again. And then a third time. We had seen him go in only a minute earlier.

'Could there be something wrong?' I asked Jack and Tollers.

I tried the door handle – it was unlocked, so I pushed the door open and walked in. The room was deserted. The lights had been left on, as it had become overcast in the last half-hour, but there was no one there.

'Where has the blighter got to?' Jack said in a puzzled tone.

'Could he have ducked in and out again?' Tolkien asked.

'He hardly had time,' I objected.

'If the lights are on and the door is unlocked, he can't have gone far,' Jack said. 'We should wait.'

For the next minute or two the three of us stood, or paced, around the room.

Then, as I became impatient, I asked, 'Can you two hear that?'

'I can hear something,' Tolkien agreed. 'A sort of low, humming sound. I would have said it was an electrical humming.'

I paced back and forth, trying to locate the source of the sound.

Finally, I turned to face Tolkien and Jack and said ruefully, 'It's coming from the wardrobe, I'm afraid.'

'After your last reported adventure I understand why you'd be hesitant to draw our attention to the wardrobe,' said Jack. 'But, on this occasion at least, I believe you're right.'

I pulled open the large, heavy doors of the old wardrobe. The humming became louder. I pushed back the hanging clothes to expose the bare oak panel at the back of the wardrobe. I leant forward to feel around, but it was a large piece of furniture and I had to put one foot on the base of the wardrobe to reach the back. When I did – it happened again.

I found myself falling forwards. I stumbled several steps, and dropped to my knees. When I looked up I found myself back in the white room I had seen before. Slowly, I rose to my feet and looked around. Jack and Professor Tolkien were standing beside me.

'We saw you disappear,' said the professor, 'and we thought we should follow.'

On the far side of the room there was a mechanical creak as a chair spun around. We were not alone. Seated at the desk filled with electrical control equipment on the opposite side of the room was David Bracken.

He stared at us and his jaw dropped. I think my jaw also dropped. I stared at Bracken, then I turned to look at Jack and Professor Tolkien. I was astonished to see they were both smiling.

'This is wonderful, simply wonderful,' Tolkien said. 'An impossible space in some other sort of dimension or on a different material plane. Wonderful!' He was clearly delighted – like a child who has just discovered fairyland or an elvish kingdom.

'It's just as you described it, Morris,' said Jack calmly. 'Tollers and I talked about your previous adventure. We decided you were too honest and too unimaginative to have made it up and too well balanced to have hallucinated the experience. So we came to the conclusion that this place you claimed to have found must really exist. And here it is. Now, Mr Bracken will, undoubtedly, offer us some sort of explanation.'

Bracken started to run his fingers through his hair as he muttered, 'This is terrible. Terrible. This is the end of everything. I won't be allowed to continue after this.'

'Now, Mr Bracken,' said Jack sternly. 'Pull yourself together. Why don't you begin with an explanation? Surely you owe us at least that?'

Bracken rose from his chair. He seemed unsteady on his feet and I thought for a moment he might collapse. Then he seemed to pull himself together.

'Yes, yes, of course. An explanation. What can I tell you?'

'How about the truth, young man?' said Tolkien. 'That would be the simplest.'

'I suppose so,' Bracken muttered dejectedly. 'I suppose it can't be helped. It's gone beyond hiding or explaining away, hasn't it?'

At this remark Jack actually hooted with laughter. 'Ho, ho, ho! It's far too late to hide things from us now, so why not just explain what this room is, where it is, and what's going on?'

Bracken, coughed, spluttered, and then began.

'This room,' he said, 'is a time chamber.' He gave us a moment to absorb this, then continued. 'I really am a student – a student of history.'

'So you are from our future, then?' Jack asked. 'And we are your past – the history you are researching?'

'Something like that,' Bracken admitted with a hangdog expression on his face.

'How does it work?' I asked.

'I don't understand the science. I'm a historian. The technicians tell me it has something to do with time and relative dimensions in space. But I have no idea how it really works.'

'Why the long face, Mr Bracken?' Tolkien asked.

'This will mean the end of my research. The last time I left the time chamber unshielded and Morris here stumbled into it, well, I had to report back to my supervisor. There was a lot of debate in the department over whether I should be allowed to continue. I pleaded with them, and I was. But this puts a lid on it. They won't let me continue after this.'

He sank slowly down on his chair, looking for all the world like a dejected puppy dog who's been left at home alone while his whole family has gone on an outing.

I was walking slowly around the room. 'There are no doors,' I said.

'There's one door,' Bracken replied, 'the one you came in through. In this time zone it interfaces with the Magdalen room, but when I return to my own time zone I step out of the same door and find myself in the history department laboratory.'

'What a wonderful way to research history!' Tolkien enthused. 'Just imagine, Jack, if we could go back and learn Old Norse from the original speakers of the language.'

'Or imagine having Catullus correct my pronunciation of Latin,' Jack boomed with delight.

'Well, it's all over for me,' moaned Bracken.

'Why?' Tolkien asked.

'We're not supposed to reveal ourselves. It's the strictest rule of historical research. The people of the past must never know they've been visited from the future. The time zone we go into must be completely unaware of our presence. And that's the rule I've broken – the biggest rule of all.'

'What are you researching, by the way?' Jack asked.

Bracken's face closed up, and it was clear we weren't going to get a real answer. 'Oh, this and that,' he said, 'just this and that.'

Professor Tolkien scratched his chin and then said, 'But no one from the future knows that we've discovered your secret. So surely you can continue?'

'But you'll end up telling someone. Or writing about it in a letter or a diary. If not now, then years in the future. And, of course, those documents will be discovered and known in my own time, and I will be disgraced and sent down from my place in the university, and lose my research scholarship.'

'Which university?' I asked.

'Oh, Oxford. I really am an Oxford student from . . .'

'Don't tell us,' Jack interrupted. 'It's probably best that we don't know exactly when you're from. And, Mr Bracken, I believe I can speak for my two friends here when I say that neither of us will ever breathe a word. Not a spoken word, nor a written word. Your secret is safe with us.'

'Really?' Bracken could hardly believe his ears. 'You mean you won't ever . . . ?'

'Of course not!' snorted Tolkien. 'We'll tell no one. We know students, and you strike us as a good sort. We wouldn't want anyone fouling up a research project by one of our students, and we won't foul up yours.'

'That's very decent of you, sir,' Bracken said, relief flooding his face. 'Very decent of you gentlemen. Very decent indeed.'

'Now, how do we get out of here?' Jack asked with a cheerful smile on his face.

Bracken told us to press on the grey, metallic panel on the wall behind us, and then walk confidently into what appeared to be a wall.

We did that, and a moment later the three of us were standing side by side in a room in Magdalen north quad in March of 1936 – exactly where (and when) we'd started from.

None of us said a word. It was almost too breathtaking to talk about immediately.

Once we were downstairs and out in the open air again, both Professor Tolkien and Jack lit up their pipes.

'How could you two take that so calmly?' I asked. I was astonished at how sanguine they had both been. It was my second visit to the 'time chamber', but they had seemed entirely unshaken by their first. How had they done it?

'We were prepared, in a way,' said Jack quietly as we walked back towards his rooms. 'In the first place, as I said, Tollers and I had decided that you had told the truth, and that something very strange was present in Bracken's room. And in addition, we're both Christians – we both know that this physical world around us is not the only plane of existence, not the only world there is. So we were ready for something, even though we didn't know what it was. But it was still a surprise, wasn't it, Tollers?'

'Yes, it was still a surprise. Quite startling, in fact. But I found our whole adventure, our very small adventure, beyond the mundane quite delightful . . . delightful and stimulating.'

TWENTY-SIX

~

It took me hours to get to sleep that night. Jack and Tolkien had cheerfully fallen into a debate over whether their experience supported McTaggart's philosophy of the 'unreality of time'. I dropped behind as they wandered off deep in conversation over the possibility of 'simultaneity' and whether time was an object or an environment.

Jack turned and said over his shoulder, 'This is to be discussed only among us three, remember? That's our promise to young Bracken.' Then he went back to his debate with Tolkien.

And that night I, as I said, lay awake and stared at the ceiling for hours. The paradoxes of time travel where whirling around in my brain.

It seemed to me that the three of us were certain to keep our promise of secrecy to Bracken, because if we let the secret slip – even much later in our lives – and left evidence of that, such evidence would already exist in Bracken's time and he would never have been allowed to commence his research in our time period in the first place.

Then I tried to go over that confusing concept again.

Yes, we must keep our secret, otherwise Bracken would not be here at all. Unless, something could happen to a time traveller that could change events before they happened.

Or something of that sort.

I was getting very confused. And I was also getting a headache from trying to understand all this. I got up, swallowed two aspirin, went back to bed and finally fell asleep.

The next morning I was walking out of the Hall after a late breakfast when Warnie appeared, coming from the direction of Jack's rooms.

He hurried towards me looking for all the world like a sheepdog that has just spotted the wandering sheep it was after.

'Loose ends, young Morris,' he puffed, slightly out of breath. 'Let's you and I tie up the loose ends.'

I asked him to explain, and he said, 'Let's track down what really happened to the Missing Milton. You and I have all the pieces in our hands, young Morris. Let's put them together and tie up the loose ends. What do you say, my boy?'

Naturally, I said yes – this was dear old Warnie, after all. And then I asked what specific project he had in mind.

'William Hare – that snarky, suspicious antiquarian bookseller. Let's get back to his little shop and ask him the tough questions. Give him the "third degree", as they say in those American films. Mind you, I'm not too sure what the first and second degrees are – presumably something less unpleasant than the third degree.'

This was down-to-earth and practical, and something I could believe in without making an effort to suspend doubts, confusions and questions. So after yesterday's strange excursion it was exactly what I wanted.

'Let's do it, Warnie,' I enthused. 'Let's interview Mr William Hare and see what he lets slip.'

We walked swiftly to the narrow back lane, near the centre of Oxford, and there we found the dingy and rather sad-looking little shop. I walked down the few steps from street level and tried the front door. It was locked.

'Locked,' I said to Warnie, pointing out the obvious (well, I am a journalist, after all).

He joined me and we peered in through the grimy windows. All was dark within, and we could see nothing but piles of mouldering books.

I raised my fist to knock on the door, but Warnie grabbed my wrist and said, 'Let's not alert him to our presence. At least, not just yet. Let's go around the side and see if there's another window.'

The shop was on a corner, and this gave us another side of the premises to investigate. It looked disappointing – just a plain brick wall, with a small, solid door set into it. Then I spotted a fanlight above the door. Creeping quietly up to the door, I stood as I tall as I could, on my toes, but the fanlight was still well above me.

Turning to Warnie I whispered, 'Make a step.'

He got my meaning at once, and came up and placed his back against the door. Then he bent his knees slightly, ready to take my weight, and cupped his hands. I lifted one foot, and stepped into Warnie's clasped hands. I straightened up and he lifted as far as he could. This brought me level with the fanlight.

Inside it was so dim that at first I could see nothing. As my eyes adjusted, I saw that the wizened little old man we had met in the shop was sitting at a desk with his back to the door. There was a single small, yellow light bulb illuminating the desk top where the man was working. It was all so dusty, dark and crowded that it might have been an illustration to a scene from Dickens – one of those crowded, busy drawings by Phiz full of shading and cross-hatching.

The glass of the fanlight was so covered in dust and grime, and the interior of the shop was so dimly lit it took me some time to work out what Mr William Hare was up to.

When I did, I leapt backwards out of Warnie's clasped hands, stumbled slightly on the cobbles, and quickly put my finger to my lips to signal silence. Warnie straightened up, rubbed his sore back, and followed me halfway down the lane.

Once I was certain we were out of earshot I said, 'He's cutting up a book. He's using a razor blade to very carefully cut the pages out of an old book. It's an octavo-sized book, so just the right size for the stolen Milton pages to be glued or sewn into.'

'Got him!' cried Warnie joyfully. 'Nothing is better than catching the villain in the act. If we get the police here quickly, they'll catch him red-handed. Although why "red"-handed, I wonder? Why not some other colour?'

'Originally,' I said, 'it referred to catching a man with blood on his hands.'

'Oh, yes, of course, that makes sense. Well, let's get moving, young Morris.'

Warnie and I walked quickly up to Carfax Square and turned down St Aldates, heading towards the police station.

As we passed Pembroke College, Professor Tolkien emerged from the college gates.

'Tollers!' Warnie called. 'I say, Tollers, old chap – have you got a few minutes to spare?'

In a rapid flow of words he quickly explained the situation.

'So,' Warnie concluded, 'we need to get the police to act quickly – to raid that dubious bookshop and catch that villain before he finishes what he's doing. And they'll be more likely to believe our information and act at once if we're backed up by your authority. This is Oxford – the title "professor" carries a lot of weight here, even with lumbering, slow-witted constables. What do you say, Tollers, old chap?'

Tolkien checked his wristwatch, then said with a warm smile, 'I'd be delighted, Warnie – delighted. And congratulations to you two on your successful sleuthing.'

We hurried down the street, past Christ Church and past the Broad Walk to Oxford Police Station.

At the front desk our distinguished-looking friend introduced himself as, 'Professor Tolkien of Pembroke College – and I have information to lay before you, information that needs to be acted upon immediately.'

Tolkien told the story, with Warnie constantly interrupting to provide corroborative details. The constable in front of us scribbled down notes then hurried to fetch a sergeant and we had to go through the whole performance again. But, thankfully, twice was enough. The sergeant announced that he and three constables would accompany us to the shop.

Five minutes later we were gathered, our colourful group of half a dozen, in front of the modest shop of 'William Hare, Antiquarian Books and Collectibles'.

The sergeant tried the door and found, as we had earlier, that it was locked. He then pounded loudly on the glass panel of the door and shouted, 'Open up in there! Police!'

This performance had to be repeated before a light came on inside, and the snaky William Hare slithered to the front door and unlocked it.

'Yes?' he asked, opening the door a bare six inches. We could see a mere slice of his face – looking like an ill-tempered owl with a touch of weasel blood.

'An information has been laid with us, sir, that you may be engaged in a criminal activity upon these premises,' the sergeant announced.

Where do they learn to speak like that? Is there a course at Hendon Police College called 'Stilted Official Speak 101'?

'I must tell you, sir, that it is our intention to enter these premises for the purpose of searching same. Now, I must ask you to step aside and allow us to enter, sir.'

'Do you have a search warrant?' hissed the villain, squinting at us all with venomous eyes. The man was looking so serpentine at that moment that he would probably have been able to hide behind a spiral staircase.

'Under the Commission of Crimes Act, nineteen twenty-seven, we do not need a search warrant when we have reason to believe that a crime is currently being committed. Furthermore, a professor of this university has laid information with us that leads us to believe that such is the case. Now, will you please stand aside, sir?'

As he uttered these words the sergeant beckoned one of his constables to his side. This was a young man who bulged out of his uniform – appearing to be a solid six feet in every direction. Hare took one look at the young man and stepped aside.

Our party wove its way through the perilously balanced piles of books that covered most flat surfaces, including the floor, and entered the small, dark back office. I was close behind the sergeant as we did so, and I was disappointed to see that the surface of the desk had been swept clean. There was nothing there.

'He's hidden what he was doing,' I said. 'As soon as he heard you at the door, he hid everything. But it can't be far away.'

The sergeant set one constable to stand guard at the front door of the shop, another to stand beside Hare to ensure he didn't flee, then he and his remaining constable began a careful search.

The first result of this action was to send clouds of dust into the air. But the second result – as they slid open the drawers of the desk – was to produce the old, leather book cover I had seen Hare working on.

'Is this what you saw, sir?' the sergeant asked me.

It was, I said, and the sergeant then asked Hare to explain himself. The bookseller wiped his fingers on his grubby cardigan and then said he was just doing some bookbinding. 'Nothing unusual or illegal in that, is there?'

Professor Tolkien urged the police officers to make a thorough search for the cut pages of the first edition Milton. And they did.

It was a long, slow search and quickly became quite dull for the spectators. Tolkien sat down on the only chair in the room, Warnie balanced himself precariously on a pile of old encyclopaedias and I found a seat on the bottom step of a narrow flight of stairs that, presumably, led to living quarters above.

But however boring it was for us, it was very thorough and, eventually, it paid off. The constable lifted a small cardboard box from the top of a tall bookshelf, opened it and found a thick wad of old printed pages inside. He handed this to the sergeant, who handed it to Tolkien.

'This is it,' the professor said with delight. 'Not a shadow of doubt. These are the pages that were cut out of the first edition of *Paradise Lost* at the Bodleian.'

'Mr Hare,' said the sergeant, 'I must inform you that it is our intention to take you to Oxford Police Station, where you will be charged with handling goods knowing them to be stolen. You do not have to say anything but anything you do say may be taken down and used in evidence. And I must inform you that you have a right to ask for legal representation.'

And that was how the Mystery of the Missing Milton was solved. I have to say that most of the credit must go to Warnie, who was relentless in his pursuit of the matter.

As William Hare was led away and his shop locked up, Warnie, Tolkien and I headed to the nearby Mitre for a pint to celebrate.

Professor Tolkien paid for the first round, and he brought the tray of glasses over to our corner table beaming with delight. As he sat down, his coat flapped open, revealing a silk waistcoat of a startling blue colour. I have never quite become accustomed to Tollers' dazzling array of waistcoats.

Tolkien insisted that he toast Warnie and I for our 'detective triumph' and then asked the question that was hovering at the back of all our minds: 'What does this crime have to do with our other mystery – the Headless Corpse?'

'Well,' I replied hesitantly, 'if we're right about Nicolas Guilford's involvement in this book racket, there must be *some* connection. Guilford is dead, and appears to have died by the same hand as took Willesden's life. So *some* connection, then. But as to what that connection is? Well . . .'

TWENTY-SEVEN

~

Warnie and I barged in to Jack's room ready to loudly advertise our triumphant conclusion to the Case of the Missing Milton.

'You're completely in the clear, Jack,' Warnie proclaimed as he burst into the room – rather in the manner of Peter Rabbit announcing his escape from Mr McGregor's vegetable patch. 'The missing pages have been recovered . . .'

He stopped suddenly at this point because Jack had a guest: Detective Inspector Gideon Crispin of Scotland Yard, and the two appeared to be deep in conversation. Their brows were furrowed, and they probably resembled Plato and Socrates when talking over what to put into that Republic of theirs.

Jack, of course, turned to face us and grinned from ear to ear. The brothers were very close and enjoyed nothing better than celebrating each other's triumphs.

'Warnie, you are a wonder,' Jack boomed. 'An absolute wonder! You didn't bring Tollers back with you to celebrate?'

'He had to meet someone at the Sheldonian,' I said. 'Good morning, inspector, please don't think we're ignoring you, and we do apologise for interrupting what is clearly a serious discussion.'

'Have you come to consult Jack's Giant Brain?' Warnie asked, and I could hear the capital letters clearly enunciated as he spoke.

'I've come to show him a piece of evidence.' With these words Crispin picked up an envelope that was lying on the table and shook out the contents with the flourish of a magician producing the flags of all nations from a small matchbox. What actually slid out of the envelope was a pair of glasses, with a cracked lens and generously smeared with dirt.

'We have confirmed that these are Willesden's glasses,' he said.

'They were found,' Jack explained, 'in the garden just below Willesden's window.'

'I must admit,' I said, 'that I had noticed Willesden's glasses were missing when we saw his head in that cricket bag on the riverbank. But I thought nothing of it. I assumed they could have fallen off at any point in . . . well . . . in whatever awful proceedings took place.'

'We made the same assumption, Mr Morris,' said the Scotland Yard man, 'until the gardener – a nice old chap by the name of Alf – brought these to one of my officers. He found them embedded deep in the soil by his roses.'

I stooped to pick them up and then hesitated.

'It's all right,' Crispin said. 'You can touch them, they've been fingerprinted. The only prints were Willesden's. So at least we can say the glasses were not removed from his face – either before or after separation from the rest of him – by the murderer.'

'Or the murderer was wearing gloves when he did so,' Warnie suggested. 'All criminals know about fingerprints these days. They probably learn about them in the introductory course they do before joining the Black Hand or the Purple Gang.'

We all examined, or in Jack's case re-examined, the glasses, and talked about them for the next few minutes. At least Crispin, Warnie and I talked. Jack fell strangely silent. I knew what that meant. When Jack fell uncharacteristically quiet, with a thoughtful expression on his face, it meant his brain was racing like the Flying Scotsman on a downhill run with a tailwind. It was in moments like these that Jack had solved impossible puzzles in the past.

'A penny for your thoughts,' I said. Jack stirred from his deep reverie and replied with a laugh, 'They would be vastly overvalued at that price.' So, whatever was going on in that inventive mind, he was not ready to share it just yet.

Tolkien came to lunch that day. Warnie stayed behind in Jack's rooms to eat a sandwich as he continued his work on the Lewis Papers, so it was just the three of us who ate pork pies and drank bitter at the Eastgate. And it was as we were leaving following our leisurely meal that we heard rapid footsteps behind us. We paused until David Bracken had caught up.

'I just want say,' he began, then he had to pause to catch his breath. 'I just want to say how grateful I am to you gentlemen for yesterday.'

'Think nothing of it, old chap,' Jack boomed. 'Always happy to do what we can to help a serious student. We just wish all of our students were as serious as you are, don't we, Tollers?'

Professor Tolkien agreed, and then I asked the question that had been troubling me ever since my bout of insomnia the night before.

'Willesden's murder,' I began, then I stopped to ensure that we could not be overheard – this was a question just for those of us 'in the know'. 'Willesden's murder – could it have involved time travel in some way?'

We were now standing on the pavement of a largely deserted High Street, in the quiet lull that often marks early afternoon, and we were well away from prying ears.

'What did you have in mind, Morris?' Jack asked.

'Well . . . we saw how Bracken's "time chamber" thingy opened into his room. Could another time chamber operated by one of Bracken's fellow time travellers have opened into Willesden's room? That might explain how his dead body – and only his body – was found in a room that was locked and latched from the inside.'

'I don't think there is anybody else operating in this time zone,' Bracken said hesitantly.

'Well, *you*, then,' I said accusingly.

'Me?' Bracken glared at me like a curate who's discovered a choir boy sucking a gobstopper during divine service.

'Yes, you. I take it your "time chamber" can be relocated in space as well as in time?'

'As I told you – I'm not a technician. Other people, more expert people, set the controls before I'm allowed to operate the thing. But, yes, of course these chambers are only useful as transportation devices because of their mobility in both time and space.'

'Then,' I said, turning to Jack and Professor Tolkien, 'don't you see what follows from this?'

'I do,' said Tolkien in his quiet, quick voice. 'Can you assure us, Mr Bracken, that you had nothing to do with Willesden's death?'

'Nothing at all,' said Bracken in an urgent whisper. He appeared outraged. 'I don't know what you're suggesting.'

'Young Morris here is suggesting,' Jack said, 'that you could have relocated your time chamber to Willesden's room, materialised there, murdered Willesden using whatever technology was used, and then dematerialised, leaving the room locked and latched and taking the head with you. I'm not sure I agree with him, but that is Morris' suspicion.'

I nodded in agreement, and Bracken shook his head in angry protest.

'But why?' he argued. 'Why would I do such a thing? I had no reason. I only arrived in Oxford a week ago. I have no history with Willesden. I have no quarrel with him. Why would I murder that poor young man?' He was flapping his hands in a vigorous protest – rather like a motorist trying to persuade a sceptical policeman that he really had been driving under the speed limit.

'Perhaps,' I suggested, 'Willesden uncovered your secret? Perhaps he heard the humming of your time chamber and stumbled across the whole thing?'

'But . . . but . . .' Bracken's voice was rising to an upper register of indignation – his usual baritone turning into a squeaking tenor. 'You did that! You stumbled across my secret! And I didn't kill you! I was honest with all three of you! Why would I be honest with you if I'd killed Willesden for making the same discovery?'

'In that case,' Tolkien said, 'we have to ask the question: could someone else have committed the murder using this amazing, magical technology of yours?'

'I can test for that,' Bracken replied, calming down and taking deep breaths. 'I can test for that. I can give you a clear and definitive answer.'

'Let's do it, then,' said Jack. 'Come along to Willesden's room, run your test and tell us what you find.'

It took only a few minutes for Jack to once again borrow the key to Willesden's room from Murray, the head porter, and for the three of us to climb staircase three to the scene of the crime.

'Here we are, then,' said Tolkien as we stepped into the room. 'So how do you run this test of yours?'

Bracken pulled a small, odd-looking object out of his jacket pocket. It was a small metallic, tubular, hand-held device with switches at one end, and tiny, flickering lights at the other.

'What does that do?' I asked.

'A wide range of things. It's a very flexible device. But what I'm going to use it for now is to test for random chronos particles. If any time travel has occurred in this vicinity at any time in the last little while, there will still be stray chronos particles drifting about, and this little device should detect them.'

'How does it work?' I asked.

'As I keep saying – I'm not a technician. But I believe it uses sonic waves or something of that sort.'

He pressed one of the buttons on the bottom of the tube, and varicoloured lights began flashing at the other end. Then he waved it slowly through the air – pointing it in turn at each wall, at the floor, the ceiling, and each item of furniture.

'I know it looks odd,' he said as he focussed all his attention on the tube, 'but it's just a hand tool, that's all it is. A type of hand tool quite common in my time.'

'You mean,' I asked, 'like a spanner or a screwdriver or something like that?'

'Something like that.'

We all waited in silence as a minute and then two minutes ticked by.

Finally, Bracken said, 'Clean. All clear. The walls, the floor, the ceiling, the furniture – all of them are uncontaminated by random chronos particles. There has been no time travel in this vicinity – I would say ever!'

'Well, does that settle your question, Morris?' Jack asked.

'I suppose so . . .' I began, and then I stopped. In fact, we all stopped to look again at Bracken's strange little tube, which had started to beep and flash a tiny, brilliant white light. Bracken looked startled. He waved the device around to try to detect the source that was causing it to behave like an over-excited, yapping Pekinese.

As he moved, the small machine flashed and beeped rapidly when he brought it closer to Professor Tolkien, and more slowly when he moved it away. Bracken repeated these movements several times so that the results could not be uncertain.

Jack found this vastly amusing. 'Ho, ho, ho!' he bellowed. 'My dear Tollers, you turn out to be a creature out of time. We always knew there was something special about you.'

'Hang on, hang on,' Bracken insisted. 'Seriously, there is something here. Not in Professor Tolkien himself; rather, it's something he's been in contact with fairly recently.'

'What sort of something?' Tolkien asked.

'Something alien. But I can't tell from these readings if that something "alien" is not of this time, or not of the Earth, or both. Where have you been recently? What have you brushed up against? What might you have touched?'

Tolkien explained that before having lunch here at the Eastgate, he'd been out and around Oxford that morning.

'But where was the last place you were before you came to lunch?' Bracken persisted.

'At the Sheldonian Theatre. I'd arranged to meet a student in front of the Sheldonian, and then we were going to walk across the road to Blackwell's. He was rather late, so I just lounged in front of the Sheldonian – leaning against the plinth of one of the Sheldonian heads.'

I knew what he was talking about – the giant stone heads that decorate the wall in front of the Sheldonian Theatre.

'We need to go there,' Bracken said, sounding quite urgent. 'We need to check this out. There is something there . . . but just what . . . well, I'm not a technician, so I can't be sure.'

Tolkien, Bracken and I had turned to go when I noticed that we didn't have Jack's full attention.

He had that look of concentration on his face again as he stared into the far distance. He looked so much like *The Soul's Awakening* he would have fooled any passing art critic.

As I watched, he walked over to the sash window, put his hand into his top pocket and pulled out the envelope containing the glasses recovered from the garden. I was surprised to discover that Crispin had left this piece of evidence with Jack. Perhaps Crispin didn't regard it as very critical evidence? Jack tipped these dirt-smeared spectacles into his hand – all the time shifting his gaze from the window to the glasses and back again.

'Jack, are you coming with us?' Tolkien called.

'I most certainly am, old chap,' Jack replied heartily, slipping the glasses back into their envelope and back into his pocket. 'Let's go and find this alien whatever it is.'

But we didn't go straight to the Sheldonian Theatre. As we passed through the porter's lodge, Jack returned the key and he also scribbled out a note on a slip of paper which he handed to Murray.

'Can you get one of the scouts to deliver this by hand, please?'

'Certainly, Mr Lewis.'

'It's fairly urgent.'

'I'll get the boy to do it at once, sir.'

Only then did we leave the college and head up towards the Broad and whatever alien artefact was awaiting us at the Sheldonian.

TWENTY-EIGHT

~

The Sheldonian Theatre is set back from Broad Street behind a stone wall with steel railings and is decorated with impressive giant stone heads. Each of these is actually a head-and-shoulders sculpture of a male, placed on a tall square stone pillar. They all have beards and sour expressions. I've never been particularly fond of them myself.

There were four of us standing in front of these stone heads with their strange, staring eyes and bulging faces – Jack, Professor Tolkien, David Bracken and me.

'What do you know about these?' Bracken asked. 'What are they statues of?'

'That's a very good question,' Jack said, 'to which there is not a clear answer. One theory is that they are "termains", or boundary markers, named after Terminus, the Roman god of boundaries. No one knows for certain who the heads were meant to represent. They've been variously called the Apostles or the Philosophers, but most commonly they're called the Emperors. A former student of mine – a young chap named Betjeman – once told me he thought of them as the "the mouldering busts round the Sheldonian". They're not in very good shape, are they?'

'You'll recall, Jack,' said Professor Tolkien, 'that the official name for these heads is "herms". I remember learning that as an undergraduate.'

'That's right,' Jack concurred, 'from Hermes, the Greek equivalent of the Roman god Mercury – one of whose roles was to be the god of boundaries.'

Perhaps, I thought cynically, these heads were not meant to represent ancient gods or philosophers or anything more intellectual than a history of beards – since each had a different style of beard?

'So which one were you leaning up against while you were waiting?' Bracken asked, directing his question to Professor Tolkien.

In response the professor walked over to one of the largest and most unpleasant of the heads. The image's worn, stone visage looked like a plug ugly from one of those Warner Brothers gangster movies – and its mouth was half open in a nasty scowl. This was clearly someone I wouldn't want to meet in an alley on a dark night. If this stone head really did represent an emperor, then it was one of those cheerful ones whose idea of after-dinner entertainment was feeding a few peasants to the lions.

'This one here.'

Bracken walked to Tolkien's side, whipped out his strange metallic, tubular gadget and started scanning the giant stone head. Immediately the buzzing began – sounding like a small, angry wasp trapped in a bottle.

'So does that thing tell you who carved it?' I asked. 'And how much he was paid for his work? Or perhaps if the bill is still outstanding?'

Bracken didn't reply right away, but focussed on concentrating as he waved his futuristic gadget about.

After a good deal of buzzing – occasionally accompanied by beeping and those small flashing lights – Bracken eventually replied, 'No one carved it.'

He let us absorb this odd statement, and then added, 'This is not a carving. This is a petrified head.'

Now, I know what you're thinking – you're thinking that there was probably a nice, quiet padded room waiting for David Bracken in the Home for the Terminally Confused, and that we should just humour him until medical assistance arrived. I would have thought exactly the same thing a few days ago. But in the interim I had been – not once but twice – inside a strange white room filled with even stranger electrical controls, a room that should not be physically possible. A room that should not, could not, exist inside a wardrobe in an Oxford college room. Certainly not in Magdalen. Perhaps in Balliol (who knows what goes on in Balliol), but not in Magdalen.

I had *seen* his strange room – the one that Bracken called a 'time chamber' – with my own eyes. Which is, you must admit, an absurd expression. I couldn't have seen it with my own ears, now could I? Or with someone else's eyes? But I did see it, and so did Jack and Tolkien. And so we were less inclined to dismiss Bracken's extraordinary claim out of hand. Because of that experience, I was not inclined to pop down to the covered market and buy him a nice, comfortable straitjacket.

A petrified head, eh? Well, that's a possibility that hadn't occurred to us before. Probably an idea you won't find in any of the Oxford tourist brochures.

Bracken was now walking down the length of the Sheldonian's stone wall running his scanning device slowly over each of the giant heads of philosophers, or emperors or whatever they were, in turn.

Having got to the end of the row, David Bracken rejoined us.

'Well,' I prompted, 'what have you found out?'

'They're all the same,' he said, tapping on his little handheld gadget as if doubtful as to the readings he was getting. 'According to this, they're all petrified heads.'

I was encouraged to discover that Bracken was finding this as surprising, and as difficult to come to terms with, as we were. It's one thing when someone peddles a weird notion with wild, wide-open eyes and a crazy expression. It's an entirely different experience when the same weird idea is offered by someone as surprised by it as you are yourself.

A long silence followed this pronouncement, broken, finally, by Tolkien, who said, 'But look at the size of them! If these are real heads – albeit now petrified into solid stone – they must have come from the shoulders of giants, or of stone trolls, or of something equally extraordinary and unknown to us.'

Jack walked over and laid a hand gently on one of them, almost as if he suspected that now that it had been found out it might suddenly come to life and snap at him.

'But they are weather worn, just as ordinary stone becomes weather worn. How can that be?' Tolkien asked.

'Because they *are* now stone,' said Bracken. 'One of my fellow students – back in my own time zone – was collecting petrified remains from the very early earth, and when some living thing goes through the petrifaction process what it becomes is stone – real stone. Such things then, of course, weather like real stone.'

'Yes,' I agreed. 'I read about it in one of the Sunday papers. In the petrifaction process organic material is converted into a fossil through the replacement of the original material and the filling of the original pore spaces with minerals.'

'So, let me be clear about this,' said Tolkien. 'These are real giant stone heads now, but they were once organic giant heads, part of some living, organic being – a very large living, organic being? Is that what your buzzing, beeping, flashing little machine is telling you?'

'More or less,' Bracken admitted.

'Could it be wrong?' Jack asked.

'I've always found it very reliable,' Bracken insisted. 'And it was tested and set by technicians before I began this expedition.'

'How did the heads get here?' I asked.

'I certainly don't know the answer to that,' Bracken said. 'Presumably the designer of the Sheldonian ordered some stone heads or stone figures to decorate the stone fence.'

'That would have been Christopher Wren, I presume,' Jack said. 'He designed the Sheldonian.'

'And he would have placed his order with a stone mason,' Bracken continued. 'Perhaps to the stone mason these heads were "found objects" – and it was much easier and quicker to supply them than to get to work with chisel and hammer and make new ones.'

'But in that case we have to ask – "found" where exactly?' Tolkien said. 'And how did they come to be wherever they were found?'

By way of reply Bracken just shrugged.

'Perhaps they were dug up?' I speculated. 'If they were under-ground for many centuries – or even many millennia – that would explain their age, and why they only turned up when Wren was looking around for decoration for his building.'

'So, how much does your little machine tell you?' Jack asked. 'What else does it reveal about these giant stone heads?'

'Well, it informs me that they were originally organic, as I've said,' Bracken explained. 'Also that they are very old, and they are alien in origin. They belong to some other, quite ancient, time zone. And they are not *homo sapiens*.'

'What, then?' Tolkien asked eagerly.

'Either not from the earth, from elsewhere, or possibly from a race that died out long ago – before *homo sapiens* came to dominate this planet.'

Alice would have been right at home here, and would have remarked 'curiouser and curiouser' as an appropriate editorial comment.

Tolkien's eyes, I noticed, were lighting up with deep interest. 'So . . . "a race that died out long ago" . . .' he quoted.

'There were giants on the earth in those days,' Jack said, adding, by way of explanation, 'Genesis six.' And then he continued the quotation: 'the same became mighty men which were of old, men of renown'.

'So, Mr Bracken,' Tolkien said, 'you have thrust this remarkable discovery upon us. How do you explain it? Where *might* they have come from?'

Bracken started muttering to himself, almost as if he had forgotten we were there, and he was totally absorbed in solving the puzzle: 'Many millennia old? Alien in nature? Remnants of Atlantis, perhaps?'

Tolkien almost leapt out of his skin. Not that he made any sudden, physical movement, you understand – he was too dignified for that. But he looked to me as if a million-volt lightning bolt had just shot through him.

'You mean there really was . . .' he began, but he stopped when he realised how embarrassed and awkward Bracken was now looking.

Jack, Tolkien and I surrounded Bracken – and without saying a word made it clear by our determined body language that we expected him to speak, and to speak some sort of sense.

He squirmed in silence, like a snail sprinkled with salt, and then, eventually, spoke: 'I've already said too much. I should have been more careful. We're not supposed to tell people in this time zone about discoveries that have not yet been made. There is a level of deep ocean exploration in my time zone that is scientifically not possible just now. So data levels from the two time zones are quite different. Is there any chance that you could just forget about everything I've just told you?'

'I'm not sure I want to,' Tolkien said quietly. 'Not that I would ever reveal your secret, or your presence among us, Mr Bracken – but this information is too good to forget. Jack, earlier this year you and I were lamenting that there is too little of what we really like in stories.'

'And as a result,' Jack said, 'we decided we'd tackle writing the sort of stories we like ourselves. I would try a space-travel story and you would try time-travel.'

'Well, this is the starting point for that – for my time-travel story. I can start by building on the destruction of Atlantis – as it's called in the myth as Plato recorded it – and create a time-travel story that goes back across the western sea to the Land of the Far West. I can see possibilities in that.'

Bracken was beginning to look alarmed, so Tolkien turned to him and said soothingly, 'All written as fiction, old chap. None of it can reflect back on you.'

'Wonderful idea!' Jack boomed. 'I've already begun my space-travel tale, so I encourage you to pursue your idea – and pursue it vigorously.'

'And it ties in,' Tolkien added, 'with my dream – what I call my "wave dream".'

Seeing the puzzled looks on our faces he explained, 'It's a dream I've had repeatedly over the years. In my dream I see a vast, towering wave, many hundreds of feet high, foaming white at the top, and about to crash down into a green, surging ocean. Sometimes in the dream there is a steep, dark, rocky coastline about to be drowned by the giant wave. Sometimes there is a white tower on that coastline, rising to a slender, elegant pinnacle and standing directly in the path of that massive wave.'

This was fascinating. I could see the creative process beginning inside Tolkien's head as he shared this vision with us. And even I, a dull journalist, could see the fictional possibilities of recapturing the downfall of Atlantis, in some form, in a time-travel tale. No wonder Tolkien's creative juices were flowing.

TWENTY-NINE

~

'Just so long as no one else ever finds out,' Bracken was saying nervously. 'I've broken all the rules they teach us before they allow us into the time chamber. *All* the rules – every one! If my course supervisor ever finds out . . . Well, those rules aren't like exam questions, you know – "Five only to be attempted" – I'm supposed to keep *all* the rules!'

Jack told him soothingly not to worry – we would all keep our word to protect his secret, and whatever Tolkien wrote would be published as fiction. No one would suspect a thing.

'So there's really nothing to worry about, old chap,' Jack concluded comfortingly.

The conversation continued along this line for another few minutes, with reassurance upon reassurance being poured upon the anxious David Bracken.

This was interrupted by the loud, cheery hail of Warnie as he approached us down the Broad: 'What ho, what ho, you chaps! What are you up to?'

Since Warnie was not one of the three who knew about the time chamber, Professor Tolkien promptly changed the direction of the conversation.

'We're finished here,' he said, 'and we were just debating whether or not to amble up to the Bird and Baby for a pint.'

'Well, if I may join that debate, I vote in favour,' Warnie said with a chuckle.

And our little group, now numbering five, was about to head towards St Giles when another newcomer waddled up to us.

Professor Mallison had emerged from Blackwell's bookshop trying to balance two brown paper parcels and an umbrella, and immediately headed in our direction.

'Gentlemen, gentlemen,' he said, beaming at us short-sightedly through his thick-lensed glasses. 'How goes your investigation? Are your friends in the police force on the verge of making an arrest?'

'Early days yet,' Jack said. 'Nothing to report.'

'Really? Really?' muttered Mallison in his usual vague manner. 'But they brought in a Scotland Yard man, did they not? I thought all that high-octane detecting power would mean an early result. Oh, well . . . if you say so . . . no doubt this is a puzzling matter . . .'

He put his head down and was about to walk away when Jack, in an act of generosity for this lonely old man, said, 'Would you care to join us for a drink at the Eagle and Child?'

'A drink? Oh, a drink. No, I don't think so. I'm on my way back to college. Work to do, you know.' Mallison was slowly shuffling away as he spoke.

'Actually, Jack,' I said, 'I may go back to the college myself. Catch up with you later.'

At that point, with Warnie keen to get started for the pub, we split up.

'Hold on, professor,' I called after Mallison. 'I'll walk with you to Magdalen.'

What I had not said to the others was that I wanted to track down Penelope and mend some fences.

'Professor,' I said as we turned down Turl Street. 'There's a friend of mine who, I have just discovered, is a niece of yours.'

'If you say so, young man,' muttered Mallison, 'if you say so.'

'Her name is Penelope . . . Penelope Robertson-Smyth. I take it you *are* her uncle? I've got that right, haven't I?'

'Uncle? Well, yes, I am as it happens. Since you ask, I am young Penny's uncle. And what is your connection with my niece?'

'Well . . . just social, that's all, just social. We knew each other a few years ago – before we graduated. Now we've moved on, and we've just reconnected, as it were . . . just recently.'

'Very nice for you, I'm sure.'

'I have, though, rather put my foot in it with her. Unintentionally, of course. We were talking about the murder – the Willesden business – and I just happened to mention that anyone who knew Willesden, or had any dealings with Willesden, or any reason to dislike Willesden, was still on the police list of possible suspects. Not because such a person might be inherently sinister, but just because the police haven't yet eliminated anyone from the list yet. Well, Penelope rather took offence at this, because she and Willesden had been friends – as I'm sure you know. Then they split up, which gave Penelope cause to resent Willesden. And I was rather wondering if you could put in a word for me with Penelope. You see . . .'

'So you're telling me,' Mallison said, blinking at me in that vague way of his, 'that anyone who had any dealings with Willesden, or reason to dislike that young man, is on some sort of "suspects list" with the police?'

'It's just how they operate, that's all,' I said hastily. 'I suppose they'd call it "procedure". So there was no need for Penelope to take offence, you see . . .'

'I suppose I must be on that list, too,' Mallison murmured, gazing off into the distance.

'Yes, I suppose you must be – living on the same staircase as the victim. Which is all the more reason for Penelope not to be upset . . .'

Mallison had come to a complete halt in our slow walk back to Magdalen, and he now resumed his waddling amble as he interrupted me again: 'So what *exactly* have the police found out? Why can't they start eliminating names from their "suspects list", eh? Why not? Tell me that. What do they actually know about this murder?'

'What do they know? Not much, to be honest. At least, as far as I can tell, they don't seem to know very much at all. They know how Willesden died, of course. Beheading is a pretty obvious cause of death.' I was babbling now, because I was finding Professor Mallison disconcerting to talk to, but I still wanted to get onto his good side in the hopes that this would improve my chances with Penelope.

'And, of course, they have the head,' I continued.

'Yes, I read about that in the *Oxford Mail*,' Mallison said. 'Tell me about finding the head.'

'I don't really know more than you would have read in the newspaper. It was found in a cricket kit bag.'

'Do they know whose cricket bag?'

'I don't think so. They asked me if there was much difference between cricket bags and I said no. But no doubt the forensic scientists will put it under the microscope and they may discover something. So that's one thing that rules Penelope out – because girls don't play cricket, you see, so it can't be her bag.'

'She might have borrowed it,' Mallison muttered in that faint, drawling voice of his. 'Might have borrowed it from a male friend.'

'I suppose so,' I admitted reluctantly.

Professor Mallison stopped abruptly and turned to face me. 'You're quite fond of my niece, aren't you?'

'Well, if I was being honest, I suppose I'd have to admit . . .'

'And from what you're saying, you're still not on the best of terms. Have I got that right?'

'That part is certainly true.'

'Come up to my rooms, then,' Mallison said. By now we were passing through the gates into Magdalen College. 'There's a book of mine she wants to borrow. I'll give it to you to deliver. That'll give you another excuse to visit her. How would that be? Would that help? Eh, what do you think?'

Of course it would help, so, of course, I said yes at once. And a minute later we were both climbing staircase three to Mallison's rooms on the top floor of the north quad building.

'What else have they discovered?' the professor asked me, over his shoulder, as we climbed the narrow staircase.

'They've found the murder weapon,' I replied.

He froze where he was, with one foot in the air. He slowly lowered the foot and turned around to look at me.

'Have they indeed?' he said. 'Now, that wasn't in the newspapers. How interesting.'

'I'm probably not supposed to have told you that. I keep forgetting that because I'm Jack's friend and Jack is Inspector Crispin's friend I know things I'm supposed to keep to myself.'

As we resumed our climb Mallison said, 'Of course, of course, I wouldn't want to get you into trouble. I won't mention it to a soul.'

Once we reached his rooms he fussed around for a while, taking off his coat and his scarf – he was, I thought, rather overdressed for a warm spring day – and then put down his parcels and umbrella and busied himself at one of his bookshelves.

'So what sort of weapon was it?' he asked, as he hunted through the shelves. 'Now, that book I promised Penelope must be here somewhere. Let me see . . .'

'Well, I suppose since I've let this much slip it won't hurt to say more. It's certainly an odd weapon – a flat sheet of timber, rather heavy, with a sharp metal blade attached at the bottom edge. Warnie thinks it looks like part of a guillotine. Rather like that one, in fact,' I said, pointing at the engraving on Mallison's wall. The picture illustrated the French Revolution at the height of the bloodletting. 'Yes, pretty much exactly like that.'

I walked up to the picture, leaned forward and looked at the guillotine very closely. 'In fact, the guillotine blade in that picture could be the brother of the one the police fished out of the river. This engraving could have been the model, or plan, on which that blade was built.'

Mallison appeared not to be paying much attention, but continued fussing over which book he had promised to lend his niece. Failing, apparently, to find it on a shelf, he began hunting through the untidy piles of books on his desk.

'Penelope will be quite annoyed if I can't find it,' he said. 'She did ask for it particularly. Go on, my boy, go on. What else do the police know?'

'That's about it really,' I murmured thoughtlessly as I wandered over to the windows of Mallison's room. One of the sash windows was open and I leant out.

'Do they believe,' Mallison asked, 'that young Willesden was killed inside his room or outside?'

'I don't really know,' I said honestly, 'But I suspect Jack has a theory. When he was asked exactly that question he said something like "Why not both?", which didn't make any sense to me at all.'

I leant a little further out of the window as I said, 'That's where Willesden's broken glasses were found – down there. Just exactly beneath this window. And it's where poor Alf's roses had their roots chopped as well.'

Turning back to the room I said, 'You should offer to help the police with their inquiries.'

'Me?' said the professor, looking startled. 'Me? Why me?'

'Because if Warnie is right, some sort of guillotine was used to kill Willesden and if anyone is an expert on guillotines in this university, it must be you. With your knowledge of the French Revolution I imagine there's no one else in England who knows more about guillotines than you do. You could probably give them some hints that might help . . .'

My voice trailed away. Mallison was looking at me strangely, and I felt a sharp chill strike me. It was as if a snowball had hit me in the back of the neck.

I still had no idea *how* he did it, but somehow I knew at that moment that I was looking at Willesden's killer. The snowball was now melting and icy water was trickling down my spine.

I began edging towards the door.

'Look, don't worry about that book just now,' I mumbled. 'Why don't I pop back after dinner and I can pick it up then, and . . . well . . . I can take it to Penelope tomorrow . . . how would that be?'

Mallison moved faster than I thought him capable of, and in a stride he was between me and the door. We stood facing each other in silence.

It was a long, painful silence. Finally, Mallison spoke. 'You've guessed, haven't you?'

'Guessed what? No, I haven't guessed anything. I'm not very good at guessing. From childhood I've been hopeless at guessing games. Ask my friends. Ask anyone.'

'I don't know how much you actually *know*. Probably very little. But if you've guessed, then I can't really allow you to leave here, can I?'

When I was in school I used to read those American pulp magazines. They were always full of mad professors. They usually wore white dust coats and conducted disgusting experiments in bubbling test tubes in secret underground laboratories. Mallison didn't have the white dust coat, or the bubbling test tubes, or the secret underground laboratory – but in every other respect he was the classic mad professor.

The bumbling, absent-minded exterior had fallen away, and there was a mad, wild gleam in his eyes.

'Well, if you'll just step away from the door, please, Professor Mallison,' I said, trying to make my voice sound as normal as possible, 'I might just slip out and catch up with Jack and the others at the pub.'

Mallison said nothing, but he shook his head. 'No, no, no, my young friend. You may not know much, but you've guessed far too much. I'll have to work out what to do with you.'

One hand came up to scratch his chin as he muttered, 'The problem will be disposal.'

At that moment I took a sudden step towards the door. But I was not fast enough.

Mallison's right hand shot out to the chest of drawers by his side. In a second he had the top drawer open and a large, wicked-looking knife in his hand.

Now, I'm not an expert in knives, but I would have described it as a wide-bladed chef's carving knife. In fact, that's exactly how I did describe it later in my statement to the police.

Why Mallison had such a deadly weapon ready to hand in his college rooms, I have no idea. Perhaps it's just something homicidal maniacs do. Perhaps, if I stayed long enough, I'd also discover his secret stash of razors, acid and revolvers. Although, to be honest, the one knife I was looking at was quite enough to be going on with.

The knife blade looked to be razor sharp – or was that just my terrified imagination?

There was no doubting that the point was extremely, well, pointy, and Professor Mallison could make a very nasty incision with just one thrust into my chest cavity.

THIRTY

~

The point of the blade was about two inches from my chest – so if Mallison decided to take an anti-Morris view of the situation, he didn't have very far to move.

One short, sharp, swift, hard thrust would stop me from making a nuisance of myself.

We stood facing each other like a strange tableau in Madame Tussaud's Chamber of Horrors – probably with one of those little caption thingies saying 'The killer about to strike'.

In his eyes was the wild gleam of a homicidal maniac. I am most reluctant, as a rule, to pass judgement on my fellow man, but no other label than 'homicidal maniac' seemed appropriate just at that moment.

I had guessed right: he had killed Willesden – for what reason, and with what method, I had no idea.

He had clearly thought that killing Willesden was a Job Well Done, and was feeling a warm sense of satisfaction sloshing about in his veins by the gallon. Then I came along and guessed his secret. That warm flood of satisfaction had now curdled and gone quite cold. And if I guessed, others might guess, too.

That careless, evil glint in his eye suggested that if he was about to appear before a judge who put on the black cap and suggested he be 'hanged from the neck until you are dead', then he might as well rack up a good score before he went.

Then I stupidly opened my mouth and blurted out, 'And Guilford – you killed Guilford too, didn't you?' Why couldn't I have kept my mouth shut? And why had he killed Guilford? Despite what I later discovered was my accurate guessing, I remained as puzzled as ever. I still felt like Dr Watson on the second last page of a Sherlock Holmes story.

Mallison's chubby face crumpled into a scowl. He now looked like a bad-tempered bulldog with a serious case of indigestion, a splitting headache, and murder on its mind.

I stepped back, and he stepped forwards – leaving us pretty much where we were before: balanced on opposite ends of his wicked-looking and extremely large knife.

When I was a boy I read in Arthur Mee's *Children's Encyclopaedia* how Roman soldiers dispatched their enemies using a short sword. It seems that the trick was to press the point of the sword home just below the breastbone, then make a sharp upward thrust into the upper thorax. At the time, I wasn't too sure what an upper thorax was, but I was certain a short, sharp thrust into it would not be a good thing.

I now regretted that I had ever paid attention to Mr Mee's helpful information on Roman military tactics, or that I remembered what I had read, since Mallison appeared to be working from the same drill manual.

Any Roman drill sergeant seeing how he was holding his massive knife, and how the point was resting just below my breastbone pointing upwards, would have said, 'That's it, laddie, well done, laddie, that's the spot, now finish the job – just one short, sharp jab.'

I was sweating profusely and poised to jump backwards the moment the knife moved in the direction of my upper thorax when there were several rapid taps on Mallison's door.

Without waiting for a reply or a friendly 'come in', Penelope swung the door open and entered, her stunning profile displaying a sunny smile.

'Hello, Uncle Alec – about that book . . .' she began. Then she spotted me and greeted me cheerfully: 'What ho, worm, what you are doing here?'

Then she spotted the knife and added, 'Be careful with that, Uncle Alec, it might go off.'

'Get over there,' snapped Mallison, 'beside your boyfriend.'

'Here's not my boyfr—' Penelope began, but then she focussed on the size of the knife Uncle Alec was waving around and submissively sidled over to where I was standing.

Mallison was not a tall man, but he was solidly built, and he was standing in front of the two of us – between us and the door – waving the point of his large, chef's carving knife back and forth. Not that he looked at all indecisive. His mad eye told me he had already decided on murder. The only decision he was still wrestling with was who to butcher first.

I slipped an arm around Penelope's waist as a comforting gesture. Penelope brushed this away as unnecessary and bristled at her mother's brother standing in front of us.

'Uncle Alec!' Penelope protested. 'If you do this, Mother will never forgive you.'

Somehow the thought of how his sister, Penelope's mother, might react seemed to carry little weight with our local neighbourhood homicidal maniac.

The wheels were clearly spinning around inside that homicidally maniacal brain – probably slipping a few cogs, and grinding erratically, but spinning none the less.

But before he could reach a decision on who should be Victim Number One and who should be Victim Number Two, we were interrupted.

Coming up staircase three towards us we could hear a series of rapid, solid, thumping sounds. These culminated in the door bursting open and a dog thundering joyfully into the room. This dog was roughly the size and shape of the Hound of the Baskervilles. Spotting Penelope, it made straight for her, brushing Mallison aside as it did so.

It leapt up, placed its giant forepaws on her shoulders and proceeded to lick her face enthusiastically.

'Mortimer! Mortimer!' Penelope protested, pulling her face away from that slavering tongue. 'Stop that. Down, boy, down.'

Mortimer obeyed this command, and then spotted another member of the family in the room. The dog spun around and leapt up on Professor Mallison to repeat its wet, slobbering greeting. By now I had worked out that the only threat this dog posed to the human race was that someone might be licked to death.

Professor Mallison, as I have said, was solidly built but not tall. As this vast canine placed its forepaws on his shoulders, it knocked over the professor and pinned him to the floor.

At the same moment the knife fell from his hand.

I rushed forward and scooped it up. Then, just to ensure that it didn't remain in the room to give the professor any ideas when he got back on his feet, I walked rapidly over to the open window and dropped the knife out.

From somewhere below I heard a cry of 'Oy! What do you think you're up to?!?'

Looking out of the window, I spotted Alf in the garden below, and the knife embedded in the soil at his feet.

'Sorry, Alf,' I called out. 'I'll explain later.'

'You better had, Mr Morris, you better had,' he called in reply. 'Look what you've gone and done to my roses!'

I turned back to the room to discover that our numbers were once again being swelled. This time striding in through the door was Penelope's eight-year-old nephew, Bertie.

'Sorry, Aunt Penelope,' he was saying. 'Mortimer got away from me. I tried to hold him but he was too strong for me. I say, Uncle Alec, what are you doing on the floor? You shouldn't be there, you know. You'll get your clothes all dirty if you crawl around on the floor, that's what Mother is always saying to me.'

Perhaps encouraged by these wise words from young Bertie, Professor Mallison scrambled back onto his feet.

'Now, I think I'm owed an explanation here,' said Penelope, putting her hands on her hips and a stern expression on her face. 'What on earth was going on when I walked in here?'

'Your Uncle Alec is the murderer,' I said, hoping to clear the air. 'He killed both Willesden and Guilford, and he was planning to kill me next.'

'What?' Penelope exploded. 'I've never heard such rubbish in my life. How dare you stand there and accuse dear old Uncle Alec, the most harmless of people, of such a crime. And in front of Bertie, too!'

'Don't mind me,' Bertie said. 'This is jolly interesting.'

'Have you forgotten, Penelope, my dear . . .' I began.

'Don't you "my dear" me,' responded the smouldering, annoyed young glamour puss.

'. . . that just a moment ago,' I continued, 'your Uncle Alec was pointing a large knife at you?'

'Golly! Did that happen?' Bertie squeaked. 'Gee, I miss all the good stuff.'

'Don't be so silly, Morris,' Penelope resumed. 'Uncle Alec is an eccentric professor, and eccentric professors do all sorts of odd things from time to time.'

'Such as murdering Aubrey Willesden and Nicolas Guilford,' I explained as calmly as I could.

'You've finally gone off your rocker, Morris,' Penelope thundered. 'Totally, completely and utterly off your rocker.'

'Is that true?' Bertie asked. 'Wait till I tell the boys at school that I've seen a real, live madman.'

'I'm not a madman,' I tried to explain. 'I'm not off my rocker. It's your Uncle Alec who's the homicidal maniac.'

'Don't listen to his delusions, my dear,' Mallison said, having regained his composure. 'He's a journalist, and journalists have these brain spasms from time to time. I believe it comes from having to write headlines containing only very short words.'

At this point I began to splutter, 'But . . . but . . . but . . .' when I was interrupted by another arrival in the room.

It was Harman, the scout who serviced staircase three.

'This dog can't stay in this room,' he puffed, having apparently just run all the way up the staircase. 'Dogs are not allowed in the rooms. I did allow you, miss, to walk your dog through the quad, because you promised you would not linger. And now I find it in one of the rooms. The dog will have to be removed at once.'

'I'm sorry, Harman,' Penelope explained. 'I left Mortimer in the care of my nephew, Bertie, who failed – or so it seems – to take proper care.'

'It wasn't my fault,' wailed Bertie. 'Mortimer's too big for me.'

And all the time I was standing there wondering what I should do about the multiple murderer who was only a few feet away. Should I attempt a citizen's arrest? Or would Penelope and Bertie jointly overpower me if I attempted to do so – on the grounds that I was the one who was off his rocker?

This problem was taken out of my hands by a clatter of footsteps on the stairs, heralding two more arrivals in what was already a very crowded room.

The first to appear was Detective Inspector Gideon Crispin of Scotland Yard, closely followed by Sergeant Henry Merrivale of the same august establishment.

Crispin glanced around the room – which was now looking like the cabin scene in *A Night at the Opera* – and seeing Mallison, walked briskly across to him and said, 'Professor Alec Mallison, I arrest you for the murders of Aubrey Willesden and Nicolas Guilford. You do not have to say anything, but anything you do say may be taken down and used in evidence. Merrivale – cuff him!'

'Gee!' squeaked Bertie in delight. 'A real arrest! With real handcuffs.'

At this point Mallison exploded, struggling, unsuccessfully, against the strong hands and even stronger arms of Sergeant Merrivale. Clearly Merrivale had years of experience in slipping handcuffs on people who didn't want handcuffs to be slipped anywhere near them, and Mallison's loud protests, and vigorous struggles, were all in vain.

'What do you two think you're doing?' demanded Penelope at her haughtiest. 'Unless you unhand my uncle at once, you will both find yourselves facing disciplinary proceedings. My father is a friend of the Chief Constable and when I tell him what you've done, you will both be in serious trouble.'

'That's extremely unlikely, miss,' Crispin said politely.

'I don't care if your father knows the Lord High Chamberlain,' Merrivale said, less politely, still straining to hold the struggling prisoner. 'We've just arrested a multiple murderer. And if you don't believe us, you can take a front-row seat in the public gallery at his trial.'

Penelope opened her mouth to protest again, but a shadow of doubt flickered across her face and she chose silence instead.

'I'll bet our first essay back at school,' enthused young Bertie, 'will be "What I Did in My Holidays" – it always is. And won't I have a ripper of a story to tell! Gee, just wait till Mr Hardcastle reads *my* essay!'

There came the sound of more steps, rather more sedate ones this time, on staircase three, and Jack arrived, having taken the stairs at a more leisurely pace than the two police officers.

'Are you safe, Morris?' he asked, genuinely concerned. 'You've come to no harm?'

'It looked dodgy there for a moment,' I said, 'but no harm done.'

THIRTY-ONE

~

Crispin and Merrivale departed with their prisoner – who was still protesting loudly. Penelope turned to Harman, the scout, now standing there with his mouth hanging open in astonishment.

'Harman,' she commanded, 'take Mortimer and Bertie downstairs and wait with them in the quad. I intend to find out what's been going on here, and why. And I expect Mr Lewis to have the decency to explain everything.'

'Gee, why do I have to leave whenever it gets interesting,' Bertie moaned.

'Downstairs! Now! At once!' Penelope barked in a voice that would have made any European dictator green with envy.

Bertie accepted his defeat and headed for the door. 'Come on, Mortimer,' he said, 'let's go down and see how many people you can knock over in the quad.'

The huge dog and the small boy trotted off down the stairs followed by Harman. Then Penelope turned her attention on Jack.

'It seems to me,' she said in a cold, firm voice, 'that an enormous blunder has been made here. You are, I am told, a friend of that officious Scotland Yard man, Crispin. Have you any explanation to offer?'

'Why don't we all take a seat,' Jack said, in his warmest, but firmest, voice. 'The story gets a bit complicated in parts.'

I quite happily collapsed my trembling frame into an over-stuffed armchair, while Penelope chose the ottoman and Jack took a seat in Mallison's own leather armchair. He was about to begin his explanation when we heard more footsteps on the stairs.

Mallison's sitting room had become, I decided, Paddington Station, and we could expect more passengers and announcements over a loudspeaker at any moment.

The new arrival was Warnie.

'I finally caught up with you,' he gasped, catching his breath. Then he pulled up a chair and sat down.

'Can you begin,' I said to Jack, 'with why you're here? And how you knew there might be a problem?'

'We were just sitting down to our drinks in the Bird and Baby,' Jack replied, 'when I recalled the sight of you striding off to join Professor Mallison. I became concerned, not so much at what you knew, but at what you might guess once you spent any time in Mallison's company and in conversation with him. If you guessed well – and you are not good at hiding what you think, young Morris – then it would be dangerous for you to be alone in the company of a murderer.'

'Rest assured, Jack, I've spent very little time alone with Mallison. The pedestrian traffic in this room could only be rivalled by The Strand on a busy Saturday.'

'I'm quite relieved to hear that. None the less, I was concerned for your safety. So I used the publican's telephone at the Eagle and Child and called Crispin. He decided that for everyone's safety it was time to act – so he set out, with Sergeant Merrivale, from the police station. Then I left the others in the pub and started here on foot.'

'Followed, a short time later, by me,' Warnie added.

'Very well,' Penelope snapped. 'We now understand every-one's movements over the last hour. Quite fascinating, I'm sure. But that's not what I want to hear. Mr Lewis – what is the case against my uncle? If, indeed, there is any sort of case?'

Jack said that the best place to start was at the beginning, and that, he said, was ten years ago.

That was when Professor Mallison's wife died, leaving the professor to raise their only child, Judith, on his own. The two, father and daughter, became very close and very dependent on each other. It's not too much to say that his life revolved around her.

Then she died in a car accident. The manner in which Judith died was particularly unpleasant.

'Her throat cut by flying glass from the shattered windscreen,' said Penelope.

'More than that,' Jack said. 'Crispin showed me the police file, which confirmed what I had already guessed: the flying glass actually decapitated her; which, out of consideration for her father, was kept from the public at the time.'

Jack went on to explain that there had been a coroner's inquest into the death. The young man driving the large and powerful Lagonda that smashed into the girl's small car was the Honourable Aubrey Willesden. He came from an old and wealthy family, who hired a London KC to represent him at the coronial hearing. The local magistrate was rather overawed by the London KC and young Willesden got off with a fine.

Mallison was furious. But he is a quiet, self-contained man and he gave no sign of this at the time. Instead, he began plot-ting to kill Willesden. He decided that what Willesden needed was a judicial execution. Murderers, he thought, should not just be killed: they should be properly executed – and, being a scholar of the French Revolution, the form of execution that seemed most appropriate to him was decapitation by guillotine. This struck him as also being a kind of poetic justice, given how his daughter died.

'Yes, that's all very well,' Warnie interrupted. 'And we've found the blade of the guillotine – but where's the rest of the thing? Where's the tall frame in which the blade slides down to do its deadly work?'

'There isn't one,' said Jack. 'It doesn't exist. Mallison came up with the idea of using what might be called a "flying guillotine". That is to say, a free-falling blade, so well-aimed, and so well-weighted, as to do the same job that a blade sliding in a proper frame would do.'

Jack explained that Mallison built the blade that the police recovered from the river in the workshop of his home in north Oxford. Then he tried it out one night in the deer park.

'The deer that had its throat cut!' I said. 'Neck almost severed, I was told.'

'Exactly,' said Jack. 'Mallison had crept into the deer park in the early hours of the morning, climbed one of the old oak trees, and then, when an animal strayed underneath, dropped the blade he had built. He was more than satisfied with the results, and he snuck back to his room with no one the wiser as to what he'd done. Then, convinced that his device worked, he needed to make it work here.'

'Naturally, the death of the deer,' I muttered, 'was put down to yahoos from the town. Sorry, Jack, I interrupted – you carry on.'

What made all this possible, Jack explained, was that Willesden lived directly below Mallison on staircase three. The execution obviously had to be carried out in the dead of night. It was not Mallison's intention to be caught. To achieve his planned execution, he needed Willesden to put his head out of his window in the very early hours of the morning when it was pitch dark. To that end, he spread the story of Judith's ghost appearing on the Magdalen lawns.

'So when he told me that,' Penelope said in a quiet voice, 'he was using me?'

'I'm afraid so, my dear,' Jack said. 'And once the story had spread widely enough, he knew he would be able to lure Willesden into the position he wanted.'

It seems, Jack told us, that the police had discovered a strange apparatus in the gardeners' shed. It was a framework of very thin, light bamboo sticks, with flimsy white material draped over them. When Mallison thought the time was right – the rumour of the ghost was certain to have reached Willesden's ears – he stole downstairs in the dead of night and set up this apparatus on the lawn facing Willesden's window. Fluttering white linen in pale starlight was enough to suggest a ghost to a suggestible mind. Then Mallison lowered down, from his own window, a small bolt tied to a piece of fishing line.

'That strange thing Crispin was showing us!' cried Warnie. 'By Jove – he may be evil, but this Mallison man is certainly ingenious. He thought of everything.'

Jack agreed that he had been remarkably thorough. Willesden was woken by the sound of the bolt tapping lightly on the glass and opened his window to investigate. He immediately saw the 'ghostly' apparition dimly on the lawn. He was, as we all know, short-sighted. He may have taken one look at the ghost and, still half asleep, leant back into his room to put on his glasses, then leant further out for a better view. When his head was well out of the window, Mallison dropped his 'flying guillotine'.

Willesden's head fell into the garden, and his body fell back into his room. The sash window fell closed and latched. The door of the room was, of course, already locked and bolted, since that was how Willesden usually slept.

Mallison then hurried downstairs and cleaned up the lawn and the garden. The 'ghost' apparatus he stuffed into the back of the gardeners' shed. The head he put into an old cricket bag. Then he took the bagged head and the blade down to the Cherwell and dropped them into the river.

'That's why Willesden's glasses were found in the garden,' I said. 'They fell off at the moment he was killed. And it was Mallison's "flying blade" thingy that chopped the roots off Alf's beloved roses.'

'All quite correct,' said Jack.

'I'm not sure I believe any of this,' Penelope said bitterly. 'And anyway, what about Nicolas Guilford? Uncle Alec had no reason to murder him, did he?'

'Sadly,' Jack said, 'Guilford had the mind of a petty criminal. He tried to blackmail Mallison. Mallison agreed to meet him, late at night, on the banks of the Cherwell. But instead of bringing money to pay Guilford, he brought a large spanner from his workshop – hit Guilford over the head and pushed him into the river. That was the second murder.'

'Hang on, go back a step,' I interrupted. 'You said Guilford was attempting to blackmail Mallison. How did that come about?'

'Guilford was one of Mallison's pupils. Once a term Mallison was in the habit of inviting a group of his students to his north Oxford home – for sherry and biscuits and to debate some issue relevant to their studies. Guilford was one of those who went. And being a compulsive snoop, he went snooping around Mallison's workshop while Mallison was busy with his other guests. What Guilford found in the workshop was the blade – almost complete in its construction. It meant nothing to him at the time, but later he guessed that it had something to do with Willesden's death, so he tried his hand at blackmail.'

'With fatal results,' said Warnie, shaking his head sadly.

Penelope suddenly leapt to her feet and walked towards the door. 'Well, I think you're all positively foul,' she snarled. 'Uncle Alec is a lovely man. He was left heartbroken by that fiend Willesden. His life was destroyed when Judith died. The court system let him down. He was entitled to his revenge. And the world is a better place now that disgusting rat Willesden is dead. You should have left the whole thing well alone. If the case remained unsolved, that would never have hurt anyone. Willesden dead: good thing. Uncle Alec at peace and left to live his own life: good thing. And you've spoiled all that.'

Her eyes glistened with tears of anger as she strode over to where I now stood, poked me firmly in the chest and said, 'And as for you – I never want to see you again.' Then she was gone.

Jack looked at me sadly and said, 'I think, this time, she meant it, old chap.'

'That's all right,' I said. 'I'm over her now. She can't seem to understand that murder became a habit with her dear old Uncle Alec. Guilford may have been a thief and a blackmailer, but those offences don't carry the death penalty.'

Jack agreed, pointing out that revenge is dangerous in the hands of individuals, and punishment should be left to the proper authorities.

'And . . . and . . .' I added by way of vehement protest, 'he was about to kill me . . . me! If that doesn't bother Penelope, then some other chap can spend his life admiring her profile.'

'Just a moment,' Warnie said, with a puzzled look on his face. 'There's still one small thing that I don't understand.'

Jack asked him what that was and Warnie said, 'Why did Willesden's window slide down and latch – giving us the false impression that he'd been killed inside a locked and latched room? I know the sash was broken, but you know what these windows are like, Jack – if you push them up with your right hand, you can latch them in the open position. So why didn't Willesden do that in the middle of the night, on the night he died?'

'Because, Warnie old chap, as you yourself pointed out, you need to use your right hand to do that, and Willesden was left-handed. As I said earlier, some of my pupils are adroit and some are sinister. You, Morris, are adroit – from the French for right-handed. Willesden, on the other hand, was sinister – from the Latin for left-handed.'

THIRTY-TWO

~

It was Thursday night, it was the weekly meeting of the Inklings and once again we were in Jack's handsome large sitting room – high ceilings, oak panelling, windows looking out onto the deer park, and modest, rather shabby furniture. Old Tom at Christ Church had long since ceased its nightly chiming.

There were, however, slight changes in the personnel since the last meeting of the Inklings just a week earlier. The usual suspects were still there, of course: Jack, Warnie, Professor Tolkien, Adam Fox, Nevill Coghill and even Hugo Dyson had managed to arrive on time. Once again I was there as a guest, as was Detective Inspector Gideon Crispin of Scotland Yard, at Jack's insistence.

In place of the departed Aubrey Willesden was David Bracken – barely able to control his excitement at being allowed to attend a meeting of the Inklings, and sitting quietly in the far corner where Willesden had sat a week before. Bracken made almost no contribution to the conversation for most of the night, but I did see him scribbling furiously in his notebook. No doubt those jottings would become the basis for some sort of dissertation, or part of a dissertation, in his history course.

Jack was just finishing retelling the tale that Warnie and I had heard earlier in the afternoon: the story of Professor Mallison's tragic obsession, and the ingenious, if awful, plot that flowed out of it.

Jack ended his tale with the story of Nicolas Guilford, the naive would-be blackmailer, who became the second victim.

When he fell silent there was a hush in the room, broken by Warnie saying, tell them about the window with the broken sash – why it latched itself, making the whole room look locked from the inside.

So Jack, who would do anything to please his brother, did so – explaining how easy it was to latch these sash windows open with your right hand, and how difficult with the left, adding that Willesden was left-handed. He ended with his comment about 'adroit' and 'sinister' students.

Inspector Crispin then added a coda to Jack's symphony, saying, 'A lot of this began to emerge in our own investigations, but I must say that I consulted Mr Lewis often – and his suggestions as to the direction our investigations should take were invaluable. Without Mr Lewis' giant brain at our disposal, I'm not at all confident we would have solved the case.'

'Very impressive, old chap,' said Dyson, grinning broadly at Jack. 'I could never have worked that out in a month of Sundays. The puzzle you faced would have struck me as one of those impossible exam papers – you know the ones I mean: you turn over the paper to begin and discover none of the questions make any sense. You've prepared for entirely the wrong exam and you haven't a clue how to answer. As a young man I once spent three hours bluffing my way through one of those.'

'How well did you do?' Coghill asked.

'Well, I threw in everything I knew that might be vaguely relevant and kept quoting the words of the questions at frequent intervals to make it appear I was addressing the right topic. And I passed. Only just – but I passed.'

This brought laughter to the room and lifted the dark mood the tale of obsession and murder had introduced.

'And how about you, young Morris?' Professor Tolkien asked. 'Have you been sufficiently impressed by Jack's Sherlock-like qualities?'

'It's not the first time I've seen them on display, but, yes, this time he was particularly dazzling,' I replied. 'And the whole story has made me think again about death.'

'With what results?' asked Tolkien, looking more wizard-like than ever as he leant forward in the yellow lamplight, puffing furiously on a long-stemmed pipe.

'Well . . .' I began, then I paused to gather my thoughts. 'Mallison decided to kill Willesden and triumphantly succeeded. The same with Guilford – Mallison decided on death, and produced death. But looking at those deaths has made me realise how different such deaths are from a voluntary, sacrificial death that saves others.'

'Aha!' Fox said with a triumphant grin. 'So you've decided to join us on the believing side of the fence, have you?'

'No, not yet,' I was quick to say. 'I've got a long way to go before I get as far as that. But I can see that not all deaths are alike. And I can also see the finality of death.'

'Finality is a good word, young Morris,' Fox responded. 'This world is rather like prep school. Death is the final door that shuts us out of prep school for ever, and shifts us from the preparation stage to the larger world beyond. So, yes, the "finality of death" is important to grasp.'

'Death is also triumphant,' I resumed. 'In the deaths of Willesden and Guilford, there is a sense in which death has triumphed over their rather sad lives. But not all deaths are like that. Or need to be like that; because a sacrificial death steals the triumph from the Grim Reaper. His sickle still does its work, but a courageous sacrificial death must wipe the smile off his face.'

'Excellent!' cried Jack with delight. 'That is a great image, a great insight, and a great truth, well worth learning.'

'Know exactly what you mean, old chap,' muttered Warnie thoughtfully into his beer. Then he wiped the foam off his moustache and added, 'When I was in Sandhurst there was an incident. I'd forgotten all about it until just now when you said what you said. One Thursday morning it was. Outside the main gates of the base there was a small child, just a toddler who'd slipped away from his mother. This little tyke was wandering across the road when a lorry came roaring around the corner. Chap on duty at the guard house dropped his rifle, ran out onto the road and pushed the child to safety. Chap died under the wheels of the lorry, but the child was saved. That's no triumph for death. That's a triumph for courage, and self-sacrifice.'

Then Warnie looked down into his beer, self-consciously, as if he'd revealed something that he found too moving to want to talk about any further.

'Precisely,' roared Jack with delight. 'Warnie, as always you have hit the nail exactly on the head. It's like that old hymn we sing sometimes in chapel: "Oh death, where is thy sting? Oh grave, where is thy victory?" You remember it, don't you, Foxy?'

'Of course,' said Adam Fox. 'The hymn writer took those words from St Paul's first letter to the Corinthians, chapter fifteen.'

'Indeed,' Jack said joyfully. 'His point there is that "death is swallowed up in victory". Hence the title of that book by one of the old puritans, John Owen, *The Death of Death in the Death of Christ*.'

'And Warnie's little story paints exactly the right picture,' Fox added. 'On the cross Jesus was pushing his people to safety, out of the way of danger, and allowing the lorry loaded with all that is wrong in our lives to crush him instead of us. That's the real meaning of the cross.'

'You chaps are galloping miles ahead of me, but, yes, I now see that point,' I said. 'All I'm trying to explain is that seeing these two violent deaths, and understanding that not all deaths are alike, has brought me to a comprehension of your symbol – The Cross. And I now agree with you that Christianity is not a "death cult" but a "life cult" – much along the lines Mr Fox just spelled out. That's the point I've got to.'

This brought a cheer from the Inklings, and they raised their beer mugs to me in a salute.

It was after midnight when the meeting finally came to an end. Most of the guests had left – only Tolkien and I remained – when David Bracken emerged from his distant corner where he had sat so quietly throughout the whole of the night as to be almost forgotten. Warnie had wandered off to his own room saying he had a few things to tidy up.

I noticed Bracken slipping his notebook, now fat with entries, into his pocket, when Jack asked quietly, 'Are you allowed to tell us anything about the future in which you live? Or is that against the rules?'

'Certainly nothing detailed,' Bracken replied, looking a little nervous, as if he was about to be cross-examined.

'What about larger patterns?' Jack asked.

'Yes, from your vantage point "higher up the mountain", as it were,' Tolkien added, 'are there patterns that emerge? What do you see from the broad sweep of history? You are a historian, after all. What can you tell us without breaking the rules?'

'What do you mean by patterns?' Bracken asked.

'This age in which we live,' Jack explained, 'sees human history in essentially materialistic terms and, hence, as being largely meaningless and purposeless. The materialists tend to see history as a tale told by an idiot, full of sound and fury, signifying nothing.'

'Oh, well, I suppose I can tell you that in my time a sense of meaning and purpose has been recovered. We tend to have a sort of "pendulum" view of history – with the pendulum swinging sometimes in the direction of a narrow view of human nature and the point of it all, and sometimes swinging back the other way towards a broader, more meaningful Christian worldview.'

'Which is dominating at the moment?' Tolkien asked. 'In your time zone, I mean?'

'Oh, definitely the latter,' Bracken said with certainty. 'In the time when I live the pendulum has swung. Not before some very difficult times, of course, but I mustn't tell you about those.'

'Why the wardrobe?' I asked. Bracken looked at me blankly, so I explained, 'Why does your time chamber look like an old-fashioned wardrobe? Surely that's a rather odd appearance to give to such powerful technology?'

'Oh, it's not permanent,' he explained. 'The time chamber has a thing called a "chameleon circuit" and the technicians set it to something that won't look out of place in the time period we're travelling to.'

'And can you tell us anything – anything at all – about the reason for your visit?' Tolkien said. 'We don't want you to violate any confidences, or step over the line. But can you tell us the purpose of your study visit? Or give us a hint?'

David Bracken looked doubtful. He hesitated for a long minute, and finally said, 'Well, all right, then. I'll tell you just one thing – and you must promise not to ask any more questions about this. The truth is . . . the truth is . . . I've actually come here to study *you*!'

'Who?' I asked.

'Mr Lewis and Professor Tolkien.'

Jack and Tolkien looked at each other and grinned. Then they both laughed.

'Can you believe that, Morris?' Jack hooted. 'Studying us? Oh, dear me, dear me!'

Both Tolkien and Jack once again laughed heartily at the thought that they would be the subject of future study. Then I started clearing up the supper things.

A few minutes later Jack and Tolkien had lapsed back into chat about English Department politics, when I thought of another question to ask Bracken.

I looked around – and he wasn't there.

'Bracken's gone,' I said.

'Probably just slipped off to his room looking for a good night's sleep,' said Jack.

'I don't think so,' I said firmly. 'When I say he's gone, I mean he's *gone*.'

'Gone back to his own time zone, you mean?' Tolkien asked.

I suggested that we go and find out.

After some initial reluctance from Jack and Tolkien, the three of us plunged out into the cool night air, walked briskly down the long straight path from the New Building to the north quad, and climbed staircase two.

As we approached Bracken's landing we heard a deep humming coming from inside his room. It gradually became louder and more rhythmical. Then it stopped altogether. Completely and quite suddenly.

I tried the door and it swung open. All three of us walked into the room, where Jack turned on the light switch.

The room was empty.

Bracken was gone.

And so was the wardrobe.

Where the wardrobe once stood there was just an expanse of bare wall.

Tolkien chuckled with delight as he relit his pipe and said, 'Our visitor from elfland has returned to the magic kingdom from whence he came.'

'Come on,' said Jack. 'Let's head back to my sitting room. The fire will still be burning, and the room still warm.'

We all clattered back down staircase two, and walked out into a world turned into fairyland by the brilliant blue of the moonlight – the moon having just emerged from behind dark, rolling clouds.

But halfway back to his rooms in Magdalen's New Building Jack stopped abruptly, and turning to Tolkien said, 'Whatever could it be, Tollers? Whatever could we do that could possibly interest the future? I can't begin to imagine . . .'

AUTHOR'S NOTE

~

This book, like the others in this series, is by way of being a homage to C. S. Lewis. But this time Lewis is on home ground – back in Oxford and in residence at his college, Magdalen.

Also joining him in this thought-provoking romp are other members of the Inklings – among whom J. R. R. Tolkien, creator of Middle Earth, is especially prominent.

Scattered throughout the text are references to the world of 1936 that might be a little obscure to some modern readers.

Therefore, here are a few things worth noticing:

- The Bird and Baby/The Eagle and Child – the pub called The Eagle and Child in St Giles Street, Oxford, was a favourite of Lewis and the other Inklings, but they often referred to it by their preferred nickname, The Bird and Baby.
- *Spindrift* by Florence Craye – a non-existent book which is central to the plot of P. G. Wodehouse's novel about Bertie Wooster and his valet, Jeeves, *Joy in the Morning*, and just the sort of thing Penelope Robertson-Smyth would enthuse about.
- The *Oxford Mail* is a real newspaper; however, the character of Mr George Rainbird represents no editor of that august journal, either living or dead.

- Warnie: Warren Hamilton Lewis (1895–1973) – the older brother of C. S. Lewis. He served in the Royal Army Service Corps from 1913 to 1932, retiring with the rank of Captain. He was granted the rank of Major when recalled to active service at the outbreak of the Second World War. I have decided to honour him with the rank of Major throughout this series.
- Nevill Coghill (1899–1980) – Oxford literary scholar best known for his modern English version of Chaucer's *Canterbury Tales* – also a theatrical producer and director with the Oxford University Dramatic Society.
- Reverend Adam Fox (1883–1977) – Dean of Divinity at Magdalen College; from 1938 to 1942 he was Professor of Poetry at Oxford; later he became a Canon of Westminster Abbey, where he is buried in Poet's Corner.
- John Ronald Reuel Tolkien (1892–1973) – philologist, writer, poet. At the time this story is set he was Professor of Anglo-Saxon at Oxford. Best known, of course, as the author of *The Hobbit, The Lord of the Rings* and *The Silmarillion* (nickname 'Tollers').
- Hugo Dyson (1896–1975) – English academic. At the time of this story he was at the University of Reading (but visited Oxford often); from 1945 he was a fellow of Merton College, Oxford.
- VC – Victoria Cross: the highest military decoration, awarded for valour 'in the face of the enemy'.
- Minto and Maureen – 'Minto' was C. S. Lewis' nickname for Janie Moore; Maureen was her daughter. Mrs Moore's son Paddy was Jack's friend, and when Paddy died in action in the First World War Jack kept his promise to care for Paddy's mother and younger sister. Jack, Warnie and the Moores shared a house at Headington Quarry, a suburb of

Oxford, where Mrs Moore functioned as housekeeper (and Jack's surrogate mother – his own mother having died from cancer when he was ten).

- Detective Inspector Gideon Crispin appears (together with Sergeant Henry Merrivale) in the earlier books in this series: *The Corpse in the Cellar*, *The Country House Murders* and *The Floating Body*.
- 'Persian Monarchs' is a salute to P. G. Wodehouse's delightful old card shark 'Uncle Fred' (Lord Ickenham).
- Barfield – Owen Barfield (1898–1997), a friend of both Lewis and Tolkien. He worked as a solicitor in London, so was only an occasional visitor to the Inklings.
- H. Rider Haggard (1856–1925) – author of *King Solomon's Mines* and similar romantic adventures.
- Sapper (pen name of H. C. McNeil, 1888–1937) – author of popular crime thrillers, featuring 'Bulldog Drummond' as their gang-busting hero.
- Ironclad – an early name (from 1866) for battleships built from steel.
- 'time and relative dimensions in space' – the initials, of course, spell 'tardis': a humble salute in the direction of the greatest time traveller of them all, Doctor Who.
- Betjeman 'a former student of mine' – John Betjeman (1906–84) was a pupil of Lewis' some years before this story is set. He later became Poet Laureate. They did not get on well; Betjeman thought Lewis unfriendly and Lewis thought Betjeman lazy.
- Arthur Mee's *Children's Encyclopaedia* – Arthur Mee (1875–1943) was a British journalist, writer and educator. His *Children's Encyclopaedia* began publication in 1908 as a fortnightly magazine. It was later republished in eight bound volumes.

- *The Hound of the Baskervilles* (1902) – the most famous of Sir Arthur Conan Doyle's Sherlock Holmes novels. One of the central characters in the story is Dr James Mortimer, a country physician who lived in the village of Grimpen, on Dartmoor. It was Mortimer who brought the problem of the 'giant hound' to Holmes' attention. It may have appealed to Penelope's sense of humour to name her giant dog after him.
- The cabin scene in *A Night at the Opera* – Marx Brothers movie (1935) – the crowded cabin scene during a trans-atlantic ocean crossing is one of the classic scenes in the movie. (If you haven't seen it, get the DVD!)
- Lagonda – a British luxury car brand, first established in 1906.

ACKNOWLEDGEMENTS

~

My thanks go to:

David Bratman (of the Mythopoeic Society and the Tolkien Gateway website) for his intelligent reading and sympathetic criticism; Ron Bind (who as a child knew both C. S. Lewis and Douglas Gresham) for a delightful meeting in the Eagle and Child, and for his reminiscences and insights; Lucy York for her editing skills; Alison Barr for her constant encouragement; and my wife, Barbara, for her endless patience.